That Irresistible Poison

Calluvia's Royalty #2

Alessandra Hazard

Table of Contents

That Irresistible Poison

Prologue

Everyone said that he was lucky.

To be betrothed to the heir to a throne, to the most politically influential man on the planet...Everyone said Seyn was lucky.

Seyn didn't feel lucky. He hated that man more than anything.

* * *

When Seyn was a child, he loved bedtime stories about kings and queens, brave princes and princesses, and their exciting adventures. There would be nothing special about it—he couldn't be the only child who liked such stories—but Seyn was a little special, after all. Seyn was a prince himself, and there was a story about him, too. It was his favorite.

"Very well, my love," the Queen said with fond exasperation, tucking a strand of silver hair behind her four-year-old son's ear. "But this is the last time. And then you will sleep."

Seyn nodded, beaming at his mother and looking at her expectantly.

"Once upon a time," the Queen started in her soft voice. "There was a beautiful little prince. He was born two months early—"

"To save another prince's life!" Seyn interrupted excitedly. "I did it!"

"Yes, darling," the Queen said with a smile, leaning down to kiss his forehead. "You saved another prince's life. And not just any prince's—it was the life of a very special prince—the Crown Prince of the Second Grand Clan."

Seyn nodded.

He was old enough to know that there were twelve royal families on Calluvia, and some princes were more important than the others.

"His name was Prince Ksar, and he was very ill," his mother said.

Seyn frowned, for the first time feeling curious enough about the mysterious illness to ask. "Ill?"

"You're probably too young to understand," his mother said with a slightly pinched expression on her face. "Prince Ksar's bondmate had died from a very rare telepathic disease, and it made Ksar's telepathy dangerously unstable. He needed another bondmate to stop hurting. But there were no other unbonded boys or girls of royal blood, so Ksar's parents asked us to bring you to this world early so that you could be bonded to Prince Ksar."

"And I saved him!"

"You did," the Queen said with an affectionate smile. "And now you're bonded to Prince Ksar and will marry him when you turn twenty-five. It's a great honor and privilege, my darling."

Probably feeling his uncertainty through the familial bond that they shared, she smiled at him.

"Don't worry, my love. He will cherish you and treat you well. You're bonded for life. The bond between you and Ksar will make him predisposed to like you. That's how the bond works."

Seyn stared at his mother with a frown. "But I'm not bonded to anyone, Mother."

Queen Janesh smiled and shook her head. "We bonded you to him right after your birth. You're just young and your telepathy isn't fully developed yet. I'm sure you'll feel him soon."

Seyn nodded, accepting the explanation and figuring that his mother was right. As far as Seyn was concerned, his mother was always right.

But years passed, and gradually it became obvious that his mother had been wrong—or there was something wrong with *him*. He didn't feel his bondmate at all, no matter how hard he concentrated.

By the time Seyn turned fourteen—the age people's telepathic abilities fully developed—he was sure that there was something wrong with his bond. Other children his age were happily bonded, and the way they described their bonds was completely unfamiliar to him.

"It's like having a best friend at the back of my mind," his older brother, Jamil, told him, his expression softening. Jamil and his bondmate were getting married in a few months, and they were nauseatingly sweet together. "It's a special connection like no other." Jamil looked at him curiously, with green eyes that mirrored Seyn's. "Why are you asking that, kid? Isn't it the same for you?"

Seyn made something up, successfully hiding his growing uneasiness and uncertainty. There was nothing but silence at the back of his mind.

No friend, no bondmate, no special connection. Nothing. Even when he spent hours meditating, all he could feel was a vague connection that led *somewhere*, but his every attempt to communicate was met with silence.

He didn't know what to do. He considered telling his parents, but he was too embarrassed. He didn't want doctors and mind adepts poking at him—and declaring him defective.

So instead, Seyn decided to research the bond.

The amount of information was a little overwhelming, and most of it was boring as hell, but Seyn was able to find something that might explain why his bond was so weird.

The thing was, bonding was supposed to be easy and uncomplicated. It had been over four thousand years since Calluvians had started practicing childhood bonds. It had been supposedly scientifically proven that bonding children's telepathic cores made their telepathy more stable. There had also been political reasons for introducing the Bonding Law, but Seyn found himself skimming the boring bits.

Every Calluvian child was bonded at the age of two or three, usually to a child close to their age. Seyn was an exception: he had been bonded right after his birth and his bondmate was eight years older than him. Apparently, Prince Ksar's first bondmate had been infected by a deadly virus while she was on another planet. The cure hadn't been found in time, the disease damaging her telepathic center irrevocably, and she had died a slow, painful death. That left a wound in Ksar's mind, his broken bond bleeding and damaging other parts of his brain.

The best mind adepts of the planet, known collectively as High Hronthar, had come to the conclusion that Ksar must be bonded immediately again to stabilize his mind and telepathy. But there had been no unbonded children of royal blood close to Ksar's age, so the Second Royal House had asked Seyn's parents to take their unborn child out of the artificial womb early for the sole purpose of bonding Seyn to their heir.

It looked like the circumstances surrounding his bond were very different from other children's. Seyn had been the only premature baby in history who had been bonded right after his birth. The age difference between him and his bondmate probably wasn't helping the situation, either. Maybe it would get better as he grew older. Maybe it would get better once he actually met his betrothed.

But then, a few months later, when Seyn finally met his bondmate at the ball Seyn's family was hosting to celebrate Jamil's marriage, that hope was completely crushed.

* * *

"His Royal Highness Crown Prince Ksar'ngh'chaali of the Second Grand Clan."

Seyn turned around and looked toward the double doors, excitement and anxiety making his heart thud painfully against his rib cage.

Finally.

Come to think of it, it was more than a little strange that he'd never met his betrothed before. He'd met Ksar's younger brother, Harht, quite often, and Seyn considered him a good friend, but Ksar had always been either out or "busy" every time Seyn had visited the Second Royal Palace. Seyn had tried not to take it personally—technically, until he turned twenty-five and married Ksar, his bondmate had no obligations toward him.

Seyn tried to tell himself that he would have no interest in some kid eight years younger than him, either, but he was only partly successful at convincing himself. Coupled with his weirdly weak bond, the lack of interest from his betrothed made him feel…a little insecure. Seyn normally wasn't insecure or shy by any stretch of imagination—he had lots of friends, and everyone seemed to like him—but his bond had always made him anxious.

That was why Seyn stared curiously at the tall man making his way through the crowd, drawing stares from all over the ballroom. Ksar was dressed formally, in gray and black colors of the Second Royal House, his white cravat the only bright touch. Ksar's long, midnight blue hair was tied back, drawing one's gaze to his sharp jaw and austere, handsome features. He looked more mature than his twenty-two years.

For the first time, Seyn wondered if those rumors about Ksar's parents genetically engineering him were true. Although genetic engineering was frowned upon, it wasn't forbidden. Ksar definitely seemed too…perfect.

It wasn't his physical appearance.

Ksar wasn't as startlingly handsome as Jamil, but he had something Seyn's brother didn't: the air of quiet authority and the calm, kingly dignity.

Despite the fact that there were no fewer than four kings and three queens present, it seemed as though he was *the* king—which should have been ridiculous.

And yet…

Seyn had seen Ksar's pictures before, of course. He'd known what he looked like. But the pictures hadn't prepared him for the self-possessed, commanding air about Ksar or for his cold, haughty expression that suddenly made Seyn self-conscious of how young and imperfect he was.

Shaking off his self-consciousness, Seyn straightened himself to his full height. He might be just fourteen, but he was Prince Seyn'ngh'veighli of the Third Grand Clan, not some farmer's kid.

Schooling his features into an expression of neutral politeness, Seyn made his way toward his mothers and Ksar.

When he reached them, Seyn stared at Ksar's back uncertainly.

He opened his mind, still hoping that his weird bond would finally start *working*.

There was still nothing.

"Your Highness," Seyn said.

Ksar's shoulders tensed up a little.

Slowly, he turned around and looked at Seyn with silver eyes that gave nothing away.

Remembering his manners, Seyn gave him a bow. It wasn't a deep one—he might not be the heir of his clan, but he was still a prince, and etiquette dictated that a shallow bow was enough.

Ksar didn't bow back, of course.

As the heir apparent of the Second Grand Clan, he only had to bow to the monarchs of the twelve grand clans and to the heir of the First Grand Clan. Unlike Seyn, he didn't even have to bow to the royal consorts. When Ksar became the king, everyone but the monarch of the First Grand Clan would bow to *him*. And although technically the First Grand Clan was a little larger, the Second Grand Clan was far more powerful politically.

"I believe you haven't seen Seyn'ngh'veighli since he was a tiny, red newborn," Queen-Consort Faryda said, glancing at Seyn with a mild but indulgent smile. "I think our boy has changed quite a bit since then, don't you think?"

It was probably blatantly obvious how much his mothers doted on him, and Seyn flushed from embarrassment. As the youngest in the family, he'd always been the focus of his mothers' doting love, which Seyn shamelessly used to get his way, but it was mortifying when they coddled him in front of an audience. Especially when the audience was his seemingly perfect betrothed. He didn't want to look like a *kid*.

Ksar's gaze swept slowly over Seyn's less-than-formal attire. He raised his eyebrows a little.

Seyn narrowed his eyes. "Yes, Mother," he said, refusing to look embarrassed. It was none of that ass's concern what he chose to wear. There was nothing wrong with his clothes, anyway. He was fourteen, not forty, and he didn't have a stick up his ass. "We have never met. His Highness seems to be a very busy person. He's *always* otherwise engaged when I visit his brother."

Queen Janesh cleared her throat, breaking the awkward silence. "Seyn..."

Seyn could perfectly hear the warning in his mother's voice. He could feel his mothers' disapproval through their familial links to him. He ignored it. He glared at Ksar, who stared back at him impassively, as though Seyn was a strange, irritating creature that had just performed an unexpected trick.

Ugh! Seyn's hands practically itched to…to mess up that perfectly tied cravat, or maybe punch that top-lofty ass in the face; anything to wipe that superior expression.

"You will make no such scene," an unfamiliar voice said in his head.

Seyn froze, staring at Ksar, wide-eyed. He had never spoken to Ksar, but that voice could belong only to him. Only bondmates could communicate in actual sentences through telepathy—or if one was a high-level telepath, but since both of them were mere Class 2 telepaths, the bond was the only explanation for his ability to hear Ksar's voice.

Despite his shock, a very large part of Seyn was relieved. His bond actually worked. There was nothing wrong with him.

"He has indeed changed," Ksar said aloud, his voice a deep monotone that sounded nothing like the scathing voice in Seyn's head.

Seyn did a double take and frowned slightly.

He wasn't an expert on telepathy, but as a rule, people's telepathic voice sounded exactly like their real voice.

Weird.

"He definitely isn't quite as red," Ksar said in the same flat voice, and Seyn's mothers laughed, as though Ksar had said something incredibly witty.

Ha fucking ha.

Seyn had no idea how to communicate through their bond—it wasn't like he'd had any practice—so he thought as loudly as he could,

"Very funny. And don't talk about me like I'm not here."

Ksar flicked his gaze to him for a moment before returning it to Seyn's mothers. He engaged them in some small talk that gradually shifted into a more serious discussion about politics.

Seyn scrunched up his nose.

Ugh, politics.

Boring.

"Aren't you supposed to be a prince? Perhaps you should try paying attention."

Seyn flinched. *"Are you eavesdropping on my thoughts?"* He glowered at Ksar's profile. One would never guess Ksar was anything but attentive as he listened to Queen Janesh. *"Also, I could never hear you before. Why?"*

There was a small pause before Ksar replied.

"Your mind is undisciplined and chaotic. Your excited childish gibberish has always been extremely distracting, so normally I block you."

Seyn took a deep breath and counted to ten, telling himself that murdering the Crown Prince of the Second Grand Clan would surely start another Great War.

"Why does no one know what a two-faced asshole you are? A perfect gentleman, my ass!"

"That's the last time I'm letting you get away with such language, boy."

"Don't you call me boy! And you aren't the boss of me. You are in my house, not yours. I will talk how I want, I will dress how I want, and I will—"

Ksar pulled out of his mind.

It was such a strange feeling. Suddenly he was just aware of the *absence* of something that he hadn't even noticed until then. Glaring at the asshole's nape, Seyn focused hard and tried to follow the mental footprints that Ksar had left in his mind. It took an incredible effort, but finally, he managed it.

He wished he hadn't.

Because now he could feel it: a thick, impenetrable wall, blocking the way and making him physically nauseous and dizzy every time he touched it. It emanated *wrong-not wanted-keep away*.

Seyn staggered back, hurt and rejection welling up in his chest and making it hard to breathe.

Ksar turned his head. Something flickered in his eyes before they became unfathomable. He could undoubtedly see that Seyn was crushed by his rejection, and Seyn fought the tears of anger and utter humiliation threatening to spill from his eyes.

I hate you, he thought with feeling, holding Ksar's gaze, something dark and ugly taking root in his heart.

I hate you, I hate you, I hate you.

Chapter 1

Nine years later

Calluvian Society Gossip

Prince Seyn in the spotlight of intergalactic mass media...Again.

Daughters and sons of the Third Grand Clan have always been known for their exquisite beauty and charisma. Many of them caused wars that shaped world history. But few flirted with scandal as often as Prince Seyn does.

It is common knowledge that Prince Seyn of the Third Grand Clan is quite the social butterfly. The twenty-three-year-old prince attends countless balls and soirees, not only on Calluvia, but also on other worlds of the Union of Planets. Nowadays, no one is surprised by the growing number of foreign admirers Prince Seyn has, admirers who refuse to give up despite Prince Seyn being unavailable. The whole Union knows that Prince Seyn is betrothed; no one seems to care, least of all Prince Seyn. Although, to our knowledge, the prince has never done anything completely inappropriate, he certainly doesn't discourage his admirers from wooing him.

However, it was Prince Seyn's recent trip to Planet Rugora that raised our eyebrows. [For those unaware: Planet Rugora is infamous for its gambling facilities and pleasure houses.] The prince was spotted by the tabloids in the company of several high-ranking members of the court.

One wonders what our esteemed Lord Chancellor thinks about his bondmate's escapades…

As a matter of fact, we have managed to get hold of Prince Ksar, but he didn't appear very concerned. "He likes to see new places and meet new people," he told us curtly, looking rather bored and distracted, no doubt in a hurry to return to the Council's session.

But we wonder: is Prince Ksar as unbothered as he seemed? And if he is, one has to wonder about the implications…

There has never been a dissolution of a childhood bond — it is forbidden by law — but we imagine if it were possible, Prince Ksar and Prince Seyn would be the first in line for it.

We can't think of a less suitable couple…

* * *

"I wish there really was a way to dissolve this stupid bond," Seyn grumbled, closing the article and setting his interactive multi-device down. "Then I would be rid of that asshole."

Prince Harht of the Second Grand Clan looked at his friend and suppressed a sigh.

He loved Seyn like a brother, but Seyn could be so unreasonable when it came to Ksar.

Seyn also tended to forget that Ksar was his brother and that Harht loved his big brother, no matter how standoffish Ksar could be. Harht was convinced that Ksar was a good person—deep down—but every time he tried to convince Seyn of that, Seyn just scoffed and told him that he was too kind and naive, and that Ksar didn't deserve to be defended.

"You're talking about my brother," Harht reminded Seyn gently.

Seyn grimaced. "Sometimes I genuinely forget. Really, it's amazing that someone like you can be related to such a vile, arrogant ass." Seyn gave him a rueful smile that didn't reach his eyes. "But yes, I get it. I'm sorry for putting you into such an awkward position."

Harht sighed. It always upset him when Seyn badmouthed Ksar, but it also upset him that Seyn was so miserable because of the bond to his brother.

"There's no way to dissolve the bond," Harht said patiently, trying to project fondness and understanding instead of exasperation. "I don't understand why you can't just accept it. The bond isn't bad. I like my bond and my bondmate."

Seyn scoffed. "Because your bondmate isn't an asshole. I would have been fine with being bonded to someone like Leylen—okay, *mostly* fine." Seyn heaved a sigh, sagging back against the couch and running his hand through his long, silver hair before starting to coil it into a complicated braid. The jerkiness of his fingers as he twisted the long strands betrayed his frustration.

"You really don't understand, do you?" Seyn said after a while.

Harht shrugged. He honestly didn't.

Seyn smiled faintly. "You're just very sheltered. You've never been on other planets. You haven't seen societies—much healthier societies—that don't shackle their children to some stranger for life. People can actually choose who they want to be with on other planets, Harht! Can you imagine that?"

Seyn straightened, his green eyes brightening. "Other races can actually fall in love. Hell, they can have sex with anyone they want! They don't have to wait until they're twenty-five and they'll be finally allowed to fuck the person who's been forced on them since childhood! Amazing, isn't it?"

Harht gave a shrug, a little embarrassed by Seyn's vulgar language, but used to it enough not to comment on it. "Personally, I'm completely fine with waiting until I'm twenty-five. It's not like I want sex."

"Precisely!" Seyn said. "This stupid bond messes with our biology, making us practically asexual until our marriage and even then we can't want anyone but our bondmate! It takes away our agency."

Rationally, Harht understood where Seyn was coming from; he did. He just…He didn't feel particularly bothered. It was hard to miss or want something one never had. It surprised him that Seyn felt so passionately about it.

"I just hate this," Seyn said, deflating, his pale lips turning down at the corners, and his eyes losing fire. Even his braid looked kind of crooked and sad.

"I'm sorry," Harht said softly, projecting as much sympathy and comfort as he could. He wasn't a very good empath—Seyn was much better at empathy—but he did his best.

"Me, too," Seyn murmured.

The palace AI's voice cut in. "Excuse me, Your Highness?"

"Yes?" Seyn said listlessly.

"His Royal Highness Crown Prince Ksar'ngh'chaali is here and wishes to see you."

Seyn jumped to his feet so fast it almost made Harht dizzy. A flush appeared on Seyn's cheekbones, his eyes glinting with almost feverish intensity. "What does he want? Never mind, I can guess. Let him in."

After a few moments, Ksar strode into the room, looking as though he owned it. Harht had always been a little envious of that ability of his brother.

"Have you gone completely stupid?" Ksar said, glaring at Seyn as he walked into his personal space. "Stupider than you already were?"

Seyn lifted his chin and held his ground, not looking intimidated at all.

"What have I done now, Your Highness?" he said with such venom in his voice that Harht barely recognized it.

"Do you make it your life's mission to make yourself—and me— the laughingstock of the entire Union?" Ksar bit off. "A pleasure planet? Really? What next? Are you going to get caught naked? You're a fucking embarrassment."

Harht gaped at his brother.

He had honestly never heard Ksar swear—or lose his ironclad composure in such a spectacular manner, for that matter. Ksar wasn't a hothead. He didn't rage and he didn't *do* yelling matches. When he was angry, he got dangerously quiet, not *this*.

This...Harht wasn't sure what this was.

To make matters worse, Seyn smirked right into Ksar's face. "Sorry, I can't hear you over the sound of your ego. Go fuck yourself. I can do whatever I want. You don't actually own me, you controlling piece of shit—"

Harht cleared his throat, deciding that he should interfere before things got ugly.

Or rather, uglier.

"Calm down, both of you."

Ksar's gaze snapped to him, a frown appearing on his face. It made Harht wonder if his brother had even noticed that he was in the room.

After what felt like a very long moment, Ksar stepped back from Seyn, his face devoid of any emotion. He was once again absolutely composed. It was almost like looking at a different person. This Ksar was far more familiar to Harht than the one who had looked like he was one moment away from inflicting violence on Seyn.

"What are you doing here?" Ksar said, in his normal voice that held very little inflection. "Shouldn't you be with Sanyash?"

Harht averted his gaze guiltily.

He really was supposed to be with their sister, and he had been, until she had caught him peeking into her memories through their familial bond. She had been so furious at him for violating her privacy that Harht had fled the palace, hoping that she would calm down. Their mother, the Queen, wouldn't be amused if she found out.

"What did you do, Harht?" Ksar said, fixing his gaze on him.

"Maybe you should stop sticking your nose where it doesn't belong," Seyn cut in.

Any other time, Harht would have rolled his eyes.

Seyn just couldn't live with being in the same room as Ksar and not picking a fight with him. Sometimes it seemed like he couldn't live without fighting with Ksar about everything and nothing.

"Maybe you should try following your own advice," Ksar said coldly, without even glancing at Seyn.

Harht sighed exasperatedly. Ksar knew perfectly well how much Seyn hated being ignored and Harht was pretty sure his brother did it on purpose. They both were absolutely incorrigible.

"Harht," Ksar said, reminding him that he was still waiting for an explanation.

Harht hung his head. "Sanyash has been teasing me all afternoon that she had some exciting news, but she wouldn't tell me anything. I was curious, and she was right there."

He shrugged, embarrassed by his impulsive decision to sneak a peek into her memories.

The thing was, he hadn't even thought that he would be successful. He was just a Class 1 telepath, his mind-reading abilities very weak against other telepaths. But his touch-telepathy was pretty strong, and coupled with the familial bond between him and Sanyash, he had been unexpectedly successful at catching a glimpse of her memories.

"I peeked into Sanyash's memories and found out that she's pregnant," Harht said and immediately winced. Was he supposed to tell Ksar that?

"You peeked into her memories," Ksar repeated flatly, ignoring the pregnancy news.

Harht squirmed under his heavy gaze.

"Last time I checked, that was a crime," Ksar said. "Punishable by as much as ten years in prison—unless you access memories of your bondmate. Violation of privacy is no joke."

"She's his sister, not some stranger," Seyn said.

"No one asked for your opinion," Ksar said, without looking at Seyn. "We're going home, Harht." He turned on his heel and walked out of the room, clearly expecting Harht to follow him.

Of course Harht did. When Ksar gave an order, people did as they were told—unless they were Seyn.

"Don't worry, it'll be fine," Seyn said, sending a wave of comfort and reassurance his way. "Do you want me to come with you?"

Harht shook his head. Having Seyn around was the last thing he needed. For some reason, he always brought out the worst in Ksar.

"I'm sure it'll be fine," Harht said with a confidence he didn't really feel.

It should be fine. Right?

He was a prince.

What could his parents do to him?

Chapter 2

Calluvian Society Gossip

Prince Harht'ngh'chaali banished to a pre-TNIT planet!

The Second Royal House issued a press release stating that Prince Harht has been temporarily exiled to Sol III, a primitive planet half a galaxy away, as punishment for his "transgression." The press release did not elaborate about the extent of the prince's transgression, but there's no doubt that it must be something serious if Queen Tamirs and the Crown Prince have decided to punish a member of their own family so harshly...

* * *

"Your Highness?"

Ksar frowned at the report in front of him. "I've requested no interruptions, Borg'gorn," he told the AI.

"I apologize, Your Highness, but Prince Seyn'ngh'veighli is refusing to leave until he sees you."

Ksar pinched the bridge of his nose. What did the brat want?

"Very well. Let him in."

His lips thinned as Seyn strode into the room, all pale hair, flawless skin, and unnatural grace. For once, Seyn's hair was pulled into a simple side braid that looked like it would fall apart from the slightest touch.

Ksar returned his gaze to the report in front of him. "What do you want?" he said coldly, checking his mental shields and finding them to his satisfaction. Being in the same room as Seyn was always aggravating, for several reasons.

"Are you crazy?" Seyn growled, marching to his desk and slamming his hands on it. "How could you do that to Harht, you sick fuck? Don't you care about him at all?"

"Mind your foul tongue," Ksar said. "And it wasn't my decision to punish Harht that way. It was the Queen's idea."

Seyn scoffed. "As if she wouldn't have changed her mind if you disagreed with her."

"I'm flattered that you think I have so much influence over my mother, but the point is moot because I fully support her decision."

Seyn glared at him from across the desk, his eyes full of fire and hate. "Are you out of your mind? Sending Harht to a pre-TNIT planet like Sol III is a recipe for disaster! He has zero survival skills! He thinks that nasty people don't exist and he trusts everyone! He's never been on another civilized planet, and you send him to some barbarian planet half a galaxy away, a planet with inhabitants that think aliens want to abduct them or some other stupid shit! He'll give himself away or starve to death."

"Are you done?" Ksar said.

It irked him that Seyn thought he was being careless with his brother's safety.

The decision might have been the Queen's, but he had carefully chosen the planet for Harht's banishment.

Sol III, or Terra, was diverse enough for Harht's odd behavior to be written off as quirkiness. Harht had also been dropped in one of the most civilized countries of the planet. He should be fine. "First, the Queen's decision isn't up for discussion. You don't even belong to our grand clan, so our affairs are none of your concern. Second, it's a suitable punishment for Harht's transgression. We all coddled him too much. It's time for him to grow up and learn some life lessons. He's on his own now. The distance between Calluvia and Terra is too great for familial bonds to work. It will make him appreciate his telepathic bonds and never abuse them again."

Seyn met his eyes. "It's hilarious that you, of all people, are talking about appreciating one's telepathic bonds. I know our bond is pretty pathetic, but you don't exactly strengthen it by blocking me off."

Ksar held his gaze unflinchingly, wondering what Seyn would do if he knew the truth. He didn't block Seyn out of his mind. There was no need. There had never been any need to do it—because Seyn wasn't really his bondmate.

Ksar still remembered the day of their bonding, all those years ago. He had been an eight-year-old, his mind an open wound from the death of his first bondmate, his senses dazed and disoriented. He could still remember with perfect clarity the moment he had been told to take a newborn infant into his arms as the mind adepts attempted to establish a bond between them. Seyn had been a tiny thing, born premature by two months.

It had taken the mind adepts four attempts before they finally concluded that the bond had taken.

At the time, Ksar had thought they were right. He could feel the child's chaotic, mindless emotions, its need for comfort and safety. Since a child that young couldn't communicate and had next to no telepathic abilities, it was impossible to determine that the bond had taken on Seyn's end—or rather, on Ksar's. Ksar had realized that something was off only months later when it became obvious that the infant couldn't feel him at all—that and the fact that Ksar's telepathic abilities had...changed.

The truth of the matter was that their bond was one-way: Seyn might be bonded to him, but he wasn't bonded to Seyn.

Not that Ksar had any intention of enlightening his supposed bondmate about the fact. If Seyn was under the impression that Ksar was blocking him out of his mind on purpose, so be it.

Being thought of as a neglectful bondmate was better than the alternative.

"I thought we agreed that the less we interacted through our bond, the better," Ksar said.

Seyn made a mock thoughtful face. "Funny that I don't remember that conversation. Actually, I don't remember us ever having an adult conversation that didn't involve you criticizing me for every imaginary sin."

"For us to have an adult conversation both of us actually have to be adults," Ksar said, returning his gaze to the reports once again.

"I'm twenty-three," Seyn gritted out. "I'm considered an adult on most other planets of the Union."

There were several responses Ksar could think of, but he kept them to himself. All of them would have just escalated their argument. He had more important things to do than to have another pointless, aggravating argument with Seyn, no matter how tempting it was. It was far more tempting than it should have been. *He* didn't have the excuse of not being an adult.

"Don't you dare ignore me, asshole," Seyn hissed, his anger flaring through the bond.

Sometimes Ksar wondered what it would have been like to have a fully functional bond with Seyn—how much more distracting it would have been—and it was a good thing he would never know. Having a one-way access to Seyn's emotions was distracting enough already.

The most aggravating part was, he had never been entirely successful at blocking Seyn's emotions. No matter how strong his telepathic abilities were, Ksar could always feel a foreign need at the back of his mind: need for companionship, need for attention, sometimes need for comfort.

Seyn had been a very emotional and needy child, and that hadn't changed much over the years: he was an extrovert, who needed people and people's companionship and attention to feel happy.

He was Ksar's complete opposite in that regard, and receiving the secondhand emotions of some needy child had irritated the hell out of him when he was younger. Thankfully, Seyn had learned to protect his mind better and stopped giving off so much *need* after their first meeting, but it was still distracting.

More distracting than it should have been.

Sometimes Ksar was tempted to break their one-sided bond completely—he could do it easily enough—but it would be foolish to do it when the consequences were unpredictable at best. Seyn might not feel him on the other end of the bond, but he would definitely notice the sudden disappearance of the bond.

After all, connecting people's minds wasn't the primary function of the bond.

"Stop ignoring me!" Seyn said again, and even without looking at him, Ksar knew his green eyes were blazing with fury, his pale cheeks flushed, his pink lips folded into a fierce scowl. He was the only person of Ksar's acquaintance who managed to become more attractive the angrier he got.

Ksar slid lower in his seat, irritated with himself. It was pathetic. He wasn't an animal. He was more than his baser instincts. His body's reaction to that spoiled little thing was beyond irritating and inconvenient.

"Leave," he said curtly, his eyes on his work. "I have no time for you."

"You—" Seyn fumed for a few moments in silence before storming out of the room.

As soon as the door shut after him, Ksar sighed.

He had a bad feeling about this.

Chapter 3

Months later, as Ksar watched his younger brother fall apart, he knew he had been right to worry.

He still had trouble wrapping his mind around the fact that his brother—his innocent little brother—had been spreading his legs for some low-class barbarian on Terra. It seemed unthinkable, but there had been no mistake. He'd seen Harht *kiss* that Terran, shameless and needy, as if Ksar wasn't there, as if Harht's reputation wouldn't be absolutely destroyed if anyone back home found out about it.

What was Harht thinking?

More importantly, what had *Seyn* been thinking? Smuggling Harht back to Terra, encouraging him to take a human name, and encouraging his affair with the human.

"Do you even have a heart?" Seyn said quietly when Harht left to pack his things. "I hope you realize that you just broke your brother's life."

Ksar pulled out his communicator and checked to see if he had new messages. There were seventeen waiting for him.

He stared at them unseeingly.

"Cease being overdramatic," he said. "You know as well as I do that I'm right. Harht and his human have no future together."

As he thought, Seyn had nothing to say to that. Seyn could be a contrary little thing, but he wasn't a naive dreamer like Harht. Deep down, Seyn must have known that Ksar was right. Seyn knew that the Ministry's laws prohibited any kind of relationship with a member of a pre-TNIT civilization. Seyn *knew* that a romantic entanglement with a human could end only in heartbreak for Harht, and yet he had still encouraged this madness.

Putting the communicator back in his pocket, Ksar looked at Seyn coldly. "It's entirely your fault," he said, walking toward him. "He was fine until you reunited him with his human and gave him a false hope."

Seyn shot him a murderous look. "Don't you dare put the blame on me, you piece of shit—"

Ksar grabbed a fistful of silver hair, dragging Seyn's face closer. "The truth hurts, doesn't it?" he said flatly, *not* looking at that pink, pretty mouth. "It's easy to be the good one, to be all supportive and nice, but the truth is, you did more damage by bringing Harht here than I did by not allowing him to keep his delusions. And for what? Just for your own selfish reasons."

"That's not true!"

"Isn't it?" Ksar said, looking into the angry green eyes. "Did you think for a moment about Harht's feelings when you insisted on this trip? No. All you thought about is you—and me, I suppose."

Seyn flushed. He shoved at Ksar's chest. "Yes, I did it because of you. To get rid of you." He smiled at Ksar. "And you know what? It wasn't for nothing. You *will* find a way to break my bond to you—or I'll tell everyone that you aren't a harmless Class 2 telepath."

Ksar's lips thinned. "You don't want to blackmail me."

Seyn lifted his chin, the air between them vibrating with tension. "I'm not afraid of you."

The ugly thing at the back of Ksar's mind stirred, whispering that he should just take what he wanted, that it would be so *easy*—

Ksar smothered it. No.

"You should be," he said grimly, taking Seyn's wrist.

Seyn glowered. "Don't touch me."

"Don't be ridiculous. I need to be touching you—and Harht—to take you home with me."

Seyn scowled at him but let him drag him toward the room Harht had disappeared into.

Ksar pretended not to notice the tears in his brother's eyes as he told Harht to take his other hand.

Sometimes playing the role of a villain was incredibly draining.

Pushing away the useless regret, Ksar activated his transponder, and the world around them disappeared.

Chapter 4

Returning from Terra to Calluvia felt... disheartening. Seyn couldn't even look Harry in the eyes, feeling guilty, angry, and upset on his behalf.

After their arrival at the Second Royal Palace, Seyn watched with increasing suspicion and distrust as Ksar restored Harry's bond to Leylen—without the latter being present. He watched Ksar's calm, impassive face as he performed what should have been an impossible task, and felt a shiver run up his spine. He'd told Ksar he wasn't scared of him. Maybe he really should have been.

"It is done," Ksar said, stepping back from his brother and eyeing him carefully. "Can you confirm it?"

Harry gave a jerky nod, like a broken marionette, and left without saying anything.

Silence fell upon the room.

"I hope you're happy with yourself," Seyn said.

A muscle twitched in Ksar's jaw. "Enough. I'm not in the mood for your smart mouth." He turned to leave, but Seyn quickly blocked his path.

"What?" Ksar said in that infuriating monotone of his, his body language impatient and tense.

"If you can restore Harry's bond so easily, you should be able to break ours—my bond to you—just as easily."

Something flickered in Ksar's eyes. "It's more complicated than that. It's much harder to perform such procedures when it concerns one's own mind."

"But it's not *your* mind we're talking about, is it?" Seyn said, his chest tightening at the reminder that he was the only one bound by the bond while Ksar was free as a bird, had always been.

"Your mind is still connected to mine," Ksar said. "It makes it difficult for me to remain impartial enough to break the connection."

Seyn eyed him. "I don't believe you."

"You may believe whatever you wish to believe," Ksar said, stepping aside, clearly with the intention of walking away and ignoring Seyn. As usual.

Seyn grabbed his shirt. "If you think you can just ignore me and I will go away, I can assure you that will not happen!"

Ksar glanced down at Seyn's hand as though it was something offensive.

"Remove your hand," he said.

"Why?" Seyn said, stepping closer. "Does it bother you?"

Ksar's face gave nothing away, but his heart was beating fast and hard under Seyn's hand.

Confused but pleased that he was getting under the bastard's skin, Seyn moved even closer, so close their faces were a breath apart. His own heart was beating fast, his body tense and hyper-aware of Ksar's proximity. Was it fear? Probably. For all Seyn's words that he wasn't afraid of Ksar, he wasn't an idiot. If Ksar was as strong a telepath as everything indicated, he was dangerous. People were afraid of high-level telepaths for a reason.

"Step away," Ksar said, meeting his eyes. There was something dark lurking in them. "I'm warning you, boy."

Seyn bristled. "Don't you call me that!"

"That's what you are," Ksar said, his thin lips twisting into a sneer. "A little boy. Not a man. Or you would know better than to annoy me and then get all over my personal space."

Seyn glared. "You wouldn't dare do anything to me, you arrogant piece of shit—"

Ksar slammed their mouths together.

Seyn's mind went utterly *blank*. He didn't even resist when Ksar pushed his tongue between his lips.

It took him several long moments to regain his ability to think. Ksar was *kissing* him.

Ksar was kissing him, which meant...

Which meant that Ksar was attracted to him. It seemed unbelievable, but there was no other explanation for this. Kisses on the cheek, on the nose, or on the neck could mean different things on different planets. But a deep kiss on the mouth was an unambiguous sign of physical attraction, universal for most civilized planets of the galaxy.

Ksar wanted him. *Him.*

A feeling of utter glee washed over Seyn. For the first time in his life, he finally felt like he had the upper hand over Ksar. For the first time in his life, he was glad that he had his stupid bond and that he was above feelings like lust and arousal. Not that he would be attracted to an asshole like Ksar if he were capable of getting sexually aroused— Seyn was certain he would have more common sense than that—but still, he was glad that he could remain absolutely level-headed while Ksar's prided composure was nowhere to be seen. He *owned* Ksar.

Ksar wrenched his mouth away and glowered at him, his lips shiny and his skin tinged with color. "You're delusional if you think you can use this against me. This is nothing."

Seyn let his gaze travel down Ksar's body and smiled when he saw the obscene bulge in Ksar's pants. He might be sexually inexperienced, but he knew what *that* meant. He was hardly a sheltered innocent. He was aware of the most obvious physical sign of arousal. He had off-world friends who'd told him about sex in lurid detail.

Seyn returned his eyes to Ksar's stony face. He had no idea how seduction worked, but if someone as naive as Harry could do it, it couldn't be very hard, right? Even if seducing such an awful person like Ksar made him want to puke a little, Seyn could absolutely do it. It would just be a means to an end.

"If you break my bond, I'll put your…thing in my mouth," Seyn said, figuring straightforwardness was the best approach.

Ksar stared at him.

And then…and then he threw his head back and laughed, a full belly laugh that Seyn had not thought Ksar capable of.

Seyn scowled, his face warming. Did he say something funny?

"My thing," Ksar said at last, smirking in that condescending, arrogant way that never failed to make Seyn want to scream and punch him in the face.

Ksar gave him a dismissive look. "I don't put 'my thing' into little boys' mouths. I like *men* who know how to suck cock."

Seyn had never felt such rage in his life.

Screw seducing Ksar to make him break the bond. It was a matter of pride now.

He leaned in and pressed his lips against Ksar's jaw.

Immediately, he felt Ksar go rigid.

Seyn was frozen too, breathing shallowly as Ksar's faint stubble prickled his lips.

He smelled good. How could such a vile man smell so good?

Shaking off the weird thought, Seyn dragged his lips down Ksar's jawline and almost flinched when he felt a very muted rush of pleasure that wasn't his own. Ksar's shields were normally as impenetrable as a fortress, but the skin contact and the fact that Ksar's mental faculties were clearly compromised, allowed Seyn to get some faint feedback.

"Cease this immediately," Ksar bit off, his hands clamping on Seyn's wrists.

Seyn kissed the corner of Ksar's mouth and felt as Ksar's muscles tensed even more.

"You can deny this all you want, but you aren't fooling anyone here," Seyn murmured, nipping at Ksar's sharp jaw. "I know you want me. I bet that's what you always wanted: to make me shut up with your *cock*."

He knew he was right when Ksar's grip on his wrists tightened, Ksar's breath hitching.

But Ksar turned his head aside, away from Seyn's lips, and gave a mean chuckle. "You don't even know what you're talking about. You're just a little boy trying to play an adult game."

Narrowing his eyes, Seyn straightened to his full height. "You think I can't do anything the whores who sucked your cock could?"

Ksar looked at him with an expression Seyn couldn't quite place. "Stop using such vulgar language," he said with something like irritation, but not quite. "It won't make you seem like a grown-up."

Seyn clenched his fists, the urge to punch the bastard nearly irresistible.

He opened his mouth to retort, but then he thought better of it. He could totally prove to that asshole that he could do it—that he could do it far better than any filthy whore of Ksar's acquaintance.

Seyn dropped to his knees.

"Get up," Ksar said, his unimpressed gaze on the opposite wall.

"Why aren't you looking at me?" Seyn said. "Afraid you'll like seeing me on my knees too much?"

This time Ksar did look down at him. "Full of ourselves, aren't we?"

Seyn looked pointedly at the bulge under the Terran pants Ksar was still wearing and raised his eyebrows.

To his disappointment, Ksar didn't seem ashamed or embarrassed. Despite the undeniable sign of his arousal, he didn't look fazed at all.

"Very well," Ksar said, something nasty and calculating about his expression. "You want to suck my cock? Go ahead."

Seyn swallowed. He knew what Ksar was doing—he was calling his bluff and expected him to back off—but Ksar didn't know him at all if he thought he could intimidate him.

He could totally do it.

How hard could it possibly be?

Sure, the mere idea of putting Ksar's penis into his mouth seemed pretty disgusting and unhygienic, but it wouldn't kill him—and more importantly, Seyn would *win*. Seyn wasn't sure what exactly he would win, but it didn't matter. It would feel so good to prove the fucker wrong, to make Ksar lose—to make him lose it. To own him.

Seyn looked into Ksar's silver eyes. They were as cold and inscrutable as ever. It was kind of funny that Seyn's mothers thought it was lovely and romantic that Ksar's eyes were the exact shade of Seyn's hair, as if it was a sign of their epic destiny together. There was nothing lovely about Ksar's calculating, cold eyes. Seyn kind of hated the color of his own hair because of them. He would have dyed his hair ages ago if he didn't know that it would make his mothers upset.

His mothers would be more than just upset if they knew what he was about to do.

"Borg'gorn, lock the door," Seyn said softly.

Ksar's nostrils flared.

There was the sound of the door sliding shut.

Neither of them looked toward it.

Slowly, Seyn reached for Ksar's fly. His hands didn't shake. Still looking Ksar in the eye, he pulled the zipper down.

The feeling of velvety, warm skin against his hand was something of a shock—Ksar wasn't wearing anything under his Terran pants—but Seyn didn't flinch.

Ksar did. "Get up," he said, his voice sounding nothing like his usual monotone. It was hoarse and tight, ringing with tension.

Seyn smiled at him, holding his gaze. "No," he said firmly, pulling the warm, pulsing organ out of Ksar's pants.

He finally looked at it.

Seyn knew what to expect, more or less. He knew what his own crotch looked like.

But the hot, hard length twitching in his hand felt and looked nothing like his own soft cock. It was so much bigger. So much harder. Hot and oddly pleasant to touch.

Seyn stared at it in fascination. Part of him couldn't believe he had Ksar's *cock* in his hand. It just seemed so...improper. Obscene. The top of Ksar's cock was dark red, already glistening with a few drops of white fluid that would become lubricant if Ksar allowed it.

Seyn licked his lips. He was aware that males of their species could emit a lot of lubricating fluid to ease penetration, and it was...it was probably gross. He wasn't exactly looking forward to swallowing all this stuff. The whole ordeal was disgusting enough.

"Don't leak a lot," he warned, and then immediately regretted it. Now Ksar would do it just to spite him.

"Get up," Ksar repeated, his voice harsher, tighter.

Seyn looked up from Ksar's cock to his face. He nearly flinched when he saw the murderous glint in Ksar's eyes.

"Why?" Seyn said, giving the hard length in his hand a small stroke. "Afraid you'll enjoy it too much?"

He got immense satisfaction out of the glare Ksar gave him.

"I'm afraid of no such thing."

"Liar," Seyn said softly. He leaned in and gave the tip of the cock a kittenish lick. Ksar's breath hitched, and Seyn felt another rush of foreign pleasure. "I can feel it, you know. I'm a good empath. You like this. You like seeing me on my knees for you. And you like this..."

Seyn licked Ksar's cock from the base to the red tip, watching greedily for any sign of Ksar losing his composure. Ksar's body stiffened like a string ready to snap, his eyes like molten silver, bright against the dark lashes, intent, hungry, heavy-lidded with base need. His face warming, Seyn circled his tongue around the slippery cock head before slowly taking it into his mouth, a little disappointed that the taste wasn't bad.

It wasn't bad at all.

Seyn's eyes closed as he struggled to separate the muted rush of Ksar's pleasure from his own feelings.

Fuck.

He hadn't anticipated this. He wanted to find this disgusting, not pleasant. Though, it wasn't his fault that he was getting secondhand pleasure from doing something he found gross. That didn't mean *he* liked it.

Reassured by that thought, Seyn relaxed and took as much of Ksar's cock into his mouth as he could. Another wave of strange pleasure hit his senses and Seyn shivered.

"Who's enjoying it now?" said the hated voice in his head.

His eyes snapping open, Seyn glared at Ksar and thought at him, *"It's hardly my fault I'm so good at this that your shields are failing."*

Ksar's eyes narrowed.

And then that bastard let his shields down completely, and Seyn moaned as that weird pleasure assaulted his senses, making him dizzy with it, and he needed—he needed—

Seyn started sucking the cock harder, slurping all over it in an entirely indecent manner, like a filthy whore, not the prince he was.

He hated it, hated that he couldn't stop doing it, but he *needed* to do it, to satisfy that foreign, unfamiliar need. It was like being thirsty but not possessing a mouth to sate that thirst. It was immensely frustrating—reaching for something that wasn't there—and Seyn sucked the hot length in his mouth harder, needing it, needing—

Hard fingers suddenly buried in his hair and forced him to stop. Seyn whined in protest. No! He wanted—he wanted—

"Open your eyes," Ksar said. "Look at me."

Ksar's eyes were hooded, revealing nothing of his emotions, though his expression was set into tight lines. "You do look good with a cock in your mouth," he said, stroking Seyn's cheek—his own cock through Seyn's cheek. "Quiet is a good look on you."

Seyn gave him a baleful look. *"What I'm feeling is your pleasure, not mine. I can feel exactly how much you want to fuck my mouth and choke me on your cock."*

Ksar looked at him steadily. "It doesn't change the fact that right now you're dying for me to fuck your mouth and come in your mouth."

Seyn had never hated him more. Because Ksar was right. He felt nearly dizzy with that need—*he would look so pretty choking on it, all hateful green eyes, flushed pale cheeks and pink lips made to suck his cock*—Seyn moaned, confused by the overwhelming need to fuck his own mouth.

"Do it," he thought. *"Do your worst, asshole."*

Looking him in the eye, Ksar cradled his face and started thrusting, using Seyn's mouth for his pleasure. Using *him.*

It should have been disgusting.

Seyn hated that man, hated him more than anything. He should have hated such a demeaning act.

He hated that he didn't.

Seyn opened his mouth wider, greedy, and so, so hungry (*wanting to get into his throat and fuck it raw so that this mouthy little shit would feel it for days*). The foreign thought made him shiver, his eyes closing as he lost himself in the slick, obscene sounds of Ksar's cock thrusting in and out of his mouth. His jaw was aching already and his lips felt sore, but he didn't care; he felt too good to care about anything but Ksar's cock and the way it was fucking him *just like he'd deserved all along, since he'd been an annoying, mouthy little thing too pretty and young for him.*

The need assaulting his senses became worse, and Seyn whined and grabbed Ksar's hips, trying to get him deeper into him—*yes, like this, so pretty full of his cock*—and then his world shattered, waves upon waves of pleasure hitting Seyn's senses as Ksar's cock erupted in his mouth, filling him with his ejaculate.

Holy shit, Seyn thought, blinking dazedly as he swallowed the come as best he could. He felt…he felt…If this was what sex felt like secondhand, he couldn't wait to experience it himself—with someone else. Someone he didn't hate.

Ksar's softening cock slipped out of his mouth.

Licking his lips, Seyn looked up and raised an eyebrow. "Well?" he said and paused, surprised by the hoarseness of his voice. "Not so bad for a little boy, was it?

Zipping up his pants, Ksar gave him a cool look. If Seyn didn't know better, he'd never guess what Ksar had been doing just a few moments ago.

"Passable," Ksar said.

Seyn almost choked with rage. "Right," he said tightly, springing to his feet. "That would be more believable if I weren't a touch-telepath."

Ksar gave a disinterested shrug. "It's a physical reaction. Even a terrible blowjob can get the job done. I've had better."

Seyn didn't know why that infuriated him more than anything Ksar had ever said to him.

"I don't care whether this was up to your mighty standards," Seyn bit off, crossing his arms over his chest. "You'll still have to keep your part of the deal."

The bastard had the nerve to look irritated. "And what would that be?"

"You'll break my bond to you."

A muscle twitched in Ksar's jaw. "I thought we were already over this. It's not that simple."

Seyn scoffed. "Please. As if I don't know that you can *make* it simple if it isn't."

"I'm flattered you think so highly of me, but I'm not a miracle worker," Ksar said, turning away and heading for the door. "Borg'gorn, unlock the door."

Seyn glared at his back. "If you don't break my bond to you, I'll tell everyone about your telepathy. It's not a threat. I'm just telling you what's going to happen."

Ksar paused, his back to him. "I'll let you know if I find a solution."

Before Seyn could say anything, Ksar left, the door sliding shut after him.

As soon as Ksar was out of his sight, Seyn became aware of several things that he had barely noticed while Ksar was there: his knees hurt, his jaw ached like hell, and there was a strange taste in his mouth.

Seyn made a face. Gross.

"Borg'gorn, may I have a glass of water?"

"Of course, Your Highness," the AI said. "On the table."

Seyn picked up the glass that had appeared on the table. He gulped down the water, eager to erase the taste from his mouth, but it didn't work as well as he'd hoped. It was impossible to completely forget the feeling of that hot, thick length in his mouth, the punishing grip in his hair, and the silver eyes fixed on him intently.

Running a hand over his warm face, Seyn shook his head. He wasn't going to think about it. What had happened, had happened. There was no point in dwelling on it. And he certainly wasn't going to dwell on Ksar's sneered words that he'd had better.

It didn't matter. He didn't care. The asshole could fuck every whore in the galaxy for all Seyn cared. He didn't give a shit.

"Your Highness?" The AI sounded hesitant. Almost awkward.

Seyn grimaced, realizing that Borg'gorn had seen and heard everything that had happened in this room. The AI had been a witness to his humiliation. *I've had better.* The ever-present AIs normally never bothered him, but for the first time in his life, Seyn wished they didn't know everything.

"I have known Prince Ksar all his life," Borg'gorn said. "I have observed that he tends to be particularly cruel when he is bothered by something."

Seyn frowned.

The AI was right.

Ksar never lowered himself to such ill-mannered insults unless he was thrown off-balance, which had to mean that Ksar had totally enjoyed the sex more than he'd let on. Seyn had *felt* the extent of Ksar's pleasure. He shouldn't have let Ksar's words hurt him. No matter what Ksar claimed, he wanted him—wanted him enough to stick his cock into Seyn's mouth against his better judgment.

He could use that.

"Thanks for your insight, Borg'gorn," Seyn said, heading for the door, the beginning of a plan forming in his mind.

He wasn't going to let Ksar make him feel small.

Not again.

Chapter 5

Ksar struggled to maintain the expression of polite interest as Councilor Xuvok talked his ear off about the bill he intended to propose in the next session of the Council. Normally, he had little patience for the man, but the alternative—exchanging small talk with members of high society—was even less appealing.

Taking a sip from his drink, Ksar glanced around the crowded ballroom of the First Royal Palace and suppressed a grimace, catching blatant stares from all over the room. He attended such social gatherings rarely for a reason. Or perhaps the fact that he attended them so rarely was the main reason he seemed to attract more stares than any other member of the royal families. A miscalculation on his part.

"…I hope I'm not overstepping, but I have to say I admire your restraint, Your Highness," Councilor Xuvok said. "I'm not certain I'd be as indifferent if my bondmate appeared so…taken with another individual."

Ksar gave him a flat look. "I beg your pardon?"

Xuvok fidgeted, his face reddening under his gaze. "Prince Seyn has been dancing with Ambassador Denev all evening. Surely you've noticed that?"

Ksar took another sip from his drink. He didn't look Seyn's way. "Prince *Seyn'ngh'veighli* can dance with whoever he wishes to dance. It's of no consequence to me or our bond."

"Of course," Xuvok said hurriedly. "I meant no offense, Your Highness. Just…" He tugged at his tight cravat. "I hold you in very high esteem, and I strongly dislike the malicious gossip people—some other people, not me, of course—spread about Prince Seyn—Prince Seyn'ngh'veighli. I simply wanted to make sure that you were aware of it."

Ksar barely held back a scathing comment. He would have to be blind and deaf to miss all the "malicious gossip" about Seyn's behavior and their bond. It was hardly a secret that he and Seyn didn't get along. Ksar was always careful to be polite when he talked about his supposed bondmate in public, but the fact that he largely ignored Seyn when they attended the same social events certainly wasn't missed by the gossipmongers.

Ksar glanced at the other end of the ballroom where Seyn was holding court, surrounded by a crowd of admirers, and had to make an effort to keep his expression blank.

Seyn was still smiling at Ambassador Denev and touching his arm. Ksar didn't need to read the Ambassador's mind to know what he was thinking as he stared at Seyn's mouth while Seyn chatted with him animatedly. Like most people in Seyn's little entourage of admirers, Ambassador Denev was a foreigner, his biology—and sexual libido—not suppressed by the bond that most Calluvians had. One day that flirty little shit was going to end up in trouble.

But *he* wasn't Seyn's minder. Ksar wasn't his anything. Contrary to what everyone thought, he wasn't actually Seyn's bondmate. There was no reason for him to pay any attention to what Seyn was doing.

No reason at all.

Except Seyn was starting to cross the line of propriety, more than he usually did. If even an old, self-absorbed politician like Xuvok noticed Seyn's behavior tonight, it would inevitably reflect poorly on Ksar, too.

"Speaking of my bondmate," Ksar said. "I believe I promised him a dance. If you'll excuse me, Councilor."

Councilor Xuvok's eyes widened. "Of course, Your Highness, of course," he said quickly, failing to hide his surprise.

With a short nod, Ksar headed toward Seyn, projecting a mild compulsion not to engage him in conversation.

The crowd of Seyn's admirers quieted down as he approached, their emotions a mix of surprise, apprehension, and discomfort. So they did remember that Seyn was betrothed. How nice of them.

As for the object of their affections, either Seyn was pretending not to see him or he was genuinely engrossed in his conversation with Ambassador Denev. Both options were equally irritating.

Hasty bows followed by a chorus of "Your Highness!" finally made Seyn turn his head.

He stared at Ksar as conversations around them came to a halt.

After a significant pause that felt like an intentional slight, Seyn greeted Ksar with a shallow bow. "Yes?" he said, his face giving nothing away.

He somehow managed to make a single word sound extremely aggravating.

Ignoring the stares and whispers, Ksar said, "I believe you promised me a dance." Seyn had promised him no such thing, but Ksar didn't expect him to call him out on his lie in such a public setting.

Seyn cocked his head to the side, his dark-red cravat loose enough to reveal the graceful curve of his neck to the greedy eyes of his fans. The color should have made him look pale and washed out, but to Ksar's irritation, it only made those green eyes appear even deeper and more vibrant.

"A dance?" Seyn said, as if he'd never heard the word before, which was rich considering that he'd been dancing all evening with his legion of "friends." Seyn looked around demonstratively before giving Ksar a sweet smile. "Sorry, but there's no music. No one is dancing."

Ksar glanced toward the musicians and tilted his head slightly.

They scrambled for their instruments, and a few moments later, the familiar opening notes of a traditional sanguinn sounded.

"Aren't they?" Ksar said, offering his gloved hand to Seyn.

Seyn slipped his hand into Ksar's, hissing, "Arrogant ass," just for Ksar's ears.

"Language," Ksar murmured.

"Fuck you," Seyn said with a sweet smile for the benefit of the other people watching them. "You *are* an arrogant ass. This is not your grand clan. You aren't supposed to give orders here. The First Queen might take exception to your bossy attitude toward her subjects."

"I'm the Lord Chancellor of the planet," Ksar said, leading him to the center of the ballroom as other couples hurried to join them. "Technically, subjects of all grand clans are my subjects."

"I'm pretty sure it doesn't work like that," Seyn said with a snort.

Ksar settled his hand on Seyn's lower back. A sanguinn wasn't a dance Ksar would have chosen himself—it was a little too intimate—but now they had no choice in the matter.

"Since when do you dance with me?" Seyn said. "What do you want?"

"I want you to stop making a spectacle of yourself," Ksar said, leading him through the steps of sanguinn. "You were all but groping Denev all evening."

"Groping?" Seyn said. "I touched his sleeve, you insufferable ass—" He cut himself off, and stared at Ksar. "All evening? I had no idea you were paying such close attention to me."

Bowing to him, Ksar shot him a flat look but couldn't refute it, because they had to switch their dance partners with the couple to their right.

When Seyn took his hand again, Ksar said, "I don't need to pay any attention to your appalling conduct. There are always more than enough well-meaning people eager to tell me about it. You're making me the laughingstock."

Seyn smiled. "If you don't want my 'appalling conduct' to reflect poorly on you, break my bond to you."

Ksar looked over his shoulder. "It's not that simple. I already told you that."

"It's been ten days," Seyn said, gripping his shoulder harder. "You've had enough time to find a solution."

Ksar said nothing.

"You know what?" Seyn said softly. "If I didn't know better, I'd think you don't want me to be free of you."

Ksar gave a sharp laugh. The couples around them turned and stared at them, not even pretending anymore that they weren't gawking. "Yes, that must be it," Ksar said dryly. "Don't be ridiculous."

"It's not that ridiculous," Seyn said, his voice becoming honey sweet. Smiling, he met Ksar's eyes. "I have ample evidence that you want me."

Ksar struggled to keep his face expressionless. He didn't appreciate being reminded of his lapse of self-control. "On a very superficial level. No more than I would want any passably good-looking man."

"Passably good-looking?" Seyn glared at him, rage coming off him in searing waves. "I *felt* how much you enjoyed yourself when I…" He flushed, glancing around, and whispered into Ksar's ear, "You loved making me suck your cock. You loved sticking your cock in me. You can't deny it."

Ksar licked his dry lips. "I'm not a slave to my baser instincts," he said, even as his hand on Seyn's lower back tugged him closer. "I assure you I don't allow them to control me."

Warm breath tickling the shell of Ksar's ear, Seyn said in a low voice, "Are you saying that if I offer to suck your cock right now, you'll say no?"

The cock in question twitched, and Ksar felt a twinge of disgust with himself. He *wasn't* a slave of his body. He would be damned if he let his cock—and Seyn— manipulate his actions.

Seyn didn't want him.

Seyn wasn't physically capable of wanting. All he wanted was to manipulate him to achieve his goals.

Rationally, Ksar could almost admire Seyn's shrewdness. The irrational part of him wanted to wring Seyn's pretty neck for daring to play him.

"No," he said coolly, looking Seyn in the eye. "But I won't say no if Prince Aedan makes the same offer. Or Lord Zayne. Or your precious Ambassador Denev. I'm not particularly picky about where I put my cock. Even you will do."

A look of pure hatred flashed across Seyn's face. "Heavens, I hate you so much."

Ksar bowed to him mockingly and strode away as the last notes of sanguinn sounded in the ballroom.

He refused to be bothered by Seyn's words. Seyn's hurt pride was of no consequence to him. It was nothing the brat didn't deserve for attempting to lead him by his cock. That should teach Seyn that trying to manipulate him was an exercise in futility.

Ksar ignored the small voice at the back of his mind that said,

But why won't you let him go?

Chapter 6

Seyn's hands were shaking as he moved down the dark corridor. Part of him wanted to turn back and leave before he was caught. If he got caught in the Second Royal Palace so late in the night, his reputation—what was left of it, anyway—would be absolutely destroyed.

He didn't turn back. Every time he was tempted to, all he had to think about were Ksar's sneered, mocking words that anyone, even Seyn, would do. No, he wasn't turning back. He would show Ksar. He would prove to him that Seyn wasn't just anyone. He would make Ksar *beg*. Beg and crawl. And then he would laugh and reject him.

The mere thought of it—of Ksar being reduced to a pathetic, obsessed thing, crawling and begging for crumbs of his attention—was so sweet that Seyn couldn't stop himself from smiling.

It was worth the risk to his reputation. Besides, it wasn't like he'd broken into the palace or anything. He'd merely stayed after visiting Harry, stayed long past visiting hours, hiding in one of the hundreds of uninhabited rooms. Not that he'd been *hiding*, per se; he just wanted to avoid the society members and politicians visiting the Queen or the Lord Chancellor.

The last thing he needed was for people to notice that he'd been hanging around the Second Royal House at night. After the dance yesterday, he and Ksar had been the focus of enough gossip and talk without adding to it.

And if the room he'd stayed in happened to be one of the few rooms not monitored by the palace AI, Seyn could always claim obliviousness. Harry was the only person who knew better—it had been Harry who had told him years ago all the secrets of the palace—but after their return from Earth, Harry wasn't exactly in a talkative mood and he wasn't likely to tell anyone the truth. Harry had been very distant and withdrawn, actually, but Seyn figured it was normal, given the circumstances, and he respected Harry's wishes to be left alone for the time being.

In the meantime, he could deal with Ksar's bullshit.

Despite the late hour, Seyn knew Ksar would be in his study. While any normal person wouldn't be working at midnight, Ksar wasn't a normal person. He tended to return home late and then work from home until the small hours of the morning, the freak. If it were anyone other than Ksar, Seyn would feel sorry for him for having such insane workload, but it was Ksar, so he hoped that one day the asshole would get buried alive under a mountain of paperwork.

The corridors of the Second Royal Palace were eerily quiet at night. The palace seemed strangely abandoned. Seyn knew the Queen and the King-Consort lived in another wing, Harry wasn't interested in leaving his rooms, and Princess Sanyash rarely visited her childhood home these days, but still.

The creepy silence in such a grand place made Seyn a little uncomfortable.

Perhaps it was the lack of servants. The Second Royal House was one of the few royal families that had abandoned the use of servants in favor of robots. Seyn's home was nowhere near as quiet and creepy at night.

"Ahem. Do you need directions, Your Highness?" a familiar voice said.

Borg'gorn.

Seyn almost face-palmed. He should have thought of this. This corridor definitely wasn't off limits to the AI. It might be dark there, but the AI likely had multiple sensors that could detect Seyn's presence. Considering that Borg'gorn was the main security measure of the palace, of course he had means to detect intruders. Seyn couldn't believe he'd forgotten that Borg'gorn wasn't just a glorified butler like the AI at his home: he was the most advanced artificial intelligence on Calluvia. The Second Grand Clan had the best programmers on the planet and their AI was incredibly powerful. Borg'gorn could kill him on the spot with ease if he thought Seyn was a threat.

Probably just like Ksar, for that matter.

"I was visiting Prince Harry," Seyn said, figuring if he acted like there was nothing wrong about him creeping in the darkness, there was a chance the AI would let it go.

"I see," Borg'gorn said, his voice so dry it sounded amused. The AI imitated emotions so well it was hard to believe Borg'gorn wasn't a sentient being. "Are you leaving or do you have another appointment, Your Highness?"

"Actually, yes," Seyn said in his haughtiest tone. "I want to meet Ksar."

A pause.

"I do not think the Crown Prince is expecting you, Your Highness."

Seyn pulled a face. "He isn't. I won't take a lot of his precious time. Tell him I'm here and that I won't leave until I speak to him."

"Very well." There was a short silence. "The Crown Prince says he has other matters that require his attention at the moment. I was ordered to show you out."

Pursing his lips, Seyn strode toward Ksar's study.

Upon reaching it, he glowered at the locked door. "Tell him to stop being a coward."

"If I may speak candidly, Your Highness?" the AI said. "The Crown Prince will be more responsive if you appeal to his sense of propriety and duty. You are his betrothed. Perhaps you should simply tell him that you are here to discuss a matter of great urgency that requires his attention instead of trying to insult him, which is a course of action I would not recommend, Your Highness."

Seyn felt a little bewildered.

It wasn't the first time the AI had been so helpful without being asked. Seyn didn't understand why, but he wasn't about to reject the unexpected help. "All right. You can tell him that."

After a few moments, the door slid open. "You may enter, Your Highness."

"Thank you, Borg'gorn."

He slipped inside the study and the door slid shut again.

Seyn leaned against it, his heart beating faster as he stared at the man seated behind the huge desk.

"What is it?" Ksar said impatiently, without bothering to look up from whatever he was working on. "Make it quick. I'm busy."

The reminder that for Ksar he was something insignificant and bothersome only served to infuriate Seyn further. He would show him.

Beg and crawl, Seyn reminded himself. The thought strengthened his resolve.

He rounded the desk, and, pushing Ksar's chair away from it, dropped to his knees in front of him.

That got Ksar's attention.

He stared at Seyn between his thighs, the corners of his mouth turned down and his eyes narrowed. "I thought I made myself clear yesterday. You will gain nothing from doing this."

Seyn gave him a sassy smile, leaning his cheek against Ksar's inner thigh. "We shall see."

Ksar put his hands on the armrests and looked at him impassively, a disdainful twist to his lips. "You're delusional."

Leaning forward, Seyn pressed the tip of his tongue against the bulge between Ksar's legs. "It doesn't look like that from where I am." He mouthed the tip of Ksar's cock through the fabric, looking Ksar in the eye. *"I barely touched you, but you're hard already. All hard and eager for me."*

"You can suck my cock every day and it won't change anything," Ksar's scathing voice said in his head.

Seyn smiled, undoing Ksar's fly. *"Every day, huh?"*

Ksar's gaze darkened. "Don't anger me," he said flatly. "You don't want to anger me. Now get up. You look like a cheap whore."

Seyn felt his face heat up, the haze of rage clouding his mind. "Isn't that what you're into?"

Knocking Seyn's hands away from his crotch, Ksar got to his feet.

"You don't know what I'm into, but it isn't you. Now leave."

Breathing hard, Seyn glared up at that arrogant, impassive face. Heavens, he hated him. Every time Seyn thought it was impossible to hate him more, the urge to punch Ksar in the face rose to unseen levels. There was *nothing* he wanted more than to knock Ksar down a peg or two. He would do anything to achieve that.

"Let me suck your cock," Seyn said softly, looking Ksar in the eye. "I liked it. I want to do it again."

A muscle started ticking in Ksar's jaw. "You can't *want* anything of the sort when you have the bond. Do you take me for a fool?"

Trying to keep his hatred behind his shields, Seyn opened his carefully edited thoughts to Ksar, letting him see the weird, intense pleasure he'd felt when he'd sucked his cock. He'd enjoyed it. He'd hated that he'd enjoyed it but he had. It was true. It might not have been his own pleasure, but it had felt amazing. The slick heat of his mouth around Ksar's cock had felt incredible. He hadn't even known it was possible to experience that kind of pleasure.

"I liked it," Seyn said honestly. "You know I did."

He did want to do it again, just not for the reason he'd stated.

But every good lie contained a bit of truth, and it would be impossible to fool Ksar if he were lying. Granted, if Ksar bothered to push deeper than his surface thoughts, he would see right through his lie, but Seyn wasn't too worried about it—Ksar seemed to have an intense aversion for his "chaotic mind" and was unlikely to do it unless it couldn't be helped.

"Come on," Seyn murmured softly, reaching for Ksar's fly. "Please."

He'd half-expected Ksar to stop him again, but he didn't.

Seyn wet his lips when Ksar's cock sprang free, long, red, and glistening with lubrication. The sight of it seemed incredibly vulgar and wrong, considering that Ksar still had that impassive, haughty look on his face. It boggled Seyn's mind that this pulsing, throbbing organ belonged to that perfect, put-together royal.

Leaning in, he gave the cock a long lick from the base to the tip, shivering at the trickle of pleasure coming from Ksar. Fuck. He'd actually forgotten how good it felt.

"Stop."

Seyn hadn't even noticed that he'd closed his eyes until he had to force them open.

Ksar was staring at him with an intense, unreadable look. "Clasp your hands behind your back and keep them there."

Suppressing the urge to be contrary, Seyn did as he was told.

Ksar sat down in his chair, and, grabbing Seyn's hair, yanked his face down to his crotch, his cheek pressing against Ksar's cock.

"Look at you," Ksar said, his other hand unbuttoning Seyn's collar. He dragged his cock down Seyn's chin, down his neck, smearing the lubricant all over his skin, something dark and nasty about his expression, before pushing his cock between Seyn's lips.

Seyn almost lost his balance because of his clasped hands. He glared balefully at Ksar. *Do you have some weird bondage fetish?* he thought at Ksar.

"No," Ksar said, pushing into his mouth slowly, his hand stroking Seyn's throat from the outside, as if he wanted to feel his cock in Seyn's throat. "I just like the idea of forcing you to take it."

"You're sick."

Ksar's lips curled. "People can get aroused by the most outlandish, strange thoughts—thoughts they would never act on. But then again, I wouldn't expect you to know."

"Why am I not surprised that you remain the same condescending asshole even during sex?"

"Sex?" Ksar said with a laugh, even as his cock started to thrust into him and his eyes glazed over with pleasure. "This isn't sex."

"Your cock in my mouth could have fooled me."

Ksar looked him in the eye. "Sex needs at least two adult participants enjoying themselves. This is you servicing me for some misguided reason. Nothing more."

Seyn was really tempted to bite off his cock. He was also really tempted to keep sucking it, to suck it harder, just a little more—

No. He wasn't there to suck Ksar's cock. He was there to make Ksar lose his composure and leave him hanging, not to enjoy it.

Seyn pulled off.

Ksar glared at him, his eyes glassy and a flush of color high on his cheekbones. "I didn't tell you to stop."

Seyn got to his feet and smiled, clenching his trembling fingers into fists. "I've just remembered that I have other, more important matters that require my attention." Throwing someone's words back at them had never felt better.

Ksar gave him a withering look, waves of suppressed rage coming off him.

"What, you thought I was really gagging for your cock?" Seyn laughed, straightening to his full height and rolling his shoulders. "I'm a son of the Third Royal House. We don't gag for anything or anyone. People gag for us."

Smiling, he turned on his heel and headed toward the door.

He didn't reach it.

He was yanked back, turned around, and slammed against the antique bookcase. Things fell to the floor and shattered, but all Seyn could see was the cold fury in Ksar's eyes before Ksar's mouth slammed against his throat, sucking a bruise into his skin.

A wave of need crashed into him with an urgency that made Seyn whine. He gasped, fisting Ksar's hair and yanking him closer to his neck. He shivered as delicious waves of pleasure traveled from Ksar's lips to his skin—pleasure and hunger, so much *hunger* it made him moan pitifully.

He raked his fingers down Ksar's back and slipped his hands under his shirt, wanting more, and finding it as his palms roved all over the smooth expanse of Ksar's muscular back. The increased skin contact only heightened the hunger, making it overwhelming—*and he ground against the little shit's hip, wanting to fuck him up, screw him right there, against that door until Seyn was so full of his cock he could feel it against his heart.*

"Is that what you want?" Seyn said breathlessly as Ksar abused his neck. "I'll let you do it—If you break my bond to you."

Ksar went utterly still.

And then he pulled back, his face hard as stone.

Only his eyes were burning with some emotion Seyn couldn't quite put a name to. Hatred? Disgust?

"Get out," Ksar said flatly.

Looking at him uncertainly, Seyn touched the stinging skin of his neck. "Look—"

"Who would have thought," Ksar said, redoing his fly and righting his clothes. His voice was cold as ice. "Who would have thought that *a son of the Third Royal House* would be willing to whore himself out to someone he claims to loathe."

Seyn lifted his chin. "I offered it *because* I loathe you. I want to be free of you."

Ksar looked at him for a long moment, his jaw locked tight.

"You want to be free of me? Fine."

Seyn's heart skipped a beat. "Really?"

Ksar turned away and walked to the open window. "Yes. If you're that desperate, I will break your bond."

Seyn eyed his back, not trusting him one bit. "Now?"

Ksar made a scoffing sound. "Your bond isn't the only thing tying you to me. Your House signed a betrothal contract with mine. Dissolving our betrothal will be much harder than breaking the bond physically. I need time."

Chewing on his lip, Seyn watched him suspiciously. "But you can break the bond now," he pressed. "And we can work together on breaking the betrothal contract."

Ksar turned around, his expression unimpressed. "You have no idea what you are asking for. You've had your bond since birth and you have no idea what it's like to live without it. All your senses will become much better. You will give yourself away immediately."

Seyn crossed his arms over his chest. "If Harry could manage not to give himself away, I can manage."

"If my brother managed to hide it, it doesn't mean you can. Harht's a throwback. His physiology is different from yours, so there's no telling what would happen to you. And his bond weakened gradually; it wasn't forcibly removed. Not to mention that Harht is a very mild-tempered person. That's likely the reason he didn't give himself away." Ksar's lips curled into a sardonic smile. "Mild-tempered isn't the word I would use to describe you. You would be a mess—a bigger mess than you already are."

Seyn wasn't fazed. He walked over to him. "I don't care. As long as the bond to you is gone, I'll be happy. I can handle it. Do it."

For a long moment, Ksar just looked at him with a pinched expression on his face.

"Fine," he said tersely. "But don't tell me I didn't warn you."

He laid a hand on Seyn's cheek and looked him in the eye.

Seyn swallowed. "You didn't need to touch Harry to restore his bond to Leylen," he said, suppressing the urge to squirm away from the touch. Every time Ksar touched him, it made him feel...agitated.

"Harht's bond had nothing to do with me," Ksar said. "I wasn't lying when I told you that performing such procedures on your own mind was harder. Now do be quiet for once. I need to focus."

Seyn fell quiet, even though his heart felt like it was about to jump out of his chest.

He couldn't believe it was finally happening—that he was going to be rid of his hated bond and this awful man.

Time seemed to positively drag.

When Seyn started thinking that Ksar wasn't actually doing anything, he felt it. The...*something* at the back of his mind, something he hadn't even noticed until now, was weakening, thinning, stretching to the limit. It made Seyn's whole body tense up involuntarily.

"*Don't resist,*" Ksar's voice said in his head. "*Isn't that what you want?*"

It was.

Of course it was.

Seyn forced himself to relax, bracing himself for what was about to happen.

He still wasn't ready.

All his senses went overload in an instant, like a forceful current trying to fit through a tiny opening, and a low whine left Seyn's lips as he gulped the air greedily.

He was hyperventilating, Seyn realized dazedly. He was trembling all over, feeling hot and cold all at once. His clothes felt like too much, and he wanted to crawl out of them, out of his own skin. His sense of smell and his hearing seemed to become ten times sharper, and he could even hear the frantic beat of his own heart.

He took a deep breath and he could feel every molecule in his lungs, feel each one racing through his arteries.

He could feel his body as he never had before, he could feel each muscle tightening and loosening, and—

Squeezing his eyes, Seyn moaned, overwhelmed and disoriented, trying to adjust to the sensory overload.

"I did warn you."

Snapping his eyes open, Seyn glared at Ksar, whom he found watching him with mild curiosity, as if he was a lab rat.

"Fuck—you," he stuttered through his clanking teeth. "Asshole."

Leaning back against his desk, Ksar raised his eyebrows. "You must feel well enough if you can still insult me."

"I would find—strength—to insult you—even if I were dying," Seyn managed, glowering at him. The longer he stared at the bastard's face, the hotter he felt. Rage felt different without the bond, sharper, more intense, his skin tingling all over with it. Fuck, he wanted—he wanted to *destroy* Ksar, bury his hands in that dark hair and mess it up, yank it until the asshole cried out, and then—and then—

Ksar's shoulders tensed up, his disinterested body language disappearing. "Of course," he murmured, eyeing Seyn with an expression that was half-speculative, half...something else. "I should have expected this."

Seyn stepped closer to him, clenching his trembling fingers and unclenching them. "What?" he bit off. Although he'd stopped stuttering so much, he still felt too hot and shaky, his skin oversensitive. "Why are you looking at me that way, asshole?"

Ksar's lips twitched. "Your ignorance is as appalling as your language. What do you think you're feeling?"

Seyn wanted to punch him, slam into him, wrap his fingers around that muscular throat, and *squeeze.*

"Disgust and hatred."

Ksar laughed, white teeth flashing. "Hatred, maybe. Disgust? I don't think so."

"You actually think you know better than me?" Seyn bit out, shoving at Ksar's chest with his hand. "You impossible, arrogant—"

Ksar caught his forearms and flipped them over so that Seyn was the one pressed against the desk. "Is this disgust?" he said, *grinding* his hips into Seyn's.

Seyn's mouth went slack, his eyes widening and his body jerking violently as flames erupted under his skin—or at least it felt that way.

"Let me tell you what this is," Ksar said. He pushed his crotch flush against Seyn's, making Seyn go cross-eyed with weird, violent pleasure.

Ksar leaned into his ear and said,

"Desire."

No!

"I don't desire you," Seyn managed, his gaze becoming unfocused as he struggled not to grind against Ksar's muscular thigh. "I hate you."

Ksar chuckled, his grip on Seyn's forearms not loosening one bit. "Newsflash, you little fool: it's entirely possible to want someone you loathe." He pushed his erection against Seyn's, making Seyn shudder and whine. "Or I wouldn't want an annoying, spoiled little shit like you."

"Fuck you," Seyn said, even as his hips pushed back against Ksar's. It was mortifying, but he couldn't stop doing it, all but riding Ksar's thigh, needing the friction, needing it like air.

Ksar made an irritated noise and, letting go of Seyn's arms, slipped his hands down to work on their flies.

Seyn's hands were free now. He could leave. He should leave. Now.

Except his body refused to listen to the commands of his brain, fine tremors of need racking his body violently. He *wanted.* Seyn groaned as a warm, big hand closed around his aching cock—around both their cocks.

"Want me to stop?" Ksar murmured into his ear, breathing unsteadily as he rubbed his leaking cock against Seyn's. "I can stop."

"Don't you fucking dare," Seyn bit out, grabbing fistfuls of Ksar's muscular buttocks and yanking his hips closer.

Ksar's hoarse laugh was the last thing Seyn remembered before he was lost to a daze of need so violent he was shaking with it. Ksar's hand felt amazing on his cock and the velvety hardness of Ksar's erection felt even better. It felt so wrong and yet so good. It had no right to feel this good, not with this man. They both had all their clothes on, their cocks in Ksar's fist the only skin contact between them.

It felt obscene.

They rutted together like animals, and a part of Seyn was utterly disgusted by the dirty, base nature of the act. He was a prince—they both were—and yet he was whining and thrusting into the hand of a man he hated more than anything, like some kind of animal in heat. But fuck, he needed it, this filthy, base act, and before long, Seyn found himself on his back with his legs wrapped around Ksar's waist, moaning lowly as Ksar thrust against him so hard that the sturdy desk beneath Seyn creaked. Seyn didn't care. All he cared about was the pleasure fogging his mind at every thrust of Ksar's erection against his own aching cock. He was clawing at Ksar's back, trying to tug him closer, needing just a bit more—

Stars exploded behind Seyn's eyelids, pleasure like no other sweeping through his body. He groaned and went limp on the desk, breathless and shocked to his core. Vaguely, he was aware of Ksar saying something and his ejaculate spilling against his stomach, but he barely registered it.

He was floating. He felt so good. He felt like he was born anew, aftershocks of pleasure making him smile dumbly.

And then reality came crashing back.

Seyn shoved Ksar off and scrambled to his feet. His hands shaking, he fixed his fly, his stomach turning when he saw the sticky mess at the front. No, he wasn't thinking about that.

Behind him, Ksar snorted. "It's hardly the end of the world," he said in his infuriating monotone. "It doesn't have to mean anything. Stop panicking."

Refusing to look at him, Seyn stormed out of the room, confused, horrified, and disgusted to his core.

What had he been thinking?

How could he have done that—now that he was finally free?

Chapter 7

Seyn stared at his niece, watching in fascination as she played with her legs.

Three months away from birth, she was already beautiful, with perfect little fingers and toes and a cute frown on her wrinkly face. He could sense her emotions a little, even through the thick walls of the artificial womb. She was confused about something. It was kind of amusing, considering that she was playing with her own legs.

"What are you doing here?"

Seyn flinched, his body tensing involuntarily. Shit. Even after thirteen days without the bond, he still had trouble dealing with abrupt sounds.

"Just came to say hi to my favorite niece," Seyn said, turning to smile at his older brother.

Jamil snorted and sat down next to him. "She's your only niece," he said, lightly touching the womb with his fingers. "Good morning. How is my beautiful girl today?"

The baby didn't react at all, the womb's walls too thick for her to hear her father.

Jamil's expression was wistful. "Sometimes I wonder if she feels lonely in there. I know it's ridiculous. We all were born that way, and we turned out fine."

"Define fine," Seyn said with a snort, and Jamil's lips curled into a crooked smile.

Silence fell over the room.

"Maybe it isn't that ridiculous," Seyn said after a while, watching his niece pensively. All telepathic races considered casual physical touch invasive because of touch-telepathy, but modern Calluvians touched each other very rarely compared even to other telepathic species. "Maybe we aren't much for physical touch because we got used to being isolated from before our birth." It was an interesting thought. Harry was the result of a natural pregnancy and he was definitely more touchy-feely than him.

Jamil shrugged, a strand of dark brown hair falling into his eyes. He pushed it back. "Maybe." His face contorted into a smile that looked more like a grimace. "In any case, the point is moot. I'm lucky that I can have her at all—that Mehmer had preserved his genetic material just months before he…"

Wincing, Seyn sent him a wave of reassurance and comfort, not having missed the way Jamil's deep voice had cracked a little at his dead bondmate's name. Admittedly, offering comfort to his big brother felt a little awkward and strange. Jamil was generally the one who did the comforting when his younger siblings needed it, never vice versa.

Sighing, Jamil reached out to him through their familial bond. "I'm fine, kid."

Seyn hugged him back telepathically, carefully suppressing his own strength; he couldn't let his brother notice how much stronger his telepathy was nowadays.

Thankfully, Jamil didn't seem to notice anything, his mind still a little hazy and distracted, tinged with grief.

It had been only eleven months since his bondmate had died.

Sometimes Seyn wondered what it was like to have a perfectly good, functional bond and a bondmate one actually loved only to lose them in such a horrible way. It was a good thing he would never know.

"Are you, really?" Seyn said, feeling a pang of guilt for being so distracted by his own problems.

Jamil shrugged again, his firm jaw clenching a little. "I still reach for his mind sometimes, but it's getting easier, I suppose. The mind adepts said the bond would heal in time and all I would feel is absence."

That didn't exactly sound reassuring.

"I still don't get why they don't remove the bond from your mind," Seyn muttered, even though he could guess why the mind adepts refused to do that even after one's bondmate's death. On the rare occasion a torn bond compromised the health of the surviving bondmate's mind, they were bonded to someone else again, provided there was a suitable candidate available, like it had happened to Ksar.

But unlike Ksar, Jamil was too old to be bonded again, even if he wished to do so. Everyone else his age was paired up and a thirty-four-year-old man could hardly be bonded to a child.

Other widowers and foreigners were options, Seyn supposed, but it was frowned upon in their social circles. Marriage was considered to be for life, even if one outlived their spouse by many years. Widowers didn't marry a second time. Jamil effectively had little choice but to be alone for the rest of his life.

Considering that his brother had at least a hundred years to live with nothing but the remnants of his bond to a dead man, it sounded...painful. Painful and incredibly lonely.

Seyn suddenly wondered how widowed people were supposed to deal with their physical needs. With their bondmate gone, their sexual urges were no longer limited to their deceased bondmate. Did they arrange clandestine meetings with other widowers? With off-world foreigners? Or were they supposed to remain celibates for the rest of their lives?

"It's against the law," Jamil reminded him, tearing Seyn away from his increasingly inappropriate thoughts. "Besides, the High Adept said the bond had been in my mind too long and it isn't safe to remove it. It's interwoven with everything by now."

Seyn frowned. Could that be true? Ksar had been able to remove Seyn's bond without much effort, but Ksar was a fucking telepathic freak, and Jamil was eleven years older than Seyn, his bond older—not to mention that it hadn't been one-sided.

"And to be honest..." Jamil added quietly, his eyes fixed on his unborn daughter. "I want to keep my bond. I still feel him that way, a little. Like an echo. I don't want to pretend he never existed. He did."

Seyn's hand twitched, the urge to hug his brother almost irresistible. It was such a bizarre feeling. After his bond had broken, he'd been feeling constantly torn between craving and fearing physical contact. But he couldn't touch his brother, not in the state he was in. Physical contact would be too much for his senses right now.

Jamil's grief would likely overwhelm him and he would give himself away.

It wasn't that he didn't trust his brother. But the fewer people knew about his lack of bond, the safer it was. Technically, not having a bond was against the law. If something went wrong, Seyn didn't want to drag his family down with him.

"You still didn't tell me why you were hiding here," Jamil said suddenly, turning his face to Seyn.

People always said he and Jamil looked alike, except for the hair color, and Seyn had never really liked such comments. He wasn't exactly insecure about his looks, but he thought comparisons to Jamil weren't really flattering for him. While they did look alike, Seyn had always thought Jamil was better in every way. His brother's jaw was firmer, his lips fuller, and his green eyes seemed deeper, maybe thanks to his dark eyelashes. Not to mention that Jamil was taller and more muscular than him. Seyn had always felt like a smaller, paler imitation of his older brother every time people mentioned the resemblance.

But nowadays, with Jamil's face thinner than it used to be and his shoulder-length hair a bit longer, Seyn had to admit the resemblance really was uncanny.

Seyn put on his best confused expression. "I wasn't hiding."

Jamil snorted. "And I suppose you weren't declining all invitations, either."

Seyn winced. He had hoped his family had been too busy to notice that.

"Just not feeling it," he said, avoiding his brother's gaze.

"You?"

Laughing, Seyn rolled his eyes. "I can get tired of socializing, too." His mind raced as he considered and discarded possible explanations for his behavior. He could hardly tell his brother the truth: that big gatherings of people were overwhelming to his heightened senses. Granted, it hadn't been as bad in the last couple of days as it had in the beginning, but his control was still far from perfect.

In fact, Seyn was positive he was going to go crazy if things didn't get easier. He could handle oversensitive hearing, he could handle a better sense of smell and taste, he could even handle his stronger telepathy, but nothing had prepared him for how *horny* he would constantly be. It was awful.

Rationally, he knew it made sense. His body was dealing with unfamiliar hormones, basically going through the puberty he would have gone through years ago if the bond hadn't been suppressing his ability to feel arousal. So it was probably normal to get hard for no reason at all, and in the most awkward of situations, but it was a small comfort when Seyn was attending a ball and surrounded by hundreds of curious eyes as he tried to hide an inappropriate erection. Avoiding all social gatherings was kind of necessary until he figured out how to control his stupid cock.

But it wasn't exactly something he could tell his recently widowed brother. Due to their significant age difference, they had never been particularly close. Truth be told, Seyn had always felt a little uncomfortable around his happily bonded brother and his bondmate—like an outsider looking in at something that would never be his.

And now with Mehmer dead, he felt even more awkward around Jamil, feeling irrationally guilty for all the times he envied his brother's happiness, as if it was his fault that Mehmer had been killed by the rebels.

Fortunately, Seyn had a foolproof way to change the subject of the conversation. "I had a fight with Ksar," he said, his face warming a little as he tried not to think about what that "fight" had entailed. His wayward cock twitched, and Seyn crossed his legs with a scowl. "Now I'm avoiding him, because I won't be responsible for my actions if I see his stupid, arrogant face."

As he expected, Jamil heaved a long-suffering sigh. "For heaven's sake, Seyn. You should try harder to get along with your bondmate. Every relationship needs work, bond or no bond. Personally, I don't get why you dislike him. He's highly intelligent, and he's perfectly reasonable and polite—"

"To you, maybe," Seyn said with a scoff. "You're the Crown Prince of our grand clan. He sees you as his equal."

"Not really," Jamil said. "His social standing is quite a bit higher domestically, and a lot higher in the intergalactic political scene. We aren't really equals, so that can't be why Ksar'ngh'chaali is perfectly civil to me."

Seyn's lips twisted. "It isn't exactly comforting, you know."

Jamil chuckled and stood up. Grazing his fingers against the womb's outer wall again, he turned to the door but paused. "Everyone has their own version of the truth, brother. He's not a petty man. Have you ever wondered why he treats you differently from others? Think about it."

And he strode out of the room, leaving Seyn staring after his brother with a frown.

* * *

The horniness wasn't going away.

He was constantly in a state of semi-arousal, and he had no idea how to deal with it. Harry hadn't been very helpful when Seyn had stealthily asked him how he had handled it. Bafflingly, it seemed it had been nowhere near as bad for Harry after his bond had broken. Maybe Ksar had been right, after all, and Harry's different physiology made the difference.

In any case, Seyn couldn't really ask Harry in depth without explaining his own situation. The conversation had been extremely awkward and uncomfortable as it was. It was obvious that even talking about his brief time without the bond was painful for Harry, so Seyn had decided against telling his friend that he didn't have the bond anymore. It would be like rubbing salt into a fresh wound.

He felt guilty enough that he was unbonded while Harry was once again stuck with an unwanted bond.

The only other person he could ask for advice was Ksar, and there was no way in hell he would ask advice from that ass, especially not after…not after what had happened. Not that Seyn allowed himself to dwell on it too much.

What had happened in Ksar's study had meant nothing; these days a strong gust of wind could give him an erection. He had been just too messed up after his bond's breaking. That was all.

Anyway, the point was, he wasn't going to ask for advice from Ksar.

But to his utter bewilderment, Ksar contacted him himself.

Of course, because Ksar lived to make his life uncomfortable, he had unknowingly picked the least convenient moment possible.

"Um," Seyn said intelligently when the palace AI informed him of Ksar's call. He stared at the ceiling, his hands still wrapped around his cock. Ksar had never called him before. He couldn't imagine Ksar ever calling him unless it was a life or death situation.

"I will accept the call," he told the AI reluctantly, taking his hand off his cock and switching on his earpiece. "Yes?" he said as neutrally as he could. After his conversation with Jamil, he was determined to be the better person and try to be civil to Ksar. After all, Ksar *had* kept his promise. Seyn no longer had any reason to antagonize him.

"Where have you been?"

Seyn's hackles rose involuntarily at Ksar's impatient, dismissive tone. It always rubbed him the wrong way that Ksar spoke to him as if he had better things to do and Seyn was merely a nuisance he had to deal with.

"What?" Seyn said, his tone more hostile than before. Screw being civil. Ksar didn't deserve it.

"You have been avoiding all social functions," Ksar said. "People are talking."

"I'm sorry, was there a question somewhere?" Seyn said with fake sweetness. "And since when do I have to explain myself to you?"

"Since I did you a favor and broke your bond," Ksar said. "If you act suspiciously, people will watch you closely. If you give yourself away, you will give me away, too."

"I'll have you know, I've been avoiding social gatherings for precisely this reason," Seyn said sharply, annoyed that Ksar thought he was an idiot. "My control isn't perfect yet. I'm struggling, okay? I don't want to give myself away."

There was silence on the line.

It didn't last long.

"So you're admitting that I was right," Ksar said. His voice didn't sound smug or anything, just his usual flat monotone, but it still managed to make Seyn fume.

"Has anyone told you how annoying your superior attitude is?"

"You have, on multiple occasions. And your insults are getting repetitive and unoriginal."

"Screw you. Asshole."

"As I said, repetitive and unoriginal."

Seyn realized he was smiling. It hit him suddenly how immature the whole argument was and how much he missed it.

He fucking missed insulting Ksar.

It was comfortingly normal in his otherwise dramatically changed life. He felt like a mess of heightened senses and hormones these days, but hating Ksar and arguing with him felt comfortingly familiar.

He kind of…he kind of wanted to see Ksar so that he could insult him to his face.

"Is your control not improving at all?" Ksar said.

The connection was so good that Seyn could hear him drum his fingers. He was probably in his study at home. The hour was late, so his cravat was probably loose—or maybe he had even removed it. He was probably leaning back in his chair, his long fingers drumming over the armrest, his gaze tired but haughty as usual...

Seyn frowned and shook the strange thoughts off. Why was he even thinking about such inane things?

"It is improving," he replied belatedly. "But it's still not fine."

"How strong are you?" Ksar said.

Seyn's lips twisted. "How strong are *you?*" he said, incredulous that Ksar expected an honest answer when he was so tight-lipped about his own telepathy. Seyn couldn't be sure, but he was positive he still wasn't as strong a telepath as Ksar. He was much better than before, but he didn't think he could break or restore someone's bond, and certainly not as easily as Ksar had.

"I'm probably Class 4," Ksar said. "Maybe Class 5."

Seyn snorted. "Right."

"You may choose not to believe me, of course," Ksar said.

Seyn vividly imagined wrapping his hands around Ksar's throat and squeezing.

"Thanks for permitting me," Seyn said, not without sarcasm, his hand creeping down his stomach and cupping his cock. It was baffling that he still hadn't lost his erection, but then again, he'd given up on trying to figure out what made his cock hard.

"What are you doing?" Ksar said, his voice laced with suspicion.

Seyn realized too late that he was breathing too loudly and unsteadily. "Nothing," he said, but he couldn't bring himself to remove his hand from his cock. Fuck, it felt like he'd been hard for ages.

"It doesn't sound like nothing," Ksar said.

"I'm doing sit-ups," Seyn said, pressing the heel of his hand against his erection, trying to stave off his arousal until the end of the call. "You know, gotta keep myself in shape so that I can have lots of sex now that I'm free of you."

"You will do no such thing."

Seyn bit his lip and squeezed his cock, which somehow had gotten *harder* at Ksar's haughty tone. His cock was fucking weird. "Pardon?"

"You heard me," Ksar said. "You may not have the bond anymore, but as far as everyone is concerned, you are still my bondmate and *no one* will—" Ksar cut himself off and then said in a stiff tone, "Your bond wouldn't have allowed you to have sex with someone else, so that would be a dead giveaway that something is amiss."

Seyn scoffed. "What's the point of being unbonded if I'm still shackled to you?"

"That's precisely why I said I must break our betrothal contract first. You're the one who insisted on breaking the bond prematurely."

Seyn rolled his eyes, stroking his cock a little. Even getting the infuriating "you were wrong and I was right" lecture from Ksar wasn't killing his erection. Quite the opposite, in fact. It was beyond baffling. What was *wrong* with him? Did he have a thing for being lectured and humiliated?

"So how close to figuring it out are you?" Seyn said, his voice a little breathless as he tugged at his cock. Screw Ksar. Screw him. It wasn't like he'd know what Seyn was doing. "Hurry up."

"What's the rush?" Ksar said, something ugly about his tone. "Are you that desperate to get fucked?"

His cock throbbed at the word "fucked" uttered in that snobbish voice, and Seyn bit back the moan threatening to leave his lips.

"Screw you. Maybe I'm desperate to fuck someone." Not that he had a preference one way or another, since he'd never tried either, but it was infuriating how easily Ksar assumed that he would be the one spreading his legs. "I'll have you know I like the idea of fucking someone."

Ksar gave a dismissive snort.

Seyn stroked his balls. "You're such an asshole. You really think you know better than me what I'd like?"

"Yes."

Arrogant ass.

"Please enlighten me, then," Seyn said, stroking himself a little faster. He had to admit it was titillating that he was getting away with it right under Ksar's nose—but it didn't mean that he was getting off to the sound of Ksar's voice. He hated Ksar's stupid voice.

"Last time I saw you, you didn't exactly try to be in charge. You were more than willing to just lie under me and let me do all the work."

Seyn flushed, unable to believe Ksar was actually bringing that up—and speaking about it in such a casual, matter-of-fact tone, as if he was discussing weather.

"It doesn't prove anything," Seyn said. "A single occurrence isn't enough to draw correct conclusions."

There was silence on the line.

Seyn flushed, suddenly realizing how his words sounded.

"It wasn't an invitation for a repeat performance," Seyn said stiffly, glaring at the ceiling. "It was a mistake. I was just overwhelmed. If I were thinking clearly, that would never have happened. Not with you."

Ksar said nothing.

"And you're wrong," Seyn said, just to be contrary. "I would totally love to fuck someone."

Ksar made another dismissive, skeptical noise.

"I would!"

He could practically hear Ksar sneer. "Even if you get to put your cock into someone, make no mistake, you'll be the one getting fucked, be it a man or a woman, the mechanics of sex notwithstanding."

Seyn's mouth went dry as he imagined strong hands holding him down as someone rode him, using his cock for their pleasure, using *him* so well he could only beg for more. Fuck.

"But you're such a spoiled little thing," Ksar said, his tone rough and nasty. "You'd prefer to be the one getting pleasured while you do nothing but just lie there and take cock."

Seyn had to bite his hand to muffle his moan. He squeezed his cock with his other hand, imagining it: being bent over a massive desk, strong hands gripping his hips as a heavy body pressed against him from behind, a thick cock thrusting inside him. Seyn had tried fingering himself and found it both enjoyable and frustrating. A cock would probably feel so much better.

"Enjoying yourself?"

Seyn blinked at the ceiling, for a moment unable to comprehend Ksar's words.

When he did, he froze, wide-eyed.

Ksar gave a soft snort. "By all means, don't stop on my behalf."

Seyn scowled, his face uncomfortably warm. He couldn't believe Ksar knew. "Fuck you. I'm not doing it with you listening!"

"You weren't so shy when you thought I didn't know."

"I'm not shy," Seyn bit off, feeling humiliated beyond belief. It must have been so amusing for Ksar to pretend that he had no idea while Seyn made a fool out of himself. "It isn't exactly a turn-on to know that you're listening. I'm just horny all the time, okay? It has nothing to do with you— I would never be attracted to you. You're the last man I'd want."

For a long time, Ksar said nothing.

When he spoke again, his voice was hard and cold. "If you can't keep your hands off your cock even when you speak to a man you claim to loathe, your self-control is pathetic. Work on it. Come up with a believable excuse for why you aren't attending social gatherings. You will not go anywhere until you can keep it in your pants."

Seyn bristled at his overbearing attitude. "I wasn't going to—I'm not stupid. I don't need your instructions. You aren't the boss of me. It's none of your business what I do."

"Until the betrothal contract between our Houses is void and null, you're my business. If you weren't, I wouldn't have wasted my time calling you."

Agh!

Furious, Seyn switched his earpiece off, wishing Calluvians used those old-fashioned phones that he'd seen on some other planets. Slamming a phone down or throwing it away would have been so much more satisfying.

"Asshole," he said to the empty room, still shaking with anger.

Seyn scowled at his hard cock, which still refused to go down. Sighing in annoyance, he took it back into his hand and started fisting it furiously.

Screw Ksar. *Screw* him. Heavens, he hated him so much.

Chapter 8

It was all well and good to say that he would avoid all social gatherings, but there was one Seyn absolutely couldn't avoid: his sister's marriage ceremony. Gynesh would kill him if he did that, and their mothers would never forgive him.

That was how Seyn found himself dressed in the blue and white colors of his House, his hair up in an intricate hairstyle that drew attention to his jawline and lips. He looked good; he knew that.

Gynesh looked positively radiant.

Seyn smiled a little, watching wistfully as his sister's entourage fretted over Gynesh's hair.

"Ladies, she looks perfect as it is," he said, stepping into the room.

The women bowed to him gracefully with a chorus of "Your Highness."

Gynesh smiled at him, her green eyes very striking in contrast with her dark violet hair.

"You may go ahead," she told her ladies-in-waiting and walked toward Seyn. She patted his cheek with a grin. "These cheekbones are unfair to the rest of us mere mortals. You aren't supposed to outshine the bride, you know."

Seyn managed not to flinch at the touch—his control had improved that much—and smiled crookedly at his sister. "Flatterer. No one is outshining you today. Ready?"

Gynesh pulled a face. "A little nervous, but yes."

"What is there to be nervous about?" Seyn said, putting her hand on his arm and leading her out of the room, heading toward the High Hall where the ceremony would take place. "I thought you got along with your bondmate."

"Yes, but he's the King of the Eighth Grand Clan. I'll have much bigger responsibilities as the Queen-Consort than I've ever had as a mere princess."

"You've been trained for the role since birth. You'll be a wonderful queen-consort." Seyn chuckled. "And I'll have to bow to you."

Gynesh wrinkled her nose. "Ugh. I don't want my baby brother to bow to me. " She nudged him playfully. "But it won't be as weird as when I'll have to bow to *you* when you become the Second Grand Clan's King-Consort."

Seyn's smile became strained. He looked straight ahead, avoiding his sister's eyes.

Gynesh sighed. "Are you still fighting with Ksar?"

Seyn pasted on a wide smile. "Let's not talk about me today. This is your day."

Regardless of what he thought about bonding, he tried not to force his opinion on other people.

He knew most other people were perfectly happy with their bonds and the bonding ceremony was one of the most important days in their lives.

His sister liked her bondmate and was excited to marry him. He could be happy for her, even if her marriage meant that she would leave their home.

Seyn almost wished she'd married down her social status; then her husband or wife would have moved in rather than vice versa. But she was marrying a king, even if he was a king of a smaller clan than theirs.

Gynesh let out a chuckle. "My day? You've been a recluse for almost a month. Gossip is running rampant. You're fooling yourself, brother, if you think all eyes won't be on you."

Seyn made a face. "Jamil should have given you away, then."

"You know that would not be proper," Gynesh said, her smile fading.

Seyn sighed. "Sometimes I really hate all our stupid, stifling rules and customs." He wasn't even sure where the custom of widowers not being allowed to give their siblings away had come from. Perhaps it had been considered bad luck. Perhaps it had something to do with the black mourning bracelet Jamil wore as a widower.

Either way, it was stupid. If Jamil's bondmate hadn't died, it would have been Jamil giving Gynesh away, not Seyn. It was also really stupid that their mothers couldn't give Gynesh away, either: tradition dictated that it had to be a male relative, which was blatant discrimination that had no right to exist in the modern world. But no one cared, because it was tradition.

Fuck tradition, seriously. Seyn tried not to think about how it would make Jamil feel to see his younger brother taking his rightful place by Gynesh's side during the ceremony; he felt nervous enough already without adding guilt into the mix.

It would be the first time in a month that his self-control would be tested seriously.

It would also be the first time he'd see Ksar since—

Seyn pushed the thought away. It was irrelevant.

"You're shaking, brother," Gynesh said as they reached the double doors leading to the High Hall of the palace. Seyn could feel the crowd behind the doors without even focusing.

Reinforcing his mental shields, Seyn shrugged. "I don't give my sister away every day. A man is allowed to be a little nervous on such an occasion."

Gynesh didn't look entirely convinced, but, thankfully, she didn't say anything.

"Ready?" he said.

Gynesh licked her lips, running a hand over her blue and white dress that matched his attire. "I don't know."

"You do," Seyn said, taking her hand and kissing her gloved knuckles. "You're ready."

She smiled at him, straightening her shoulders. "I am."

Seyn nodded to the footmen.

They bowed and opened the heavy double doors.

* * *

The ceremony passed in a blur.

Seyn barely registered it, smiling and nodding at hopefully appropriate times, keeping his eyes fixed on Gynesh and King Farhat as they knelt before the High Adept and tied the white ribbon that symbolized their marriage bond to each other's wrists.

He could barely hear the traditional words the High Adept said as he performed the ceremony, his hands on Gynesh and Farhat's heads. Seyn tried to concentrate on the High Adept's face, and tried not to look around, focusing all his mental attention on keeping his shields up.

It still wasn't easy. It was impossible to ignore people's emotions and thoughts in a crowd that big. It didn't help that his sense of smell was overwhelmed by the different fragrances in the room, and his attention kept drifting to conversations that were happening at the other end of the High Hall. It felt like the crowd's thoughts and emotions were pressing down on him from all sides, making him shake with the effort to keep himself from being overwhelmed. Dammit, dammit, dammit—

Suddenly he felt such an unnatural, blessed *silence* that Seyn nearly jumped in surprise.

"You're a mess," a familiar voice said in his head. *"If you don't get better at controlling yourself, it's only a matter of time before you give yourself away."*

Seyn closed his eyes for a moment before turning his head toward the first row where royal members of the largest grand clans sat. He glared when his gaze met Ksar's.

"Get out of my head," he thought as loudly as he could, his eyes roaming over Ksar's formal attire. The bastard looked unfairly good in his House colors, his signet ring glinting on his little finger.

Ksar's lips curled slightly. *"I'm the one keeping you from having a very public breakdown."*

As much as he hated it, Ksar was entirely correct. The knowledge ate at him, but Seyn wasn't an idiot to reject help.

Correctly interpreting his silence for the reluctant agreement it was, Ksar told him, *"It's tiring for me to keep extending my shields to you across the room. Come over here."*

Eyeing him suspiciously—since when had Ksar offered help voluntarily?—Seyn walked toward him, ignoring some curious stares. Thankfully, most people had their eyes on the marriage ceremony and he attracted relatively little attention as he made his way to where Ksar sat with his family.

Upon reaching them, Seyn gave a bow to Ksar's family, receiving a polite smile from Ksar's father, a sharp look from Queen Tamirs and a curious look from Princess Sanyash, who looked very beautiful and very pregnant.

Finally, he turned to Ksar and gave him a shallow bow that was more like a nod. He smiled innocently when Ksar's silver eyes narrowed.

"Sit," Ksar said curtly, gesturing to the empty seat beside him.

The empty seat that shouldn't have been there, actually.

Frowning, Seyn took the seat and murmured, "Where's Harry?"

Ksar gave a slight shrug.

"You don't know?" Seyn said, incredulous. Ksar usually made it his business to know everything; he was the biggest control freak Seyn knew.

"I believe he's moping and I have no patience for that."

Seyn shook his head. "You're such a bastard. He's your brother."

There was a barely noticeable tension at the corners of Ksar's mouth.

"Our family affairs are none of your concern."

Seyn studied him, suddenly wondering if the seemingly heartless bastard was feeling a bit guilty for making his brother miserable.

Leaning close to Ksar's ear, he murmured, "Guilt is an uncomfortable feeling, isn't it?"

Ksar stiffened.

He turned his head, and a shiver ran up Seyn's spine when he felt Ksar's breath on his lips.

It was...disconcerting.

"If I should feel guilty, then so should you," Ksar said softly. "I'm not the one who dragged him back to Earth and gave him a false hope."

Seyn spluttered in indignation. "It's not the same and you know it!" he hissed, grabbing Ksar's arm. Heavens, he wanted to kill him, wanted to wrap his hands around that muscular throat and—and—

"Ahem," came a delicate cough from behind them.

Seyn flinched, only now realizing how close he and Ksar had been.

Pulling back, he looked at Princess Sanyash, who was looking between Seyn and her brother with something like bemusement on her face.

"You are making a scene, brother," she said quietly. "I can't believe I'm saying it, but behave yourself. People are staring."

Ksar gave a clipped nod without even glancing at his sister, his heavy gaze still on Seyn.

For no damn reason, Seyn *blushed,* unable to hold Ksar's gaze for more than a few moments but also unable to stop looking back at him.

What was wrong with him?

"*It's called attraction, you little idiot,*" Ksar's dismissive voice sounded in his head.

Seyn scowled at him. He had a horrible suspicion that Ksar was right, but everything in him rebelled at the idea. He couldn't possibly be attracted to that asshole. Seyn hated him, despised everything about him. He couldn't be attracted to him.

Ksar shot him a flat look. "*I told you: it's entirely possible to be attracted to someone one dislikes — or I wouldn't possibly be attracted to a mouthy, disrespectful brat like you.*"

"Fuck you. And stop reading my mind, you creep."

"*Besides,*" Ksar told him in his head, as if Seyn hadn't said anything. "*Considering that as far as your body is concerned, it's been sex-deprived for years, it's not surprising that you're eager for sex.*"

"I'm not eager for sex," Seyn hissed out, barely audibly. "Not with you!"

Ksar lifted his eyebrows a little and shifted his gaze pointedly to…to Seyn's hand, which was stroking Ksar's biceps.

Seyn stared at it, feeling absolutely mortified and betrayed by his own body. Yanking his hand away, he opened his mouth and closed it without saying anything.

Ksar heaved a sigh, and Seyn hated that he couldn't stop noticing the way it made Ksar's chest expand. Ugh. He almost wanted his stupid bond back. This was horrible.

"*Look,*" Ksar said in his mind, his mental voice laced with irritation. "*It isn't a big deal. I'm well aware that you can't stand me, which is mutual. But we wouldn't want you to give yourself away because your body has too many new hormones you have no idea how to deal with. I'll have sex with you if you want. To take the edge off.*"

Seyn licked his lips, his pulse thundering in his ears. "You don't have to make it sound like such a chore."

Ksar looked him in the eye.

A beat passed, then another.

Seyn felt heat rush toward his groin, *want* making his hands tremble and intensifying the longer he looked into Ksar's eyes.

"It won't be a chore," Ksar said in a low voice, "if you don't make it one."

"Screw you," Seyn said, barely moving his lips, only vaguely aware that everyone was rising to their feet. The ceremony seemed to be over, but it felt so very distant. "Fuck you."

Ksar leaned to his ear and said, "I'll be the one doing it. And you will like it." And then the asshole just *breathed* against the sensitive shell of Seyn's ear, making Seyn tremble violently and let out a small moan.

"My study, ten in the evening."

And with that, Ksar stood and left to congratulate the happy couple, leaving Seyn trying to awkwardly hide the giant bulge in his pants.

Chapter 9

Seyn told himself he wasn't going.

He was determined not to go.

So he had no explanation for what he was doing at the Second Royal Palace at eleven in the evening.

"You're late," Ksar said coldly the moment Seyn walked into his study.

Seyn closed the door and leaned back against it, trembling faintly and hoping Ksar couldn't see it. "Eager?"

Ksar shot him a look that would have been unimpressed if it wasn't also weirdly intense. "I'm not in the mood for your sass," he said, leaning back in his chair and loosening his white cravat. "Come here."

Seyn's heart felt like it was about to jump out of his chest. His knees were weak as he walked toward the man seated behind the desk. It felt like Ksar was the only thing in focus while everything around him seemed hazy.

He straddled Ksar's lap and leaned in. He was breathing unsteadily, but so was Ksar.

"For the record, I hate you," Seyn said, looking from Ksar's eyes to his thin, cruel lips. The urge to bite them was nearly irresistible, but *no*, he wouldn't. That would be too close to kissing, which…No. Just no.

"I fucking despise you," he said before sinking his teeth into Ksar's sharp jaw and almost moaning at the surge of *want*. Shaking with it, he ground his cock against Ksar's stomach as he peppered Ksar's strong jaw and neck with hard kisses and sucks, breathing him in. Ksar's earthy, masculine scent was doing strange things to him. And fuck, the taste of him…The secondhand want he'd felt before was nothing compared to this overwhelming need for—for *something*.

Seyn whined in frustration, hands roaming all over the expanse of Ksar's chest and arms, greedy, wanting to feel skin, wanting to feel closer to the awful man he'd hated all his life.

"Don't leave marks," Ksar said tersely, unbuttoning his own shirt unhurriedly.

Seyn sucked harder on his neck, just to spite him—and, okay, because he wanted to. No matter how hard he kissed the bastard's skin, it just wasn't enough; he wanted more.

Shrugging his shirt off, Ksar sighed and pushed him away. "If we do this, we do it on my terms," he said.

Seyn glowered at him, but then he noticed that Ksar wasn't as indifferent as he pretended to be: he was fully aroused and his muscles were so rigid with tension they looked positively delicious.

It was such a strange thought. Seyn had never thought of another person as delicious, but now, looking at the broad shoulders with muscles rippling under the smooth skin, that was the only thought he had: delicious. He wanted to consume him, lick him from head to toe, leave bruises all over his body, and—fuck, he wanted that asshole to leave bruises all over *him*.

He wanted to have marks on his skin, proof that he affected Ksar as much as he affected him, proof that Ksar wanted him.

"Why on your terms?" Seyn said, his trembling hands traveling down Ksar's chest to his hard stomach. He moved his hand lower, cupping the now-familiar bulge under Ksar's dark pants. "Stop pretending you're doing me a favor. It's not like you get nothing out of this."

Looking at Ksar's face, it was impossible to tell that Seyn was stroking his cock through the fabric. "Take it or leave it," he said testily, his thumb brushing up Seyn's throat. He gave Seyn a half-lidded, haughty look. "You know where the door is."

The most infuriating part was, Ksar's attitude was doing things to Seyn's body it had no business doing. Seyn couldn't believe his cock was actually into Ksar being the bossy asshole he normally was. There was nothing attractive about that kind of attitude. He hated it. But apparently, Seyn's cock disagreed.

Seyn's cock was stupid. Stupid, and seriously messed up.

Seyn tried not to lean into Ksar's touch too much, but he had a feeling he wasn't entirely successful. "And what are you going to do if I agree?"

Ksar looked at him through heavy-lidded eyes, his thumb stroking Seyn's earlobe, making him shiver violently.

His silver gaze didn't look away from him even for a moment, so intense it felt like a physical touch. "I'm going to strip you, bend you over my desk, and give you a thorough fucking. That's all. It's been a long, stressful day and I'm not in the mood to be imaginative."

Seyn wet his lips, his cock twitching but his whole being rebelling at the idea of giving this man that kind of control over him.

"Only if you make it good," Seyn said, feigning nonchalance.

His lips curling, Ksar pushed him off his lap and started unfastening Seyn's shirt. He didn't even glance at his own hands, still holding Seyn's gaze. "Is there a doubt?"

Seyn licked his dry lips again, feeling torn between wanting to punch that arrogant dick and sucking his dick. "If someone told you arrogance was an attractive trait, they lied."

"It's not arrogance," Ksar said, pulling Seyn's shirt off and finally looking away from his eyes.

Seyn shivered under Ksar's heavy gaze on his body. He suppressed the bout of insecurity and doubt.

He knew that by most planets' standards, he looked good. Hell, he knew he looked more than just good. He was on the lean side, but he was toned with muscle, his shoulders, pecs and stomach well defined. He looked after his body, made sure to keep it in perfect shape, a habit more than anything. Ksar often accused him of being a vain attention whore, and while it wasn't true, it…had a grain of truth.

Seyn still cringed when he remembered the phase he'd gone through in his late teens, when he'd gotten into his head that Ksar might actually start liking him if he were as perfect as him. The phase didn't last long, thankfully— he knew better now—but the habit to work out and look as good as possible had stuck.

So yes, he knew he looked good, objectively, but this was *Ksar,* the man who always found some fault in him.

Whatever Ksar was thinking as his hands traveled down Seyn's sides to his waistband, it was hard to tell. Even the skin contact gave no real clue to what Ksar was feeling: Seyn's own lust made it hard to pick up someone else's emotions through touch-telepathy.

Seyn's stomach quivered as Ksar's large hands spread over it.

"Nervous?" Ksar said, stroking his trembling stomach with his knuckles.

"Not at all," Seyn lied.

Ksar chuckled softly, hooking his thumbs on the waistband of Seyn's loose pants and tugging them down so slowly Seyn was positive the bastard was doing it on purpose, his hands stroking his tingling skin ever so slightly.

By the time Ksar took his pants off, Seyn was a wreck. A panting, flushed wreck of want. When Ksar actually got to his knees to take the shoes off him, long fingers stroking Seyn's ankles and making his toes curl, Seyn felt embarrassingly close to begging, and he suddenly hated himself more than he hated this man. At this rate, he thought he might come from one touch to his cock, which would be a whole new level of mortifying.

Ksar's eyes lifted to Seyn's as his hands finally slid up Seyn's bare legs to stroke his quivering thighs. The asshole actually had the nerve to smile a little at Seyn's hateful gaze. Granted, his hateful gaze probably wasn't particularly threatening considering that his hard cock was practically poking Ksar in the face.

"You should be careful with murderous looks like that," Ksar said in his usual monotone. "You could actually hurt someone whose shields aren't as good as mine."

Before the implications of what Ksar had just said could sink in, Ksar fucking *swallowed* his cock. Seyn's eyes rolled to the back of his head, a long, stuttered moan leaving his lips. Fucking hell.

Ksar sucked cock as aggressively and confidently as everything he did, his strong hands gripping Seyn's thighs so hard they were probably leaving finger-shaped bruises, but Seyn didn't care. All he cared about was that perfect, warm, wet mouth around his aching cock, and fuck, he was about to come into *Ksar's mouth*—

Except Ksar pulled back, letting Seyn's cock slip out of his mouth, and said, "Not yet."

His whole body burning with need and desperation, Seyn glared down at him, feeling like he wasn't even in control of his own voice anymore. He couldn't look away from Ksar's lips, which were shiny from Seyn's leaking cock.

"Turn around," Ksar instructed, his eyes roaming all over Seyn's naked body.

Seyn wished he could tell him exactly where he could shove that bossy attitude. But his cock was so hard it hurt, and his body felt like one raw nerve, ready to unravel at a single touch. So he turned and bent over the desk, arching his back instinctively, and felt a rush of vindictive pleasure when he heard Ksar's breathing hitch.

When nothing happened, he looked over his shoulder at Ksar and found him staring at his ass with a fixed, intense expression.

And then Ksar spread his cheeks and *licked* his hole.

Seyn flinched. "What the hell are you doing, you—"

Chuckling hoarsely, Ksar spread his cheeks wider and pushed his tongue inside.

A high-pitched whine left Seyn's throat, his body jerking as if electrocuted. Another deep lick had him grabbing the edge of the desk for support or he would have collapsed. Fuck. This shouldn't feel so...Such disgusting act had no right to feel so good. He couldn't believe he was really enjoying having Ksar's tongue in his asshole. Ksar's *tongue*, fucking hell.

"You'll like my cock even better," the bastard said in his head, fucking him with his tongue and then slipping in his long fingers. *"It's bigger. Thicker. It will fill you up much better. You'll be so full you'll feel it for days. And you'll like it. You'll like it and you'll come back for more."*

"Never," Seyn managed, his entire being rebelling at the idea, but his body was shaking at every little thrust of those clever fingers and tongue. Fuck, just a little more—

Seyn flailed a hand blindly backwards; it landed on the back of Ksar's head and he pressed Ksar's face forward while he pushed his ass back on Ksar's tongue, needy for it, little bitten-off moans spilling out of his mouth. Part of him was mortified—he was behaving like a wanton slut—but it felt so good. So fucking good.

He almost sobbed when Ksar pulled his tongue and fingers out.

"We shall see," Ksar said, getting to his feet.

"Never going to happen," Seyn panted out, staring dazedly at Ksar's desk and trying to ignore how unsatisfied and horribly empty he felt. He would *not* beg, and he definitely would never come back for more. A one-off with a man he loathed was foolish enough but could be blamed on his hormones. A repeat occurrence would be just plain destructive and stupid. "Just get on with it, will you? I have to return home before I'm missed."

"I don't like your attitude," Ksar said.

"I don't like your face, so we're even."

"I can't believe I want to fuck such a childish thing," Ksar muttered under his breath.

"I can't believe I want to fuck a sick bastard like you," Seyn said. "So let's just do it and forget this ever happened."

There was the sound of clothes rustling before Seyn felt Ksar's hands on his hips again. "A sound idea."

"I have a lot of them; you're just too arrogant to acknowledge—"

Seyn's words turned into a gasp as something thick, hard, and slippery pressed against his stretched, tingling hole.

Ksar's cock.

It was gratifying to know that Ksar was aroused enough to leak so profusely, except Seyn was faring no better himself, his own cock's lubricant dripping down his thighs. He was a mess. He probably looked like a whore, bent over the desk and eager for the cock of the man he'd hated half of his life.

But fuck, he wanted relief so badly he didn't give a shit about how he looked. He was so fucking empty and so damn hard.

"Come on," he gritted out finally, unable to stand the wait anymore.

When Ksar tightened his grip on his hips and pushed inside, Seyn didn't make any sound. He was unable to, his mouth opening and closing as he tried not to come.

The feeling of fullness was incredible. Incredibly gratifying in a way he hadn't expected.

The thing was, Seyn knew the biology behind sex between Calluvian males. It wasn't a fluke that Calluvian males could produce an adequate amount of lubricant to ease penetration—some of the species in their evolutionary tree hadn't been entirely heterosexual. So yes, he'd known that penetrative sex between men was enjoyable physiologically, at least to some degree.

But knowing something rationally and actually feeling the immense *satisfaction* from having a cock in him was completely another. It was satisfying on a completely other level than just having his fingers in him or his hand around his cock. It supposedly had something to do with brain chemistry and pheromones, but at that moment Seyn couldn't care less why it felt so good. It just did, but it also wasn't enough.

"Get on with it, I don't have all day," he snapped, and was immensely embarrassed by how breathless his voice sounded.

"You do realize that I can feel how much you like this, right?" Ksar said into Seyn's nape, his body big and hard behind him. "It's pointless to pretend you aren't enjoying this."

Seyn glared at the door. "It's also pointless to act all superior and shit when you're harder in me than a steel rod."

Ksar's teeth closed on the sensitive skin of his earlobe.

"I've never claimed to be perfect," he said, finally pulling out and thrusting in again.

Seyn let out an embarrassingly high-pitched sound, his eyes becoming unfocused.

Fuck.

"I'm not proud of this," Ksar said, his grip bruising on Seyn's hips as he started pounding into him, his breathing harsh and unsteady against Seyn's ear. "This is all your fault. I should have been better than this."

"Screw you," Seyn said, but it came out as a moan as he pushed back on the delicious length inside him. How could this feel so good? It should have been disgusting. Some of his thoughts were disgusting, too: the ones that were screaming that yes, this was exactly what he'd been needing, a strong man with a thick cock who knew how to make him feel good, just…like…this…

"More," he gasped, reaching back and digging his fingers into the hard muscle of Ksar's ass, urging him on.

Ksar let out a desperate grunt, and then his mouth was at Seyn's neck and he was biting it like a savage. Seyn wanted to protest. He wanted to beg for more. He did neither; he could only let out small whimpers as Ksar pounded him into his desk.

It was fast, dirty, and desperate. His whole world narrowed down to the hot, unsteady breaths against his nape, the hard body behind him, and the thick, perfect cock moving inside him, fucking him so good. He had no idea how long it lasted. The pleasure pulsed through him in waves, intense and unrelenting, taking him higher and higher, even though it felt like he was teetering at the edge all the time. Just a bit more—there—

Ksar's hand wrapped around his cock and started stroking him hard and fast, in time with his thrusts.

"Come," he said into Seyn's ear, his voice so husky it was a growl.

Seyn wanted to tell him to go fuck himself, but, to his embarrassment, his body actually obeyed.

He coated the desk with his come, whimpering weakly. In an instant, every muscle in his body seemed to shift from being tightly wound to loose and trembling. Seyn collapsed onto his elbows, blood pounding in his head, and his heart trying to climb out of his throat.

He was only distantly aware of Ksar's cock softening inside him and Ksar's come dribbling down his thighs. He hadn't even noticed Ksar coming, but he must have. Maybe they had come together. He didn't know. He couldn't think. His eyelids slipped shut and he might have blacked out for a short while.

The next thing Seyn was fully aware of, he lay boneless on the desk, still shaking with the aftershocks of his orgasm, his stomach and thighs sticky. He was pinned beneath Ksar's heavy body as they both tried to steady their breaths.

Seyn blinked his eyes open and stared dumbly at the desk. His brain still didn't seem to be working properly; that must have been the reason he felt so good and content with the world.

He felt more than heard a sigh against his neck before Ksar pulled out of him.

Seyn shivered at the sensation, his body too sensitive. The air-conditioned air hit the beads of sweat on his back, and the feeling of contentment disappeared at once.

Now he just felt awkward and weird, at a loss how to act.

Avoiding Ksar's eyes, Seyn straightened, wincing at the soreness of the muscles he hadn't even known about. His knees still felt a little weak as Seyn reached out for his discarded clothes and started putting them on, forcing himself to ignore the sticky mess on his thighs.

He could hear Ksar getting dressed too, but Seyn didn't look his way, still feeling wrong-footed and weird. How was he supposed to look at the man he hated more than anything after sharing with him the most intense, pleasurable experience of his life?

"Don't make it weird," Ksar said.

Buttoning up his shirt, Seyn forced himself to look at him.

He found Ksar already impeccably dressed, his cravat the only thing missing from his attire. His face was absolutely unreadable. The only thing that betrayed that he'd just had rough, energetic sex was the air of satisfaction that still lingered about him.

"It was just sex," Ksar said, meeting his eyes as his fingers (*fingers that had been inside him*) started tying his cravat. "It probably needed to happen. Now it's over."

"There's still the betrothal contract," Seyn said, trying to tie his own cravat—and trying to ignore the weird feeling in his gut.

"Not for long," Ksar said, returning to his seat and bringing up some graphs. "Now if you'll excuse me, I still have work to do. Borg'gorn, the records I requested."

"Here they are, Your Highness," the AI said.

Seyn turned away and left, doing his best to ignore the tight feeling in his gut. Ksar was right. They had fucked and finally snapped the weird tension that had always been between them. It wasn't more complicated than that.

It wasn't.

Chapter 10

One month later

Seyn marched through the halls of the Calluvian Ministry of Intergalactic Affairs, ignoring the curious looks he was receiving from the Ministry workers.

Ignoring their thoughts was much harder.

While Seyn's control over his telepathy had improved considerably in the past few months since Ksar had broken his bond, it still wasn't perfect. The hardest part was tuning out other people's thoughts. It wasn't much of a problem at home, but it was much harder in public places like the Ministry, where there were a lot of telepathically null Calluvians who had no mental shields whatsoever. Their unprotected thoughts still tended to overwhelm him, giving him a hell of a headache after a few hours of exposure.

Seyn couldn't imagine being around t-nulls all day long. That almost explained why Ksar was such an asshole.

Except Ksar had lived without his bond for decades.

His control over his telepathy was likely hundreds of times better than Seyn's, so being around t-nulls couldn't be an excuse for Ksar's attitude.

Seyn scowled. If Ksar weren't such a dick, he would have had the decency to offer him some tips on how to control his telepathy, but no, of course it hadn't even occurred to Ksar. The asshole was basically throwing someone who couldn't swim into the ocean and just expecting that they'd learn before they drowned.

To be fair, Ksar had warned him. Seyn knew he had asked for this, but still. He hadn't expected that adjusting to the bond's absence would be so hard. Harry hadn't seemed to struggle that much when his bond had been broken.

But then again, it was becoming increasingly obvious that he was a stronger telepath than Harry. Without the bond, Harry had probably been Class 3. Seyn couldn't tell for sure, but he estimated that he was Class 4 or Class 5. He could read people's minds so easily it was a struggle not to.

Needless to say, in the past few months, he'd learned how many people had less than flattering opinions of him, which was…eye-opening.

He'd always considered himself a friendly, sociable person, but after overhearing some of his friends' thoughts, his desire to socialize had lessened exponentially even after he had stopped feeling overwhelmed in crowds.

So far, a life without the bond wasn't what he'd hoped it to be.

"Health and tranquility," Seyn said, greeting the receptionist with a smile. "I want to see the Lord Chancellor."

The man barely glanced at him before returning his gaze to his multi-device.

"The Lord Chancellor is in a meeting. Make an appointment if you wish to see him. He has an opening in his schedule in eleven days."

"Eleven days?" Seyn said incredulously, irked by the man's attitude. It wasn't unusual for the t-nulls working at the Ministry to refuse to conform to the customs they thought old-fashioned, which Seyn could respect, but it was considered in extremely poor taste not to greet a member of a royal family at all.

"Yes, I believe I already said so," the receptionist said, his voice dripping with sarcasm.

Why was he surprised that Ksar's employees were impolite, self-important jerks, too?

"I can't wait eleven days. I need to see him now."

The man smiled only with his lips. "I'm sorry, but there's nothing I can do." His thoughts were very loud and clear: *No wonder the boss can't stand him. What an arrogant, entitled princeling.*

Seyn stared at him with narrowed eyes before turning around and striding toward the massive double doors.

"Wait!"

Ignoring his yell, Seyn pushed the doors open and marched in. "I need to talk to you."

Six heads turned to him.

"Oh," Seyn said, his face warming. "Sorry. I didn't think you were actually in a meeting."

Leaning back in his chair and ignoring the curious stares of his subordinates, Ksar met his gaze.

Seyn's stomach felt funny. He shifted from one foot to the other, suddenly hyper-aware that it was the closest he'd been to Ksar in a month.

They'd crossed paths a few times, but Seyn had managed to stay away—he'd had no reason to talk to Ksar—and Ksar hadn't approached him, either.

"Have you forgotten your manners?" Ksar said.

His cold tone made Seyn bristle momentarily before realizing that it wasn't him Ksar was addressing.

Ksar's subordinates stood hurriedly and gave Seyn awkward bows. "Your Highness," they muttered.

Feeling very bewildered but stupidly pleased, Seyn nodded to them before looking at Ksar. "I need to speak to you. This is urgent."

Ksar gave him an unreadable look and said in Seyn's head, *"I'm actually busy. I don't have time for petty, pointless arguments."*

Seyn glared at him. Just when he started thinking Ksar was being decent, of course he'd shown his true colors. *"This is really important. It's about Harry."*

Ksar frowned slightly and glanced at his subordinates. "Leave. We will continue at a later time."

He waited until they were alone before saying, "This had better be important. What about Harht?"

Seyn scoffed at Ksar's stubborn insistence not to call Harry by his preferred human name. "I can't believe you're even asking. You live in the same house. Have you talked to your brother lately?"

Ksar shot him an impatient look. "The house in question has over a hundred rooms and you know I return home late. Get to the point."

"There's something wrong with him. He looks like shit, he barely eats, he barely talks, and when he does, he sounds nothing like himself!"

"Is that all? You interrupted my meeting because my brother is still moping over his human?"

Seyn leaned over the desk, bringing their faces much closer. The smell of Ksar's aftershave hit his nostrils and it took Seyn several moments before he could gather his thoughts. "He isn't fucking *moping*," he bit out, angrier with himself than with Ksar. "Yes, at first I thought he was just depressed, but there's something very wrong with him. I don't recognize him anymore! It's like he doesn't give a shit about anything."

Ksar shrugged. "I have been led to believe it's a normal reaction in such circumstances. He fancied himself to be in love with that Terran."

Heavens, he was so heartless.

Seyn pursed his lips. "You know what he told me this morning? That he thinks he's dying. And he sounded like he was talking about weather."

Ksar stared at him.

Then, he stood up and headed out of the office.

Relieved that Ksar was finally taking him seriously but still annoyed that Ksar had been so ignorant about the problem, Seyn followed Ksar out of the room.

"I can't believe you haven't noticed anything," he said, falling into step with him. "You know I rarely leave the palace lately. That's why I haven't seen Harry in a while. What's your excuse? Do you even care about your brother? Have you really been avoiding him since we returned from Earth?"

His jaw clenching, Ksar headed toward the nearest t-chamber. He said nothing.

"A guilty conscience?"

Seyn noted that Ksar's fingers curled into a fist for a

moment before relaxing again. His face was like stone.

"I'm still not convinced that there's something wrong with him," Ksar said as they got into the t-chamber. "Perhaps it was just an excuse for you to come here."

Seyn narrowed his eyes. "What is that supposed to mean?"

Giving their destination to the computer and leaning back against the t-chamber's wall, Ksar looked at him through half-lidded eyes. "Don't pretend you have no idea what I'm talking about."

Gathering all his mental strength, Seyn gave him a telepathic punch.

Ksar didn't even flinch. The asshole actually had the nerve to look amused.

"You know perfectly well you can't hurt me that way," Ksar said. "If you want to make me hurt, you'll have to use your fists. But you won't."

Balling his fists, Seyn hissed, "And why is that? Right now it's pretty damn tempting."

Ksar looked him in the eye. "Because you're afraid to touch me."

"You—you—you arrogant, conceited—" He stepped closer to Ksar, breathing hard with fury. He wanted to *hurt* him—

The t-chamber doors opened, signaling their arrival at the Second Royal Palace.

"Compose yourself," Ksar said, straightening up. "I see your control is still as pathetic as it was a month ago."

"My control is perfect, thank you," Seyn gritted out, following Ksar out of the t-chamber. "But one can have only so much self-control when one comes across such an arrogant, ignorant ass like you!"

"You talk a lot," Ksar said, heading toward Harry's rooms. "But actions speak louder than words. And the truth is—"

"Shut up."

"The truth is," Ksar said, as if he hadn't said anything. His tone was disinterested and flat. "For someone who claims to despise me, you spend a lot of time thinking about sex when you're around me."

"Get out of my head, you creep," Seyn spluttered.

Ksar's lips curled. "I wasn't actually reading your mind, but it's good to know I'm right."

Seyn scowled at him, his face uncomfortably hot. "I fucked you only because I was horny and I had no other options. I can't exactly have sex with someone I actually want until I'm free of you officially."

Ksar's face went blank. He walked faster, looking straight ahead.

"My control over my hormones is much better now anyway," Seyn said, walking faster too.

He'd be damned if he was walking behind Ksar like some sort of servant. "What happened twenty-nine days ago wouldn't have happened if my control were as good as it is now."

He did feel infinitely more in control of his body. He was no longer a sexually frustrated wreck. He could last a whole day without getting an inappropriate erection for no reason at all. Yes, he still jerked off a few times a day to take the edge off, but he no longer felt the *need* to be touched.

All things considered, Seyn had been quite pleased with his progress.

Until today.

Seyn pursed his lips, glaring at Ksar's profile.

He hated himself for his inability not to notice his uncompromising jawline and that little expanse of his neck visible above his cravat—or the curve of Ksar's shoulders and biceps under his formal dark blue Ministry attire.

Having a libido sucked, Seyn concluded sulkily, reinforcing his mental shields.

It was a relief when they finally reached Harry's rooms.

But Seyn's relief didn't last long.

The worry he'd felt for his friend had spiked again when he saw that Harry was still sitting on the couch. Had he actually been in that position for hours? To make things worse, Harry's gaze was unfocused and distant, as if he wasn't entirely there. It was blatantly obvious that something was very wrong with him, and Seyn felt another surge of anger at Ksar and Harry's parents for not noticing such an obvious thing.

"Just look at him!" Seyn said. "It doesn't even look like he's moved from that couch since I left him in the morning! Can't you see it's not normal?"

Ksar followed him into the room with an unimpressed look on his face, as if he still thought Seyn was wasting his time.

"You shouldn't have messed with his mind," Seyn said. "You're not a professional mind adept. No doubt you fucked it up and now he's all weird and sickly!"

"I didn't 'fuck' anything up, as you so eloquently put it," Ksar said, but then he frowned, looking at Harry. "Harht?"

Harry stared at him without blinking. "What?" he said after a few moments, as if he had trouble grasping that he was being asked something.

"See?" Seyn said.

Ksar's eyes narrowed. He studied Harry carefully.

"Borg'gorn, run a full medical scan on Prince Harht," Ksar said.

Nothing prepared Seyn for what happened after that.

He listened numbly to Borg'gorn's findings, barely contributing to the conversation.

While he had thought that there was something off about Harry, he had no idea how serious the situation actually was.

Harry was sick. Very, very sick. He was in real danger of losing his mind—he was in danger of *dying*. And there was nothing Seyn could do to help. He couldn't even pretend to understand what his friend was going through. He'd completely forgotten that Harry's body had different needs from his. He'd never really thought of the importance of the fact that Harry was a throwback. Throwbacks shared common traits with surl'kh'tu, a subspecies of ancient Calluvians that had a single mate throughout their lives. Being apart from his human was literally detrimental to Harry's health.

Of course, as the cynical, skeptical asshole, Ksar was reluctant to believe Borg'gorn's findings.

"Am I supposed to believe Harht can't live without that Terran?" Ksar said, his tone like ice.

"As there are no precedents, I can only hypothesize," Borg'gorn said. "But Prince Harht's readings are most worrying. He may not necessarily die, but I do think his physical and mental health will keep deteriorating." A pause. "May I speak freely, Prince Ksar?"

Ksar gave a clipped nod and the AI continued, "I was going to inform you this evening that I had concerns about

Prince Harht's health. I have taken the liberty of observing the young prince since his return from Sol III. I have noticed that his concentration has been deteriorating at an alarming rate. Yesterday he spent six-point-three hours without moving, staring at nothing I could see. I had to say his name seven times to make him react. If the prince's awareness of his surroundings keeps deteriorating at this rate, it is very likely that he will eventually fall into a comatose state, perhaps with a very limited awareness of his surroundings. I recommend daily injections of the surl'kh'tu hormone suppressants to make him more alert and focused, but it cannot be a long-term solution. Eventually they will stop working."

"And you're absolutely certain that the cause is the throwback gene?" Ksar said.

"There is always a margin for error, but I am ninety-nine-point-two percent certain," Borg'gorn replied. "Besides the aforementioned hormone in his system, there are significant changes in the young prince's herovixu, the area of the brain that is specific for throwbacks."

Ksar's lips folded into a thin line before his gaze fixed on Harry. "Talk to me, kid. Is it really that bad?"

Harry moistened his lips, his violet eyes the only color on his pale face. "I—I don't know. I haven't even noticed that I zone out for hours. But I feel..." He seemed to struggle gathering his thoughts. "I feel like there's a hole in me that's sucking me in from the inside out."

Ksar's face was like stone. "And that's because of him? The Terran?"

Harry flinched, curling into himself, as if even the mention of his human hurt him. "Does it matter?" he said, barely moving his lips.

Ksar bored his eyes into his brother's bowed head, and Seyn shivered. Although it wasn't directed at him, he could *feel* the force of Ksar's telepathy as Ksar examined Harry's mind.

At that moment, Seyn knew without doubt that Ksar was dangerous. It was supposed to be impossible to read one's mind without eye contact.

Was Ksar Class 5? Class 6?

Class 7?

A cold shiver ran up Seyn's spine. He moved closer to Harry, wrapping an arm around him.

At last, Ksar tore his gaze from his brother, his jaw set and his expression vaguely sick.

"Your mind is a mess," he said tersely. "Some parts of it don't react to stimuli at all. Borg'gorn is right. Your mind is dying, Harht."

Harry stared at his elder brother blankly.

His heart in his throat, Seyn pulled him closer, trying to project comfort and probably failing. How could he project comfort when he felt sick with worry himself?

"You are going to do something to help him, right?" he said hoarsely, looking at Ksar.

Ksar glanced at him and said nothing.

Harry shook his head, looking dejected. "Don't worry about me," he said, his voice small. "I won't disgrace our family."

Ksar closed his eyes for a moment. "Harht—"

"I know," Harry said, biting his trembling bottom lip.

Seyn looked from Harry to Ksar, hating how useless and helpless he felt. "But can't we just smuggle him to Earth?" he said. "Like I did?"

"And then what?" Ksar said. "It's impossible to delete the teleporter's history. Sooner or later, Harht would be found, and the consequences would be much worse. And even if he wouldn't be found, he'd never be able to step foot on his home planet and see his family. Is that the sort of life you want for him? Do you think he would be happy to live like that, with all his familial links gone? Telepaths are not meant to live without telepathic communication for long stretches of time. He would be miserable."

Seyn's chin lifted. "At least he would be alive and sane. We must do something!"

Ksar went very still. "*We* won't do anything," he said testily. "*You* will go home and keep your mouth shut about everything you've heard."

"How can you be so heartless?" Seyn said, jumping to his feet. "He's your brother!"

"Yes," Ksar said. "He's my brother, and this is a family issue. You're not family. Leave. You overstayed your welcome a long time ago."

Seyn flushed with fury and humiliation and stormed out of the room.

Heavens, he couldn't wait to be free of that asshole.

He'd never hated anyone more.

Chapter 11

"Why are you always so nasty to him?" Harry said as soon as Seyn was gone.

Ksar looked at his younger brother and pursed his lips, not knowing what to say.

He knew what it looked like, of course. He was perfectly aware he behaved like a right bastard where Seyn was concerned. Partly, it was intentional. Partly, it was out of genuine irritation with the brat. Partly, it was out of frustration with the situation.

In short, it was complicated.

It always had been, though he definitely hadn't felt any animosity towards Seyn when he was a newborn infant who was supposed to become his bondmate. At the time, he'd been dizzy with pain and nausea, and he just wanted the pain to stop. The mind adepts had been confident that bonding him again would stabilize the remnants of his first bond.

They had been correct, at least in that regard. After Seyn had been bonded to him, the pain had stopped, but while the mind adepts hadn't noticed that the connection was-one sided, it hadn't taken Ksar long to figure out that something was wrong.

While his eight-year-old self hadn't exactly been thrilled to be bonded to an infant who couldn't even communicate and cried all the time, Ksar had done his part and tried to comfort the child to the best of his ability when Seyn's undeveloped telepathy reached out to him. Except it didn't work: the baby had never shown any sign of noticing his efforts to soothe it.

When he realized that the infant couldn't feel him at all and his own telepathy was off the charts, the child that was supposed to be Ksar's bondmate had become nothing but an annoying burden—and a source of constant guilt.

Even back then, Ksar's younger self had known that if he told someone that the bond was one-sided, the mind adepts could likely fix it—and the baby crying at the back of his mind would stop being so miserable and confused. But by that time, Ksar already knew what the childhood bond did to one's mind and telepathy. He hadn't been willing to be bound again.

So he hadn't told anyone.

Instead, Ksar had focused on controlling his telepathy. He raised his mental shields and did his best to ignore the needy little voice at the back of his mind. (*Are you there? Where are you? Please talk to me.*) Except ignoring it had never been easy, and he'd resorted to shielding himself from the connection completely.

At the time, he'd still been a child himself and his control hadn't been anywhere near as good as it was now, so he had been forced to shield himself from all his telepathic connections, the ones to his family included.

Although it had been his own choice, the lonely boy he had once been had resented the needy infant for forcing him to shield himself from his familial bonds, too.

Guilt was a peculiar thing. It could twist itself into irrational resentment and dislike quite easily.

He had managed to avoid the young Prince Seyn for as long as he could: fourteen years.

Meeting him in person for the first time had been an unwelcome reminder that the needy, hurt presence at the back of his mind was a real person—a teenager with huge green eyes full of resentment and hope, whose mind *still* begged for his attention.

It had been aggravating. Ksar had thought he was no longer capable of feeling guilt, and it had been irritating when the sharp-tongued boy proved him wrong in that regard. Guilt wasn't an emotion Ksar had ever been particularly fond of.

But it wasn't irritation that had made him be rude to the brat. His rudeness had always been carefully calculated. Seyn couldn't find out that there was something wrong with the bond, so making Seyn think that Ksar had been neglecting their bond—and Seyn—on purpose all these years had been the only course of action he could have taken.

Acting like an asshole was also supposed to discourage Seyn from wanting to be anywhere near him, which would reduce the chances of his learning the truth.

It had worked the way he had planned. His condescending, borderline rude attitude ensured that Seyn wanted nothing to do with him and remained oblivious about the state of their bond.

But there was a factor Ksar hadn't taken into account, something he hadn't expected at all: as Seyn grew older, *he* had trouble ignoring Seyn as he was supposed to.

Ksar had watched uneasily as his bondmate transformed from a mouthy boy into a beautiful, spirited young man.

It was incredibly ironic that the brat who had been the bane of his existence, the one person who could ruin his life and career, the one person who hated him more than anything, the one person who would never look at him with something other than rage and hatred even if he knew the truth, was the personification of everything Ksar wanted—and couldn't have.

It didn't exactly help that with each passing year that brought them closer to Seyn's twenty-fifth birthday, Ksar could no longer avoid thinking about what he was going to do when the time for their marriage ceremony came. He'd always known that his options were very limited. In fact, he had exactly one feasible option: to mess with Seyn's mind—and the mind adept who performed the bonding ceremony—and make Seyn think their marriage bond was perfectly functional.

The thought had never failed to put Ksar in a foul mood. Although he had never claimed to be a good man and had done his share of manipulating people for political gain, he'd never been keen to manipulate *Seyn's* mind. It had always been an option he'd ignored.

He could have manipulated Seyn's memories and made him think that Ksar had been a perfectly nice, considerate bondmate all along, which would have been the path of least resistance if he hadn't found the idea so distasteful. It was enough that his perceived rejection made the boy feel neglected; he wanted to avoid outright manipulating Seyn's mind unless it absolutely couldn't be helped.

Forcing Seyn to believe that they had a marriage bond—and forcing him to share Ksar's bed as a result—had never been something he looked forward to. He might not be a good man, and sometimes he might have been infinitely tempted to stuff that mouthy little shit with his cock, but he wasn't a fucking rapist. And for all intents and purposes, that would be rape. Brainwashing and rape. A man's sexual fantasies had nothing to do with reality.

And the reality of the situation was that Seyn had always made him feel like one sick bastard for everything he had done to him, everything he would do, and everything his body wanted to do to him. Needless to say, he'd always felt conflicted and snappish whenever Seyn was around.

But now Seyn knew the truth.

Seyn was no longer bonded to him.

There was no need to ever brainwash him—because there would be no marriage.

It should have been a relief.

It *was*.

And it wasn't.

Ksar pushed the thought away, suppressing his frustration and irritation. One would think that breaking Seyn's bond would stop making him feel so conflicted, but it had made things more complicated, just in a different way.

But it was neither the time nor the place to be thinking about Seyn.

He also wasn't going to think about the way Seyn had looked at him a little while ago: with that disgusting *faith* in his eyes, as if he believed there was nothing Ksar couldn't do if he put his mind to it.

That faith might have been subconscious, but it was still there. Seyn had no business looking at him like that when he claimed that he couldn't wait to be completely free of him so he could have sex with people he actually wanted.

For someone who loathed him, Seyn had too much faith in his ability to perform miracles.

And it would take nothing short of a miracle to find a solution for Harht's situation.

"That's irrelevant," Ksar said. "We have more important things to discuss."

"What important things?" Harht muttered, looking down at his hands. They were shaking. They were shaking so badly Harht didn't seem to be able to stop the tremors even when he clasped his hands.

Ksar eyed him with a small frown. Harht didn't seem to be all there, lost in his mind, misery coming off him in waves. Ksar could catch snatches of his thoughts without even delving into his mind again, and soon it became obvious Harht was working himself up into a panic attack, his breathing getting labored and his eyes dazed and lost.

"Harht," Ksar said sharply. "Breathe. *Harry*!"

His brother flinched, opening his mouth and closing it, trying to breathe and failing.

Dammit.

In a few long strides, he was by Harht's side and was pulling him into his arms. Harht clung to him, his eyes squeezed shut, tremors racking his body.

Ksar held him, his throat uncomfortably tight, his unseeing gaze fixed on the opposite wall.

It had been years since he'd last hugged the kid.

Harht had probably been seven or eight, a tiny thing with huge violet eyes full of trust and hero worship for his big brother.

He'd always looked at Ksar like he could do no wrong.

And he'd let him down.

His expression resolute, Ksar pulled back. He tipped Harht's face up and looked him in the eye.

"I can't promise you that it will be easy, Harry," he said, making sure to use Harht's preferred human name. Judging by the slight widening of Harry's eyes, he didn't miss it.

"It won't be," Ksar said. "But I promise you that I will find a solution." He thought about what he would have to do, and his lips twisted into something ugly and bitter. "By any means necessary."

* * *

To say the Queen was displeased by the news was to say nothing. But she didn't say anything, standing silent as her husband comforted their youngest son.

She exchanged a look with Ksar, her face blank but her eyes glinting with fury.

Ksar shook his head and said quietly, "I'll handle it."

Queen Tamirs eyed him carefully, her expression inscrutable. "Can you?"

Ksar rolled his shoulders and nodded.

A furrow appeared between her brows. "Be careful," she said.

Ksar shot her a sharp look. Sometimes he wondered if she knew about him, but he didn't make an effort to find out. If she wanted to claim ignorance, that was her choice. It was probably safer that way.

With a clipped nod, Ksar left the Queen's office. He was glad that he hadn't had to influence his parents' minds to make them more...open-minded about Harry's situation. It seemed he wasn't the only one in the family with a soft spot for their youngest member. Not that Ksar had expected the Queen to disinherit her favorite son, but he hadn't been certain that her love for Harht would be stronger than her prejudice against "lesser societies."

Granted, the Queen hadn't exactly been happy to hear the news that her youngest son had taken some pre-TNIT barbarian for a life partner, but all in all, it had gone smoother than Ksar had expected. Their parents' concern for Harry had outweighed their dismay by the situation. Harry was going to need their parents' unconditional support while Ksar solved the problem of Harry's bond to Leylen'shni'gul and the fact that legally Harry couldn't have a relationship with the human.

Ksar strode toward his office.

* * *

An hour later, as the door closed behind Lady Leylen, Ksar sagged back in his seat, staring blankly at the wall.

He told himself it was a perfect solution for everyone involved. Harry would be free and could eventually reunite with his human, Seyn would get what he wanted—freedom from him—and Ksar... He would just exchange one unwanted bondmate for another, significantly less annoying one. And he had far less qualms about manipulating Leylen's mind than he had about manipulating Seyn's.

It really was a perfect solution.

It was.

The knot of unease in his stomach was irrational, so largely irrelevant.

"Borg'gorn, tell Prince Seyn'ngh'veighli to come here at his earliest convenience."

Chapter 12

Seyn was surprised when just a few hours after he had been basically kicked out of the Second Royal Palace, Borg'gorn contacted him to tell him that Ksar was requesting a meeting "at his earliest convenience."

The nerve of that asshole.

Seyn fumed, considering just ignoring the request after the way Ksar had treated him, but in the end, his curiosity won out. What did Ksar want? Why would he request a meeting after telling him just a little while ago that he'd overstayed his welcome?

So Seyn waited until the late evening, not wanting to appear eager, and headed back to the Second Royal Palace.

"How is Harry, Borg'gorn?" he asked as strode toward Ksar's office.

"The young prince is in his quarters with the King-Consort and the palace physician," the AI replied.

Seyn perked up. "Have they found a solution?"

"I am not in a position to share with you the contents of their conversation, but I can reveal that the physician has confirmed my earlier findings."

Seyn deflated.

A part of him had hoped the AI's conclusions regarding Harry's health had been wrong, but it probably had been stupid of him: Borg'gorn had the combined knowledge of the best medical minds in history. There was no doctor on the planet who could have given a more accurate medical diagnosis than the Second Royal House's AI.

"Your Highness?"

Seyn looked up. "Yes?"

"May I ask you to be more civil when you speak to the Crown Prince?"

Seyn blinked incredulously. "More civil? Me? You should be having this conversation with Ksar, not me."

"I am aware that the Crown Prince can be rather…ill-tempered where you are concerned," Borg'gorn said diplomatically.

Seyn smiled. "The understatement of the century."

"But he has been working non-stop since you left, and I believe he is currently in a rather foul mood. Any confrontations with him when he is in such a mood are highly inadvisable, Your Highness."

Seyn rolled his eyes. "Is he ever not in a foul mood?"

The AI's silence was quite telling.

"He was not a happy child," the AI said at last. "And he is not a happy man."

Ignoring the twinge of *something*, Seyn said, "If he isn't happy, that's entirely his own doing. He's the one who keeps even his own family at arm's length." To be fair, now Seyn had a better idea why Ksar might have done it. In the past few months, he'd found that it was difficult to be honest and close to his family when he had to keep such a huge secret from them.

"Announce me," Seyn said, stopping in front of the closed door leading to Ksar's office.

"The Crown Prince is otherwise engaged right now," Borg'gorn said apologetically. "But he said it would not take long."

Unimpressed, Seyn folded his arms over his chest, glaring at the door. Did Ksar think he had nothing better to do with his time?

Finally, after what felt like forever, the door opened and Councilor Vehmer emerged. He looked pensive, but his expression changed to surprised when he saw Seyn. He bowed. "Your Highness."

Seyn nodded to the councilor, curious what he was doing here at such a late hour. "Councilor."

"The Crown Prince says you may come in, Your Highness," Borg'gorn said.

With a last curious look at the councilor, Seyn entered Ksar's office.

As the door slid shut after him, silence fell over the room.

Ksar was seated behind his desk, his expression serious and hard to read.

Seyn eyed him, something akin to trepidation churning in his gut.

"Take a seat," Ksar said quietly.

The anxious feeling became worse. Something wasn't right.

Seyn did as he was told, searching Ksar's face for clues. When he found none, he reached curiously with his senses. He could feel a vague impression of other people's emotions—it seemed there had been a lot of people in this room today—but he couldn't read Ksar at all.

When Ksar finally spoke, his voice was flat and disinterested, contradicting the sharp intensity of his silver gaze. "I've found a solution for Harht's—Harry's problem."

A relief like no other rushed through Seyn. He grinned, leaning forward in his seat. "Really?"

Ksar stared at him strangely before looking away. "Yes," he said in a stiff voice. "At least I hope so."

Seyn blinked. "You *hope* so?" It was the first time in his memory that Ksar was less than confident about his plans.

"It will require intricate political maneuvering both domestically and intergalactically," Ksar said. "It will likely take months before the laws will be passed."

"What laws?" Seyn said, feeling off-balance. He couldn't remember him and Ksar ever managing to have a civil conversation for so long without it turning into an ugly argument.

Ksar looked at him. "The repeal of the Ministry's 156th law and some changes to the Bonding Law."

Seyn felt his eyes widen, his breath catching in his throat. Surely Ksar wasn't serious? He didn't know enough about intergalactic politics to judge the chances of the repeal of the Ministry's 156th law—the one that forbade the citizens of the Union of Planets to have interpersonal relationships with members of pre-TNIT civilizations—but he was positive the Council would never do anything to the Bonding Law.

It wasn't just the t-nulls who were afraid of high-level telepaths. Even the telepaths in the Council were unlikely to support any change to the Bonding Law. It might completely overhaul the social hierarchy, which obviously wasn't in the Council's best interests.

People in power didn't want change unless it benefited them. No matter how often Seyn had bitched and whined about the unfairness of the Bonding Law, he had never seriously thought that anything would change. Fear was a powerful motivator to keep the status quo intact.

"They'd never repeal the Bonding Law," Seyn said.

"That's why I have no intention of pushing for the complete repeal of the law," Ksar said neutrally. "It would be too suspicious if such a bill passed."

Seyn stared at him. "You mean you want to rig the Council's voting." It was a statement, not a question. He didn't know why he was surprised. It wasn't like he hadn't known that Ksar had absolutely no qualms about manipulating someone's mind. A scowl twisted Seyn's lips before fading. He wished he could tell Ksar what he thought about his despicable methods, but if it was done to help Harry, was it wrong? And more importantly, did he really care about the means as long as the Bonding Law was changed?

"What do you intend to propose, then?" Seyn said.

Ksar raised his eyebrows. "No righteous indignation?"

Seyn made a face. He felt weird enough that he agreed with Ksar on something. He didn't need Ksar to rub it in. "I asked you a question," he said coolly. "If you don't intend to push for the repeal of the law, how would it help Harry?"

"The Council would be more open to a small amendment to the law," Ksar said. "A conditional clause that would allow individuals who have reached the age of majority to petition for dissolution of the bond."

Seyn's heart skipped a beat. "Anyone who's over the age of twenty-five? Why would the Council agree to it? There would be chaos."

Ksar's face remained impassive. "Passing such a law wouldn't mean that just anyone would get the approval of the Council and the High Hronthar. I'm sure it would be highly regulated." His voice became somewhat sardonic. "I don't expect most requests to be approved."

Right. Of course. Introducing a conditional clause would only ensure that the people in power remained in power.

Seyn shook his head, his mind reeling. "But Harry isn't twenty-five. He can't apply for the dissolution of the bond for another year." He frowned, looking at Ksar sharply. "Unless you think Harry can wait that long without his health deteriorating..." He trailed off, realizing what Ksar had likely meant. But it still didn't make sense. "Leylen would never petition to break her bond to Harry."

Ksar's heavy gaze on him was unmoving.

"She's already agreed to do it."

Seyn's brows furrowed, his bewilderment increasing. "She has? Why the hell would she do it? Her family is a bunch of social climbers."

"Precisely," Ksar said.

Seyn's breath caught in his throat.

He stared at Ksar blankly. "You mean..."

"Yes," Ksar said, his voice toneless. "You may not consider the position of my consort an honor, but, luckily for Harry, Leylen doesn't share your opinion."

Seyn opened his mouth, but nothing came out. He found himself blinking, unable to grasp it.

He probably looked stupid. He *felt* stupid, because while the words registered, his mind remained blank, unable to imagine Ksar marrying Leylen—unable to believe that he would be finally completely, absolutely, totally free of Ksar.

Forever.

"She can't seriously..." he whispered, barely moving his lips. "She can't..."

"Want to marry me?" Ksar said with a nasty edge to his voice. "She does. She's beyond excited."

Seyn glowered at him, jumping to his feet. "Then she's an idiot," he ground out. "Is that all? Then excuse me, I'm off to celebrate. This is the best day of my life."

Ksar's face was absolutely expressionless. "It will be months before the law is passed. But don't let it stop you."

Seyn smiled at him sweetly. "It won't. By the way, pass my condolences to Leylen. Best of luck to her. She'll need it."

Not a single muscle shifted on Ksar's face. He said nothing, so Seyn turned on his heel and strode out of the room.

As soon as he was outside, his smile dropped.

Seyn tried to put it back, but all he managed was an uncertain curl to his lips that felt nothing like a smile. He didn't know why. This *was* the happiest day of his life. He'd dreamed of being free of Ksar for a decade; of course he was happy. He was ecstatic. Thrilled. Everything was fine.

Everything was *great*.

Then what was this weird feeling knotting his stomach into a hard-packed ball?

Chapter 13

Six months later

"Announce me," Ksar said tersely and walked toward the window overlooking the royal gardens.

"Of course, Your Highness," the AI said before pausing. "Who do you wish to see? The Crown Prince is currently occupied, but the Queen and the Queen-Consort are not."

Ksar grimaced. Considering that he'd rarely called on Seyn in all the years they'd been supposedly bonded, it was probably a fair assumption that he hadn't come to the Third Royal Palace to see him.

"Prince Seyn'ngh'veighli," Ksar said, looking at the lavish gardens below.

There was silence for a while before the AI said, "The Prince will be here momentarily."

Before long, there was the sound of footsteps.

Ksar straightened his shoulders, ignoring the way his pulse had picked up.

He hadn't seen Seyn in almost six months. Either the little menace had been avoiding him or their paths had genuinely never crossed.

It wouldn't be all that surprising if it was the latter, considering that Ksar had spent most of his time on other planets and had rarely attended Calluvian social events this year. Even when he had, he had been there with the sole purpose to speak to the political figures he needed to ally with.

Still, he hadn't seen Seyn *once*.

It was...odd.

Not that he had been actively looking—Seyn would have been a distraction he didn't need—but it was just a deeply ingrained habit to seek him out with his eyes every time Ksar attended social events. A bad habit he needed to break.

Ksar schooled his face into a blank expression and turned around just as Seyn entered the room, all pale, shiny hair, porcelain skin, and wide green eyes. To Ksar's dismay and irritation, his body reacted in a very predictable way to the sight of the brat, as if he were an adolescent with no control over his body. Utterly disgusting.

Seyn halted in the doorway. "You look horrible," was the first thing he said, before flushing, for whatever reason.

"Then I look like I feel," Ksar said with a tired smile that felt like a grimace. He knew he had dark circles under his eyes. Lack of sleep would do that to anyone. He was exhausted and sleep-deprived after months of constant work and travel as he had pushed for laws that had no chance of passing without all the bribing, manipulating, and coercing he'd done.

He should have stayed away from Seyn when his mental faculties were so compromised. This conversation might have been necessary, but coming in person certainly wasn't.

He didn't know what had made him come here in person.

Liar, said a voice at the back of his mind.

Ksar grimaced inwardly.

Yes, he knew why he was here.

It was just too shameful to admit even in the privacy of his own thoughts. He was here because he'd wanted to turn his brain off and stop thinking for a little while. And apparently it meant that he wanted Seyn. It really was quite pathetic.

"I've heard how busy you've been lately," Seyn said, walking toward him. "I'm surprised you found time for me in your very busy schedule."

He came to a halt a few steps away, his eyes still zeroed in on Ksar's face with an intense look of dislike and something else. As usual, he was wearing something casual, his shirt half-sheer, his pale throat bare.

Ksar's fingers twitched.

He clasped his hands behind his back. "You've probably already heard that the amendment to the Bonding Law was passed. The 156th law will be repealed in the next session of the Ministry's Chamber of Lords. Everything is in place. Yesterday I petitioned for dissolution of my bond, as did Leylen."

Seyn's jaw clenched.

"Yes, I've already read about it in the gossip columns—as well as was informed about it by every well-wisher on the planet. It's been a highly enlightening day." His voice could have frozen fire.

"I gave you advance notice six months ago," Ksar said. "And I recall you started celebrating on that very day."

The look Seyn shot him was positively toxic. "It doesn't mean you don't have to warn me before you publicly jilt me, asshole. I'm asking for the last time: to what do I owe the dubious pleasure of your visit?" Seyn rubbed the back of his neck before crossing his arms over his chest. He averted his gaze, biting his bottom lip. "I thought the point was that I don't have to see you again."

"It's not that simple. Requesting the dissolution of our bonds is just the first step. I expect that it would take the Council and the High Hronthar close to a month to approve both requests." Ksar dragged his gaze away from Seyn's mouth, irritated with himself. "The problem is, you and I don't have a bond to dissolve anymore."

Seyn's tongue slipped out to moisten his lips. "So what? Is it going to be a problem?"

"It depends," Ksar said. "I have no way of knowing what mind adept will be appointed by the High Hronthar to break our non-existent bond. I won't be able to change the mind adept's memories if their telepathic abilities are stronger than mine."

Seyn's pink lips curled into a crooked sneer. "Is that even possible?"

"I don't know," Ksar heard himself say, once again disgusted that he had to force his eyes away from the brat's lips. It was getting beyond pathetic. "My telepathy wasn't exactly tested."

"You're stronger than me, and my telepathy is pretty damn strong."

Seyn paused, color high on his cheekbones. "Why are you all over my personal space?" he added, eyeing the tiny distance between them.

Ksar didn't know how they had ended up this close. He refused to believe that he was the one who'd moved closer. He had better self-control than that.

"Perhaps it's you who is all over mine," he said.

Seyn scoffed. "I'm not the one staring at my mouth like I want to put my dick in it."

Ksar's jaw tightened. He looked into the green eyes. "You sound like you've been thinking about it a lot."

Flushing crimson, Seyn shot him a venomous glare.

"Touched a nerve?" Ksar said, stepping closer.

He put his hands on Seyn's hips and felt Seyn tremble against him.

"Get your hands off me," Seyn bit off shakily.

"I will," Ksar said, their mouths so close he could feel Seyn's unsteady breaths on his lips. Fuck. He wanted to *consume* him. He wanted to mess Seyn up, pull at his shiny, perfect hair, yank it by the roots, and then rip his clothes. He wanted to get to Seyn's skin, wanted to fuck him until he screamed, until he was wanton and slutty, until Ksar was so far inside him he couldn't breathe, until those hateful green eyes were wide open and blind to everything except him.

Ksar said hoarsely, "If you say it like you actually mean it."

With a feral growl, Seyn buried his hands in Ksar's hair and yanked him down. "I fucking hate you." He bit at Ksar's bottom lip, making them both gasp. "I loathe you. I *loathe* this."

Ksar absolutely shared the sentiment as he finally took that infuriating, maddening mouth with his. Ksar pushed his tongue between those soft lips, nearly groaning at the sweetness he found inside.

It was highly illogical: mouths didn't taste sweet. It was all hormones and pheromones that made kissing a person one was attracted to so satisfying.

Still, kissing this particular person shouldn't have felt so damn good—so damn *right* and perfect, as if this was what he'd been craving all these months. His hands felt unsteady, his entire body pulsating like he had an aphrodisiac running through his veins where he should have had blood.

Seyn kissed back just as hungrily, threading his fingers through Ksar's hair, sucking on his tongue and making small, contented noises that went straight to Ksar's cock.

The urge to fuck, to put himself inside that pale, silky skin, was overwhelming. He was this close to shoving Seyn to the floor and taking him right there, in the middle of the Third Royal House's drawing room.

A sound from the doorway made him freeze.

Ksar tore his mouth away, and Seyn *whined*, his hands still clutching at his shoulders, his eyes glazed with desire, mouth swollen and bitten red.

With some difficulty, Ksar wrenched his gaze away to look over Seyn's shoulder, and his eyes locked with shocked green ones that belonged to Seyn's older brother.

Ksar suppressed the urge to swear.

Following his gaze, Seyn turned around and went still at the sight of Prince Jamil.

For a long moment, no one said anything.

Sighing, Ksar reached toward Jamil's mind with the intention of erasing the relevant memories when Seyn grabbed his wrist and said sharply, "Don't!"

Against his better judgment, Ksar stopped.

"How do you propose to explain to your brother why you were humping me when you aren't supposed to feel arousal at all?" Ksar told Seyn telepathically, watching the Crown Prince carefully. If Jamil decided to leave and tell everyone what he saw, he would erase his memories, regardless of what Seyn said. Erasing Jamil's memories was the safest way to ensure that no one discovered the truth. The more people knew, the bigger the chance that the Council would find out.

"I wasn't humping you!" Seyn hissed out, full of indignation.

Ksar felt his lips curl into a smile. *"Is that the most important thing you needed to address? You have strange priorities. And you were most definitely humping me."*

"You have no room to speak. I can still feel your erection against my ass."

"And whose fault is that? I'm just a man."

"You touched me first!"

"You kissed me first."

"That's irrelevant, you ass. Anyway, I'm not letting you mess with my brother's mind. He has suffered enough already. His terminated bond is still hurting, and who knows what it would do to him if his mind is messed with again.

"I can assure you I'm fully capable of—"

"Seyn!"

Seyn flinched at the sound of his brother's voice, and Ksar realized that they were still indecently close. He still had a hand on Seyn's hip while Seyn was still gripping his other wrist, all but leaning back against Ksar. He could only imagine what they must look like from Seyn's brother's perspective.

"I can't even..." Jamil said, shaking his head.

His handsome face contorted with a mix of anger, disbelief, and confusion. He seemed undecided what emotion to settle on. "What is the meaning of this, Seyn?" He glanced sharply at Ksar, his dislike obvious. "He has just publicly humiliated you by requesting the dissolution of your bond, and yet I find you all but having—" He cut himself off, his eyes narrowing as they studied Seyn, clearly noticing the undeniable signs of arousal in his younger brother's body.

Ksar had to suppress the instinctive urge to step in front of Seyn.

Instead, he looked at Jamil coldly and said, "No offense, but it's none of your concern."

Predictably, Jamil took offense. He straightened himself to his full height, his eyes glinting with anger. "None of my concern?" he said. "I have every right to demand an explanation. In fact, I've been trying to get hold of you all day. First you publicly humiliate my brother and our House, then I come across you with your tongue down Seyn's throat. Explain yourself."

As an eldest brother himself, Ksar could understand where Jamil was coming from. Except he had little patience for people sticking their noses into his business, and even less patience for explaining himself to them.

"Jamil," Seyn tried, sounding half-embarrassed, half-exasperated.

"Not a word, Seyn," his brother snapped. "I thought you hated him. I always thought your hatred for him was unjustified, but now that he's actually done something to justify it, I find you all but climbing him instead of—"

"Leave," Ksar said, his patience worn thin.

Jamil stared at him, incredulity written all over his face. "You're actually trying to give orders in my own palace?"

Ksar sighed, tired of this pointless and completely avoidable conversation—if Seyn let him erase his brother's memories.

A chuckle broke the tension in the room.

Seyn was laughing, his eyes glinting with unrestrained mirth.

"I fail to see what is so amusing," Jamil said sharply.

Ksar ignored him, staring at his younger brother instead. He didn't think he'd ever seen Seyn laugh so genuinely in his presence. The sight was...oddly transfixing.

Still chuckling, Seyn looked at Ksar. "I've been telling everyone what an arrogant, entitled asshole you are, but no one ever believed me. It's good to see you show your true colors to someone other than me. Being able to say 'I told you so' never felt better." He turned back to Jamil, grinning. "See? I told you he was a horrible, arrogant asshole."

"Seyn," Jamil said, incredulity thick in his voice. "You were just kissing him like you were trying to eat him. And now you say how horrible he is. Am I the only one noticing the contradiction here?"

No, he wasn't the only one.

Although Ksar could no longer see Seyn's face, he could feel his intense embarrassment and defensiveness.

"It was a mistake," Seyn said. "Nothing for you to worry about. Please stay out of my personal affairs, Jamil."

His brother shook his head.

"There's more at stake here than your personal affairs. He publicly humiliated our House—the entire Third Grand Clan, actually—by rejecting its scion in such a manner. There's a betrothal contract signed by our parents. Even if the Council gives him the permission to break the bond, he's still morally obliged to honor the contract. He literally owes his life to you! I don't understand how you can be kissing him after the way he publicly rejected and humiliated you. Don't you have any sense of pride and self-respect?"

"Enough," Ksar said, stepping in front of Seyn. It had nothing to do with protectiveness. He didn't feel protective. The waves of intense discomfort rolling off Seyn were simply too aggravating to his already frayed nerves.

"Stay out of it," Ksar said, looking at Jamil firmly. "This is the last warning."

Jamil's green eyes narrowed. Although the color was the same, Ksar thought they were nowhere near as expressive and beautiful as his younger brother's.

"What is that supposed to mean?" Jamil said.

"Ksar," Seyn said from behind him, a warning clear in his voice. He put a hand on Ksar's arm, as if that would stop him from doing something rash. Ksar had no intention of doing anything rash. All the touch accomplished was to make him hyper-aware of it, which just made him more irritated with the whole affair. He was done playing nice.

"It means exactly what I said," Ksar said, looking Jamil in the eye. Seyn had asked him not to erase his brother's memories; he had said nothing about not watching them.

Everyone had something they wanted to hide, even the seemingly proper, boring princes like Jamil.

Finding what he was looking for, Ksar said, "If you don't stay out of my affairs, I'll have no reason to stay out of yours."

For the first time, a hint of wariness appeared on Jamil's face. "You know nothing of my affairs."

"Don't I?" Ksar said with barely any inflection to his voice. "I think the society will be very shocked to find that the Third Grand Clan's recently widowed Crown Prince has a very...interesting relationship with a low-bred servant."

He heard a sharp inhale from behind him but didn't look away from Jamil's rapidly paling face.

"Seyn is right," Jamil said, barely moving his lips. "You're a despicable bastard."

Ksar looked at him coldly. "If I let Seyn get away with insulting me, it doesn't mean I will tolerate insults from you. Leave."

"If you think I'm leaving my brother with someone like you—"

"Your brother is capable of thinking for himself," Ksar cut him off, beyond irritated now. "He's more capable of handling me than you are. Leave before I lose my patience and do something I might regret."

Seyn's grip on his biceps tightened. "Don't hurt him."

It was extremely galling that Seyn thought he could tell him what to do. Though, if he were honest enough with himself, perhaps Seyn wasn't entirely wrong in that assumption. Seyn had the most aggravating ability to make him feel guilty and Ksar had never cared for that particular feeling.

"Is that a threat?" Jamil said, his face deathly pale.

"No," Ksar said. "It's a warning. If you stay out of my business, I will stay out of yours and no one will have to find out that their Crown Prince likes being bent over and used by a servant."

Jamil flushed scarlet.

"Stop talking to my brother in such a vulgar way," Seyn hissed into his ear, his grip on Ksar's arm becoming painful.

Ksar felt his lips curl. "If I didn't know better, I'd think you were jealous."

Seyn dug his fingers into his arm. "I'm not fucking jealous," he hissed, anger and embarrassment coming off him in thick waves. "Why would I be jealous over a man I detest?"

Ksar pursed his lips and glanced back at Jamil. "Why are you still here?"

His jaw clenched, Jamil looked mutinous, but after a long, charged moment, he said tersely, "Seyn, I'll be waiting for you in my office."

As soon as the door shut after his older brother, Seyn sighed. "Great. Just fantastic."

Ksar turned around. "You have only yourself to blame. You should have let me erase his memories."

The silver-haired prince scoffed, crossing his arms over his chest. "You violated his privacy enough already." He scowled, a slight blush coloring his cheeks. "My brother is a widowed, grown man. You had no right to shame him for what he likes in bed." Seyn narrowed his eyes. "It doesn't make him a lesser man—or a lesser prince, for that matter."

"It doesn't," Ksar agreed, shrugging.

"If he weren't already ashamed of his physical desires, I wouldn't have been able to use it against him."

Seyn shook his head. "You sicken me."

Ksar studied him for a moment before settling his hands back on Seyn's hips. "Do I?" he said quietly.

He could kind of sympathize with Prince Jamil. Being ashamed of his desires was something he'd become intimately familiar with. It was shameful that he felt so disgustingly eager—eager to touch, eager to kiss, eager to bury himself in this hostile young man who looked at him as if he was the most wretched person in the world.

Maybe he was.

A good man would leave Seyn alone after everything he'd done to him.

He wasn't a good man.

"I want you," he said, pulling Seyn closer by his hips.

Seyn sucked a breath in and put his hands on Ksar's chest. "Really?" he said with an unsteady chuckle. "Do you seriously think I'm having sex with you again?"

Ksar held his gaze. "All you have to say is no."

Seyn's throat worked.

He moistened his lips with his tongue, opened his mouth, and then closed it.

"Just say no," Ksar said, leaning in to nibble at Seyn's earlobe. He felt Seyn shudder, a gasp leaving those lovely lips.

"I hate you," Seyn whispered shakily, his fingers clutching the front of Ksar's shirt as Ksar nuzzled the side of his face.

He smelled good.

He always did.

"I'm still not hearing a no," Ksar said, kissing along Seyn's jaw, feeling far too breathless for his liking. "You can hate me all you want. We don't have to like each other to fuck."

"Charming," Seyn said with a chuckle, but it turned into a moan as Ksar kissed his way down his cheek to his mouth.

The kiss was deep and endlessly hungry. Seyn seemed to forget all his objections, kissing him back with need and aggressiveness that rivaled his own, little moans of pleasure spilling out of his mouth as Ksar's hands roamed all over his body and undressed him swiftly.

"Fine," Seyn said breathlessly, yanking at Ksar's cravat and undressing him with unsteady hands. "Fine. But this is the last time."

Ksar murmured his assent, pushing him onto the couch. He stretched out on top of him, relishing the way Seyn's athletic but lithe body felt under his much bigger one.

He was only distantly aware of Seyn's hands fumbling between them to free their erections, his gaze fixed hungrily on Seyn's flushed, aroused face: on his bitten, moist lips and glassy eyes. He looked drunk. He looked obscene.

He looked beautiful.

"Stop giving me that creepy look," Seyn said hoarsely, wrapping his hand around their equally slick cocks.

"What creepy look?" Ksar said, gritting his teeth as Seyn started stroking them.

"Like you can't decide if you want to eat me or fuck me."

That was actually quite accurate.

Bracing himself up on his elbows, Ksar looked into Seyn's glazed eyes. "I think I'll do the latter. Tell your AI to lock the room."

"You have some nerve," Seyn said before grabbing a fistful of Ksar's hair and pulling him down to bite at Ksar's lips. His shields were completely down and Ksar could feel his thoughts even without trying to read them. (*I fucking loathe you; ugh, why can't I stop kissing you?*) Seyn tore his mouth away only to command breathlessly, "Omer, engage privacy locks."

A couch in the Third Royal Palace's drawing room wasn't exactly a piece of furniture Ksar had ever expected to have sex on. It was too narrow, uncomfortable, and small for two men. It should have made this one of the most awkward, worst sexual experiences of his life.

It should have, but it didn't.

Ksar was shaking with the desire to touch too much to care about the narrowness of the couch. It was kind of pathetic, truth be told. It was pathetic how eager he was to get inside the young man under him. It was pathetic how little patience he had for preparing Seyn properly for penetration. At least he wasn't alone in his eagerness: Seyn was murmuring breathlessly into his ear that he was ready, *just do it already, get in me, want your cock, want you so much, it felt so good last time.*

The first push made Ksar groan as incredible tightness enveloped his aching cock, Seyn's thighs shaking from the half-folded position he was in. Ksar didn't think he'd ever been harder in his life, the heady lust making thinking extremely difficult. All he could think of was *finally.*

"Come on," Seyn demanded, digging his heels into his back. "Pleasure me. Harder."

Ksar felt such a violent instinct to *please* him that the unfamiliar feeling made him freeze. He stared at the naked young man under him and reminded himself he was no slave to his body. "I will," he bit out. "At my own pace." He set a very slow, thorough rhythm that was frustrating even to him, much less to Seyn.

Seyn whined. Seyn bitched. Seyn called him names. Seyn clawed at his back. The telepathic onslaught to his senses was the worst: Seyn gave off such raw need that it was extremely difficult not to give in and fuck him as hard as Seyn wanted him to.

Ksar held on, undeterred, thrusting into him so slowly that soon Seyn was whining, all but clinging to Ksar as he moaned and cursed him.

"Please," Seyn finally bit out, his voice absolutely wrecked, his hips mindlessly trying to push back on Ksar's cock. "*Ksar.*"

There was something about the way he said his name that made Ksar lose it, his self-control shattering into a thousand pieces. Growling, he slammed hard inside him, and Seyn cried out, blunt fingernails raking down Ksar's back, the spark of pain heightening Ksar's pleasure.

Yes, yes, yes, like that. Ksar wasn't sure anymore whose thought it was, his own shields coming down enough to let their pleasure and their thoughts mix as he set a hard, fast pace. He could feel how much Seyn was enjoying his cock, how much he loved being full of it, how much he loved the base nature of the act, how much he loved just lying there under Ksar's heavy body and taking the brutal fucking Ksar was giving him.

"You can stop feeling so smug, asshole," Seyn said breathlessly. "I can feel exactly how much you're enjoying yourself, too."

A laugh tore out of Ksar's throat and Seyn grinned at him dazedly.

Their gazes locked and held and Ksar felt an unfamiliar heat pull low at his gut. He resumed thrusting but couldn't quite look away, their eyes locked together.

It felt both incredibly intimate and incredibly filthy: holding Seyn's gaze as they fucked, seeing Seyn's eyes cloud with pleasure and letting Seyn see every shift in his expression.

"Want you deeper," Seyn said, fingers digging into the hard muscle of Ksar's ass. "Deeper, come on."

"I'm as deep as it gets," Ksar gritted out, his balls pressed flush against Seyn's buttocks. He pulled out and slammed in again, his frustration mounting as the desire to get deeper started driving him crazy. He glared at the young man under him. "Quit it."

"I'm not doing anything," Seyn moaned, hands trying to pull Ksar's hips closer, as if his cock could get any deeper inside him. "Come on!" he demanded, all but sobbing, his cheeks flushed and his eyes moist.

Ksar looked down at him in frustration, his body pulsing with want so strong that he felt breathless with it. He knew what was happening, even though he'd only heard of it before. It was his own fault. He'd had sex with telepaths before and he'd never let his shields down even a little, but he'd allowed Seyn to feel what he was feeling multiple times. It was inevitable that it would backlash. Now Seyn wanted—needed—telepathic connection on top of the physical one.

"I need," Seyn croaked out, writhing under him like he was possessed. He threw his legs over Ksar's shoulders, trying to get him deeper. "I need—I need—"

Swearing elaborately, Ksar undid all his remaining shields and let his mind merge with Seyn's at the same time as he slammed his cock into him.

Seyn sobbed out, their combined pleasure flooding Ksar's senses to the point of overwhelming him. It felt so good that each thrust of his cock felt like a small orgasm. He was only distantly aware of low, animalistic noises coming out of his throat as he slammed into Seyn with the urgency he'd never felt in his life, the act becoming more carnal and pure instinct.

With their minds connected, it was natural to perfectly time each thrust to satisfy the man under him, and before long, Seyn was coming—*they* were coming, wrapped around each other in a tight embrace.

Ksar collapsed on top of him, shaking with his entire body and breathing hard, his mind sluggish and dazed with pleasure. He only had the presence of mind to roll them to their sides, but Seyn made a protesting sound, clutching at his shoulders. "Don't leave me," he whispered.

Ksar opened his eyes and stared blankly at the couch cushion.

As if only just realizing what he'd said, Seyn tensed under him before shoving him off. "Get off me, you big oaf."

Ksar got to his feet and reached for his carelessly discarded clothes, still feeling more than a little shaken.

He started dressing, not looking Seyn's way as he tried to regain his equilibrium. He put on his pants and walked to the mirror with the rest of his clothes.

Ksar grimaced, looking at the fingernail marks all over his arms and back. "I look like I had a fight with a wild cat," he remarked, slipping into his shirt and fastening it.

Behind him, Seyn scoffed. "I look like I was mauled by one, so we're even."

Hooking his cravat around his neck, Ksar turned around and found Seyn in front of the other mirror. He was trying to make himself presentable and largely failing. His silver hair looked like a disaster, his jaw and neck covered in red marks Ksar couldn't remember leaving.

"That's why you should wear a cravat," Ksar said, walking toward him.

Seyn made a face at him in the mirror. "I do wear it—when I have to."

Ksar turned him around and, taking his cravat off, started tying it around Seyn's neck.

Seyn's brows pinched. "I don't wear white cravats," he said after a moment.

Ksar didn't look away from the task at hand. He didn't let his fingers graze the creamy skin, even though they itched to. It was highly disconcerting. He'd just had a very satisfying orgasm, easily the most satisfying in his life.

"Now you do," he said.

"The white color doesn't suit me."

"It does," Ksar said testily, biting back the urge to say that anything suited Seyn. "You just like being contrary."

Seyn lifted his chin, involuntarily drawing Ksar's eyes to his puffy, well-kissed mouth. "I don't want to wear anything of yours."

Ksar gave him a flat look. "You refuse to wear my cravat, but you just had my cock in you."

Seyn glowered at him, his cheeks flushing slightly. "It was a mistake. A moment of madness."

Ksar's stomach clenched.

"A rare occasion I agree with you."

"Good." Seyn crossed his arms over his chest. "Now go away. I don't want to see you in my house again."

"It doesn't matter what you want. I'll be very surprised if your brother allows me entry after what happened today."

Seyn's brows furrowed. He shot him a look Ksar couldn't quite decipher. The lack of knowledge was… jarring after they'd had their minds merged just a little while ago.

The memory made Ksar frown. What they had done was irresponsible.

Dangerous.

He should have known better. He did know better. Regardless of how good it had felt at the time, merging minds in such a way was incredibly risky. Uncontrolled telepathic merges were considered illegal on most worlds of the Union of Planets for a reason. For a very good reason.

"I have to go," Ksar said, glancing at the clock. He'd wasted enough time on an unnecessary visit as it was. "Try to come up with a believable explanation for your brother."

"Stop telling me what to do," Seyn said sourly, looking anywhere but at him.

Ksar turned to go, but paused and looked back at him. He felt…agitated, off-balance, and he didn't know why. The feeling was as unfamiliar as it was unwelcome.

"Fix your hair," he said.

Seyn just glared at him and didn't say anything, his arms still crossed over his chest.

Realizing that he was looking for an excuse to linger, Ksar turned away swiftly and headed for the door, infuriated with his own behavior.

Pathetic.

It was a good thing their non-existent bond would soon be officially broken and he would have no reason to be around Seyn. Being tied to Leylen looked more appealing by the second.

Anything was better than this disgusting lack of rational thought and self-control.

"What did you tell them?" Seyn said before he could reach the door.

Ksar paused with his back to him. "Who?"

"When you requested the bond's dissolution." Seyn's voice was very stiff. "What did you cite as the reason?"

"Fundamental mental incompatibility."

A harsh laugh left Seyn's mouth. "No one would believe that's the real reason. Everyone knows how little you think of me."

Ksar pursed his lips. He wanted to disagree. Except he knew Seyn was right. Although he'd never treated Seyn with anything but politeness in public, people weren't idiots. Their mutual animosity was widely known.

Ksar had had no time to check the media's reaction to the latest news, but he had little doubt that the gossip columns must be having a field day. His petition for the bond's dissolution was far from being the only one, but it was easily the most high-profile case out there. The most scandalous. And of course it would be Seyn's reputation that would suffer the most, not his.

The thought was...displeasing.

"Everyone knows how little you think of *me*," Ksar said. "So use it. You won't be humiliated if you don't act humiliated." And he strode out of the room, trying to shake off the crawling feeling of unease and wrongness under his skin.

There was nothing wrong. Everything was proceeding as it should.

After months of hard work, now wasn't the time to start having second thoughts.

Chapter 14

After Ksar left, explaining himself to his older brother was the last thing Seyn felt like doing, but he knew Jamil would just come looking for him if Seyn didn't go to his office. Leaving the palace wasn't an option, either; not when there was a small army of paparazzi lying in wait.

He found his brother pacing his office, a deep frown on his face. Green eyes so much like his own fixed on Seyn the moment he entered the room.

"Explain," Jamil bit off, motioning for Seyn to sit down.

Seyn remained standing. "There's nothing to explain," he said.

Jamil rubbed his temples with a pinched look. "And I suppose you are wearing his cravat because you felt like it?"

Seyn almost groaned aloud. He'd forgotten about it. He should have changed before going to see his brother.

"Look," he said, avoiding Jamil's eyes. He wasn't bad at lying, but he'd never particularly liked lying to his family.

"You have nothing to worry about. It was nothing. So I kissed him; what's the big deal? It was the equivalent of...of a divorced couple kissing for the last time for old times' sake." He ignored the uncomfortable, sinking feeling that appeared in his gut at the comparison.

"For old times' sake?" Jamil repeated, his voice laced with disbelief. "Since when do you kiss him? I thought you hated that man! And that was no chaste kiss." Before Seyn could say anything, Jamil pinned him with a hard, searching gaze. "Not to mention that you aren't supposed to be able to want such things, much less do them with the man you've always claimed to despise!"

Seyn considered lying. He considered claiming that he was one of the few people capable of feeling sexual attraction despite their functional childhood bonds—it was extremely rare, but it did happen—except he was tired of lying. He was fed up with lying to his family. He trusted his brother. He trusted him to keep his secret. He trusted him not to betray him.

So he sat down, and he started talking. He told Jamil everything, reciting the events of the months following Harry's first trip to Planet Earth. He told him about Harry's bond and Harry's deteriorating health. He told him about the solution Ksar had found to free Harry of his bond and betrothal contract. He told him that Ksar had actually broken Seyn's bond already.

He talked and talked until there was nothing left to say.

Silence fell over the room when Seyn finished, his hands clenched in his lap as he waited for his brother's reaction.

Jamil seemed absolutely speechless.

"Wait," he said at last, raking his hand through his shoulder-length hair. "Are you saying that you aren't bonded to Ksar anymore, but you've had sex with him anyway?"

Seyn cringed. Of course that would be what Jamil would fixate on. "It was just hormones and stuff," he said, looking anywhere but at his brother. "I was horny and he was the only available option. That's all."

He felt his brother's heavy gaze on him but refused to look his way, studying his hands with perhaps exaggerated interest.

"Seyn."

There was so much judgment in his voice that Seyn snapped, "Like you have room to talk!"

The silence that fell between them was the most awkward in his life.

"What is that supposed to mean?" Jamil's voice never sounded colder.

Seyn winced. He hadn't really intended to bring that up. There were some things one didn't want to know or discuss with one's older brother.

"You couldn't possibly believe that bastard's lies," Jamil said.

Seyn looked up. "He wasn't lying," he said. "He's a manipulative asshole with no principles, but I know him. I can mostly tell when he's lying or being evasive about something. He had no reason to lie about you. And your reaction proved that he was right."

A flush appeared on Jamil's cheekbones. He rarely blushed out of embarrassment, so Seyn assumed he was angry but he wasn't sure. Seyn was hesitant to use his telepathy to gauge his brother's thoughts and emotions.

His telepathic core still felt raw after merging with Ksar's, and the prospect of touching someone else just felt…wrong.

"So you trust the words of the man who publicly humiliated you over my words," Jamil said.

Seyn pursed his lips, eyeing his brother carefully. "You have no reason to be so defensive, you know. Your husband died a year and a half ago. It doesn't dishonor his memory that you…have physical needs."

"I'm not talking about this with you," Jamil said.

Seyn chuckled. "Don't be so prudish. I get it. Although it's not as bad as it had been at the beginning, I still think about sex at least five times a day."

Jamil's lips twitched in an approximation of a smile. He shook his head. "I'm still not talking about it with you. It's too…strange. I used to change your diapers, kid."

Seyn scrunched his nose up. "No, you didn't. We have servants for that. And speaking of servants…" He leaned forward, grinning. "So who is it?"

It could be anyone. Unlike the Second Royal House, their House didn't use robots to perform most tasks, and there were more than a hundred servants in the palace alone, and another hundred working in the gardens.

Jamil shook his head. "I'm not talking about it. In any case, we have other, far more important matters to worry about."

"Like what?"

Jamil looked him in the eye, his expression turning grim. "Like how we're going to handle the society's reaction to the news."

Seyn's stomach clenched.

"What do you mean?" he said.

Jamil sighed. "It's one thing to handle a few curious visitors in your own home, and it's completely another to attend social events after being publicly insulted and humiliated in the worst possible way. There hasn't been a jilted prince in thousands of years. Considering how politically influential and respected Ksar is, you'll be the one receiving the brunt of the public's scorn and pity. Do you want to avoid social functions for a while?"

You won't be humiliated if you don't act humiliated.

Seyn got to his feet. "No. I'm not hiding."

Chapter 15

"Keep your head high, darling," Queen Janesh said, a gracious smile on her lips as she accepted people's bows with a slight nod.

"And smile," the Queen-Consort said, taking Seyn's arm and looping hers through it.

"I'm smiling," Seyn said, trying to pretend he didn't see the sneers on people's faces as they turned away to whisper or, worse, snicker. He hadn't really thought it would be this bad. It felt like everyone in the ballroom was gawking at him, as if he'd grown a second head overnight. Maybe Jamil had been right and he should have stayed at home.

"Smile like you mean it," his mother said, leading him deeper into the ballroom as the Queen stayed behind to talk to someone.

Seyn tried to. But it was hard to keep a sincere smile on his face when even his friends kept a safe distance from him, as if they were afraid to become the laughingstocks too if they associated with him in public.

Maybe they weren't really his friends.

"You don't have to babysit me, Mother," he said with a wide smile that hurt his cheeks. "I know you and the Queen wanted to speak to some politicians. Go. I can handle myself."

"I'm not going anywhere," the Queen-Consort said, nodding politely to people who bowed to her. "My wife doesn't need me. My son does." A barely noticeable tension appeared by her eyes. "If we had known it would end this way, we would have never granted the Second Royal House the favor of bonding you to their heir. Your mother didn't mince words when she spoke to Queen Tamirs yesterday."

Seyn suppressed a wince. "Mother, I told you both that I'm glad Ksar did it—that's what I wanted, too. I'm not angry."

"I am," she said, her voice like steel despite her smile. "I'm allowed to be angry on behalf of my son. I swear when I see Ksar'ngh'chaali, I'll tell him what I think of his ungrateful, selfish, undeserving—"

Seyn was only distantly aware that his mother was still ranting, but his attention zeroed in on the woman at the other end of the ballroom.

Leylen.

She looked radiant, her smile blinding as she laughed with her friend about something. Her smile froze a little when she caught sight of him. Something flickered in her eyes—something that looked a lot like pity.

A white-hot rage filled Seyn's chest. He didn't want her pity. She was the one who should be pitied, not him. He was fine. He was free. He was happy. He was—

"Darling," his mother said softly. "You're hurting me."

"Sorry," Seyn said, loosening his grip on his mother's arm and putting on another smile. He ignored the looks people shot between him and Leylen, and tried to ignore the whispers, which was harder to do because of his heightened senses.

"...Have you heard? What a delightful scandal!"

"They say Ksar'ngh'chaali wants to get rid of him in order to marry her."

"His own brother's bondmate!"

"She's beautiful."

"So is Seyn'ngh'veighli, to be fair."

"He's too pale. And it's hardly a secret that Ksar detests him."

"She and Ksar will make a striking couple."

"I feel sorry for Prince Seyn, though."

"It's his own fault. I wouldn't tolerate his scandalous behavior if I were in the Lord Chancellor's shoes, either."

"There must be something seriously wrong with him. I know Ksar. He would have honored the contract if there weren't some serious flaw in his bondmate."

"I agree, there must be something wrong with Prince Seyn."

His mother murmured, "Don't listen to them, Seyn."

"I'm not listening," Seyn lied, smiling wider.

Suddenly, he felt his mother tense up. "The nerve of that man," she hissed under his breath. "How dare he show his face in public after dragging your name through the mud."

Seyn swallowed. He hadn't expected that Ksar would be at this ball: he'd barely attended any social gatherings in months.

"Don't look at him, dear," his mother murmured.

165

"Where is he?" Seyn said, making an effort not to look around.

"Over there, talking to Councilor Gfyion and Ambassador Fehtur," his mother said, her lips curling into a sneer. "Apparently *he* isn't a social pariah. Don't look at him, sweetheart," she added when he turned his head. "He's beneath your notice."

Seyn tried not to look. He did.

But it was impossible. His gaze followed his mother's glare.

Ksar was in the middle of a group of politicians, looking his haughty, cold self.

As if feeling his gaze, Ksar looked right at him.

Licking his lips, Seyn dragged his eyes away.

He glanced back a few moments later.

Ksar was still looking at him.

"Why are you clinging to your mother's skirts?" a familiar scathing voice said in his head.

Seyn wasn't even surprised anymore. Ksar seemed to think he had a right to get into his head whenever he wanted.

"Get out of my head," he snapped. *"And I'm not clinging to my mother's skirts. I'm escorting her."*

"You usually have an entourage of eager puppies following you around."

"I guess they now think there must be a fundamental flaw in me," Seyn said with sarcasm that came out all wrong.

There was silence in response and Seyn started thinking Ksar had gotten out of his head when he spoke again, his mental voice terse and annoyed.

"Are you waiting for me to reassure you that there's nothing wrong with you?"

Seyn glowered at him across the room. *"Fuck you. I know there's nothing wrong with me."*

The haughty, superior look in Ksar's eyes made his hackles rise.

"Then prove it," Ksar told him.

Seyn set his jaw.

"Excuse me, Mother," he said, tearing his gaze away from Ksar. "I see Ambassador Denev over there. I'll go talk to him."

His mother looked unsure but nodded.

Seyn strode determinedly toward Ambassador Denev, ignoring the stares and the whispers. He would be damned if he let himself be shunned and ostracized in front of Ksar's eyes.

Denev seemed partly pleasantly surprised, partly uncomfortable when Seyn approached him.

"Your Highness," he said after a moment of hesitation, bowing to him slightly. "I didn't expect to see you here, after…" He trailed off, rubbing his shoulder in discomfort, a faint blue flush appearing on his cheeks. He was a dear, really, one of Seyn's favorites.

"After what?" Seyn said, raising his eyebrows and smiling kindly, pretending to be oblivious to the fact that everyone around them was listening to their conversation with avid curiosity. "After I finally got myself free of an unwanted bond?"

Denev's face cleared up.

"Of course, Your Highness. Please forgive me for the presumption. I swear I didn't believe those rumors—I simply…"

"I didn't doubt it for a moment," Seyn said with a smile.

"Only people who don't know me would believe that it wasn't my decision to break the bond. Unfortunately, I'm not of age yet, so I discussed the matter with Ksar'ngh'chaali, and he agreed to file the paperwork."

"I see," Denev said, smiling back. "In that case, I hope I'm not being too forward, Your Highness, but I'm happy that you will be free soon."

Seyn felt a pang of discomfort. He'd always liked Denev. He was Ksar's opposite: friendly, approachable, and nice. He wore his heart on his sleeve. Denev had never made it a secret that he was rather smitten with Seyn, even though he understood Calluvian customs well enough to know that Seyn could never return his feelings in his bonded state. But it seemed now Denev was getting his hopes up.

Feeling a little bad, Seyn chewed on his lip, looking for a response that wouldn't encourage the foreigner too much and wouldn't hurt his feelings, either.

Thankfully, at that moment, two other people approached them, and Seyn put on his best smile and turned to them.

The next few hours were spent making nice with people Seyn didn't care about, putting on his most charming smile and pretending to be oblivious to their thinly veiled insults. It was exhausting. It was infuriating that he even had to do it. But it was immensely satisfying to prove to Ksar that he could totally win people to his side.

Ksar didn't leave the ball early, as he usually tended to do. Ksar didn't approach him and didn't look at him all that often, but his presence across the room energized and motivated Seyn like nothing else could.

He would show him.

By the end of the night, he would have everyone in this ballroom wrapped around his little finger.

It was early morning as a very exhausted Seyn finally allowed himself to stop fluttering from one group to another and looked around with satisfaction. He could no longer see any pitying looks directed his way or hear the derisive remarks and snickers. He'd done it. He'd proved to Ksar—and to himself—that he could do it.

Seyn looked around the ballroom, eager to locate Ksar and rub it in his face.

But he was nowhere to be seen.

Ksar had left.

He was gone.

Seyn deflated, his smile slipping as a hollow feeling settled low in his gut. The satisfaction and triumph he'd been feeling just moments ago turned into something bitter, and he hated it, and he hated Ksar for ruining everything once again.

"I'm so proud of you, dear," the Queen said on their way back. "You handled yourself admirably."

Seyn shrugged, staring at the wall of the t-chamber moodily. He just wanted to get home and feel shitty in the privacy of his room.

"Yes, it went so much better than I expected," his other mother said, squeezing his arm. "You charmed them all, sweetheart. I shouldn't have doubted it."

Seyn said nothing.

"Is something amiss?" the Queen said. "You are not pleased."

Seyn wondered how she knew; he had his shields fully up, preventing any emotional transference through his familial bonds.

But then again, she was his mother. Mothers always knew, somehow.

"He left," Seyn murmured. "I wanted to prove to him that I could win them back. But he left!"

There was a moment's silence.

"Who?" the Queen-Consort said faintly.

"Ksar. Who else?"

This time the silence lasted longer as his parents exchanged a look he couldn't quite read.

The Queen had a pinched expression on her face. "Darling," she said slowly. "Why do you care?"

Seyn glared at the wall and said nothing.

His other mother was eyeing him with open concern. "The Council is in favor of approving Ksar's request. You'll be officially free of him any day now. Why do you still care what he thinks? You have always resented your bond to Ksar. I thought you'd be ecstatic, especially now that you've managed to sway the public opinion. It's effectively over now. You finally got what you have always wanted."

Seyn crossed his arms over his chest. "Still. I wanted to prove to him that I could do it."

"Darling, you don't have to prove anything to him," the Queen said, her tone becoming incredulous. "He's nothing to you anymore. Just ignore him. Let it go—"

"I can't!" he snapped.

His mothers stared at him blankly, the sudden silence ringing in his ears.

"I can't, okay?" Seyn said tightly. He looked away, running his shaking hands through his hair.

He was immensely relieved when at that moment they arrived at the palace and he could escape his parents' stares.

They had been looking at him as though he'd lost his mind.

He was starting to wonder the same thing.

The door to his bedroom slid shut behind him with an unsatisfying soft click. Seyn strode inside and came to a halt by the table, staring at it. At Ksar's stupid snow-white cravat on it.

Seyn kicked the table, turning it over.

Something shattered and broke, but he didn't care. He threw everything he could see through his blurring vision: priceless heirlooms and exotic alien souvenirs, ancient books and top-notch electronics—nothing was safe from his rage.

A servant rushed in and stopped upon seeing the wrecked room.

"Out," Seyn growled.

The servant left hurriedly, and Seyn gripped his bedpost, collapsing against it. A sob forced its way up his throat. Then another, a horrible choking noise.

He had no idea how he'd ended up slumped on the floor. There was a sharp ache in his leg that probably meant that he'd sunk down onto some broken shard. There was a dull ache in his throat that couldn't be as easily explained.

He didn't know why his eyes were wet. There was no damn reason for it.

No reason at all.

Chapter 16

Twenty-one days later, Seyn received an official message from the Council, informing him that Ksar's petition had been approved. The date for breaking the bond was in three days.

Seyn stared at the message for a few moments before carefully putting his multi-device back into his pocket.

Jamil stopped making funny faces at his daughter and looked up. "Bad news?"

"No," Seyn said, putting on a smile and focusing his gaze on Tmynne. The four-month-old baby princess smiled back at him, her green eyes sparkling as she reached out to Seyn's hair with a chubby hand.

"Good news, actually," he said. There was no point in trying to hide the news from Jamil. As the Crown Prince, he sat on the Council himself. Every grand clan had two votes on the Council, one for the ruling monarch—or their consort in their absence—and one for the heir apparent.

Unless Jamil had missed the latest session of the Council, he likely already knew the news.

If Seyn tried to hide anything, he had no doubt it would only reaffirm his family's opinion that there was something wrong with him.

There was nothing wrong with him.

He was fine. He was better than ever. Seyn was sick of his family treating him like a fucking ticking bomb. So he had broken a few priceless heirlooms; so what? It didn't make him emotionally fragile or something.

It meant nothing.

He was fine.

"Ksar's petition was approved," he said and smiled wider. "I'll be a free man in three days."

He felt Jamil's gaze on him, but he kept his eyes on Tmynne. She finally managed to grab a lock of his hair and made a triumphant noise.

Seyn chuckled. "Fine, but no hair pulling, all right?"

Tmynne pulled at his hair, hard.

Laughing, Seyn lifted her from her crib and hid his face in her sweet-smelling hair. He could feel that Jamil was still watching him.

"Do you want to talk about it?" Jamil said at last, sounding as uncomfortable as Seyn felt.

Seyn paused. He lifted his head and looked his brother in the eye. "About what?"

Jamil gave him an unimpressed look. "I'm your brother, kid. Don't insult my intelligence by pretending it isn't a big deal for you."

"I don't really have the bond anymore, remember?" Seyn said with a soft chuckle. "It will be just a formality."

Jamil's expression didn't change. "Do you remember the Shadow War?"

Seyn's brows furrowed in confusion.

The Shadow War hadn't been a real war. It referred to the twenty-year period in Calluvian history that had taken place nine thousand years ago.

Back then, there hadn't been twelve grand clans; there had been just two, but the relationship between them, especially between their queens, had been so bad it put real wars to shame. Queen Eguiless and Queen Xeryash's mutual hatred and rivalry had been legendary; it still was.

But what did that have to do with anything?

Seyn shrugged, bewildered by the sudden change of subject. "What about it?"

Jamil looked at him hard. "The queens hated each other for so long that their sole purpose in life became destroying each other. They were obsessed with it. But then Queen Xeryash died from a heart attack, of all things. And do you remember what happened to Queen Eguiless?"

Seyn put the baby back in her crib, needing the excuse to look away from his brother's eyes. Yes, of course he knew what happened to Queen Eguiless. They said she became very strange after her archenemy's sudden death. She acted withdrawn and listless half of the time and fell into mindless rages the other half.

"Hate is a powerful feeling, too," Jamil said. "It's a passion, too, just on another end of the spectrum. Some say it's stronger than love, and that if you suddenly lose someone you hated for years, it would leave as big a void as if you lost a loved one."

Seyn chuckled, rubbing the back of his neck. "What does that have to do with me?"

"All I'm saying is that it's okay to feel strange about finally getting the freedom you've always wanted. You don't have to pretend to be happy if you aren't."

"I'm not pretending," Seyn said. "I'm happy. My life *isn't* revolved around Ksar." He hated how unconvincing and defensive his voice sounded.

Judging by the look Jamil shot him, he wasn't convinced, either.

"It'll get better," Jamil said, his expression turning wistful as his gaze shifted to his daughter. "Give it time."

Seyn looked at him curiously. Time had certainly seemed to help his brother. Jamil did look loads better. His green eyes were brighter, his complexion healthier. He'd gained the weight he'd lost after his bondmate's death and now he was almost as built as Ksar. He looked startlingly handsome, younger, and at peace with himself. He no longer gave off grief and misery.

Seyn was unsure why he hadn't noticed the changes in his brother before. Was he really as self-absorbed as Ksar said?

The thought made him frown. He'd accepted a long time ago that he had something of a tunnel vision where his relationship with Ksar was concerned, but it was no excuse for barely paying attention to his family.

"You look good," Seyn said. "I'm happy for you."

His shoulders tensing, Jamil shot him a startled look. "What? What are you talking about?"

Seyn's eyebrows crawled up. Did his brother sound flustered? No, he must have imagined that. Jamil didn't do flustered. "Fatherhood suits you. I'm glad Tmynne's birth changed your life for the better."

Jamil exhaled and his shoulders lost tension.

"She did," he said, shifting his gaze back to his daughter.

Seyn gave his brother a long look, wondering.

The door suddenly slid open and a man Seyn didn't know walked into the room as if it were his own.

The man came to a halt upon seeing him, his casual attitude changing. He gave Seyn a stiff bow, with his hands clasped behind his back—the way only servants bowed to members of the royal family.

Seyn frowned. The man was obviously a servant, but he didn't hold himself like a servant. There was nothing subservient or particularly respectful about his posture.

Seyn studied the man. He was tall, perhaps Jamil's height. He was broad-shouldered and well muscled but wiry, as if he was all raw muscle and virile power with no fat at all. His skin was unusually dark for their clan, his features sharp and strange. His dark hair was cut very close to his scalp. There was black paint peeking out of his sleeve—or perhaps it wasn't paint at all. It resembled those permanent tattoos Seyn had seen on some planets.

The overall impression the servant gave off was *wild*. He reminded Seyn of a bird of prey. A predator. What was a man like that doing as a palace servant? Actually, why had he entered the Crown Prince's rooms without as much as a knock?

Seyn glanced at Jamil, expecting him to reprimand the servant—his brother wasn't one to tolerate insolence—but Jamil just raised his eyebrows at the strange man. "Yes?"

Seyn stared at his brother incredulously.

"You're late for your meeting with the King-Consort of the Twelfth Grand Clan," the man said. He had a faint accent Seyn couldn't quite place.

"Ah, yes," Jamil said, tearing his eyes away from the other man's and picking up his multi-device from his desk.

"Let's go, Seyn. I would like you to be there, too. You know the Twelfth Grand Clan's colonies better than I do."

Seyn followed him out of the room, glancing back at his niece uncertainly as the door slid shut. "Are you seriously going to leave Tmynne with that strange man?"

"She sees him more often than she sees you," Jamil said, looking straight ahead.

Pushing aside the pang of guilt—he really should spend more time with his family instead of sulking because of Ksar—Seyn said, "Who is he?"

"My manservant."

Seyn blinked. "He looks like a thug, not a manservant!" He came to an abrupt halt. "Wait, is he the servant you let—" He cut himself off when Jamil shot him a withering look that promised death if Seyn dared finish that sentence.

Seyn grinned, shaking his head. He'd never thought his prim, proper brother had it in him. "I can't believe you! Where did you even find him? He looks dangerous!"

"You know," Jamil said in a very mild voice, "someone who keeps falling on his enemy's cock really has no room to talk."

Seyn's mouth fell open.

Jamil never used such vulgar language. It seemed he had touched a nerve.

"I don't!" Seyn said belatedly, his face warm. "It happened just a few times and is never going to happen again!"

Everything in Jamil's expression screamed skepticism.

Seyn scowled. "Anyway, it's none of your business. It's completely irrelevant to the subject at hand."

"It's not irrelevant. Have you not noticed that Ksar is the gold standard against which you measure other men?"

Before Seyn could refute that utterly *ridiculous* claim, Jamil pinned him with a look. "You do. Don't even try to deny it. You find nice, humble men boring. You naturally gravitate toward arrogant and haughty ones, the more confident the better. You judge me now because you can't imagine being attracted to someone of a lower class— someone so unlike Ksar." Jamil's lips twisted. "Start judging me when you figure out how to stop gagging for Ksar's cock."

His brother stalked away, but Seyn barely noticed it.

He stood frozen, a tight, sickening feeling settling low in his gut.

Every doubt he'd been carefully suppressing since his little breakdown after the ball, surfaced again. Was he really as obsessed with Ksar as his brother had said? Did he subconsciously think that Ksar was *perfect*?

Seyn scoffed at the mere thought. Of course he didn't consider Ksar perfect. Ksar was an arrogant, infuriating, despicable, horrible person.

But he's my *horrible person. Mine.*

Seyn closed his eyes and took in a deep breath. And then another.

It did nothing to quell the panic rising in his chest.

Chapter 17

The ancient clock on the wall sounded deafening in the utter silence of the room.

Ksar stood still, leaning back against the stone wall, his gaze on the clock.

He just wanted this to be over.

"This place is creeping me out."

Ksar tensed. It took a conscious effort to relax his muscles again. He and Seyn hadn't said a word to each other since they had been left alone to wait for the mind adept that would break their non-existent bond. Not speaking to Seyn had suited Ksar perfectly. The less they interacted, the better. The less he looked at Seyn, the better. He didn't trust himself not to do something he would regret.

"It's the High Hronthar," he said neutrally, sweeping his gaze over the stone walls.

The High Hronthar was a peculiar place indeed. Located in the middle of nowhere, in the center of Calluvia's sole desert, its architecture and culture were dramatically different from the rest of Calluvia.

The sprawling building was thousands of years old and hadn't changed much since it was built. The monks lived a secluded life devoted to mind arts, interacting with the rest of the planet only when their services were needed. Admittedly, now that the childhood bonds were breakable, perhaps their services would be needed more often.

But then again, Ksar mused, perhaps not. In the month since the amendment to the Bonding Law had passed, only three petitions out of thousands had been approved by the Council, his and Leylen's among them. Considering how much bribery and coercion had been required to get them approved, Ksar would be very surprised if more than a few petitions were approved in the future.

"How is Harry?" Seyn said stiffly, breaking the silence again.

Ksar didn't look at him, his lips thinning at the reminder of his brother's condition. Harry's condition had deteriorated to the point that he barely reacted when people tried to talk to him. Sometimes there were rare moments of lucidity, but they didn't last long. Even with the best care modern medicine could offer, Harry's health was failing at an alarming rate.

"I have heard that his and Leylen's bond was broken yesterday," Seyn said. "But obviously he isn't answering my calls. Did it go well?"

"As well as one would expect," Ksar replied. It had been a challenge to convince the High Hronthar that he needed to be present while they broke Harry and Leylen's bond. Even with Harry's forged medical records, it wasn't easy to convince the monks that Harry wasn't well enough to go to the monastery unaccompanied.

After that, the rest had been relatively easy. Unlike Ksar and Seyn, Harry and Leylen actually had a bond to dissolve; the challenging part had been to trick the mind adept who performed the ceremony into thinking that there wasn't anything unusual about Harry's mental state. Thankfully, everything had gone smoothly. The bond between Harry and Leylen had been officially broken and no one seemed to suspect that anything was afoot.

"I'm taking him off-world later today to get treatment for his illness," Ksar said, choosing his words carefully. The High Hronthar didn't use modern technology to monitor its rooms, but that didn't mean there weren't eyes on them. The monastery was old enough to have secret passageways for observing the visitors.

"Oh," Seyn said. "Good."

There was nothing "good" about it. Ksar wasn't exactly looking forward to delivering Harry to his human. He was still less than pleased about the necessity of leaving his ill brother at the mercy of a member of a civilization that didn't even believe in extraterrestrial life. Harry was extremely vulnerable in his current state. If his human rejected him, that would absolutely destroy him.

"Do you know who will break our bond?" Seyn said.

Ksar's lips thinned as he was reminded of another thing he had no control over. The mind adept who had broken Harry's bond was Class 4 at most. However, that didn't mean the mind adept appointed to their case would be as weak.

"No," he said curtly.

"*Cease talking about it,*" he told Seyn telepathically without establishing eye contact. "*We don't know who might be listening.*"

"You're worried," Seyn told him, his thoughts laced with bewilderment. *"Why? I'm sure you can do it."*

Ksar almost laughed. It was infuriating that Seyn thought manipulating a trained mind adept would be easy. And yet a part of him felt like puffing his chest out at Seyn's show of faith in his abilities.

Fucking pathetic.

He couldn't wait to be free of Seyn and the disconcerting effect he had on him.

"Mind adepts aren't just regular telepaths," he told Seyn testily. *"They're the sole exception from the Bonding Law for a reason. They might be forbidden by law from taking a position of power on the Council, but they still wield enormous power. They've been trained in mind arts from birth. Most mind adepts are probably not stronger than you telepathically, but they're far better at mind arts than you can ever dream to be. Raw power isn't everything. These people know everything there is to know about the mind—and about the bond. It won't be easy to fool them, especially if we get a strong one."*

Before Seyn could say anything, the door opened and the tall figure of the High Adept walked in.

Ksar suppressed the urge to swear.

Instead, he put on a faint smile as the High Adept bowed to them regally.

"Health and tranquility, Your Highnesses."

In his peripheral vision, Ksar could see Seyn stiffen ever so slightly; perhaps he had finally realized the seriousness of the situation.

"Health and tranquility," Ksar said, giving the High Adept a clipped nod. "It's an honor, Your Grace. I didn't expect that you would waste your time on such a trivial matter."

The High Adept looked at him steadily, his deep blue eyes betraying no emotion at all. He couldn't be older than thirty-five, very young for such a high position. His straight white hair, a shade paler than Seyn's, fell to his shoulders, almost indistinguishable from the long white robe he was wearing, but his eyebrows and stubble were oddly dark. Although his stoic face was nowhere near as mouth-wateringly exquisite as Seyn's, it was striking. He would have been an attractive man if he weren't so unnaturally expressionless.

"The dissolution of the sacred bond between scions of two royal houses is hardly a trivial matter, Your Highness," the High Adept said, coming to a halt and glancing between them. "Kneel beside me. Let us not waste our time."

Ksar felt his pulse quicken. While he wasn't nervous, per se, he disliked not being in control of the situation. Taking his chances and hoping for the best wasn't the way he did things. He didn't know for sure how strong a telepath the High Adept was, but it was reasonable to assume that he wouldn't have earned his position at such a young age if he weren't either exceptionally skilled at mind arts or telepathically gifted. Neither option was particularly reassuring.

When neither he nor Seyn moved, the High Adept looked between them blankly. "Is there a problem?"

"Yes," Seyn said.

Ksar went very still, and then, for the first time that day, he looked Seyn straight in the eye.

Chapter 18

"Pardon?" the High Adept said.

Seyn dragged his eyes from Ksar's inscrutable face and looked back at the High Adept. "I would like to have a word with my bondmate in private," Seyn said. "It won't take long."

A tiny wrinkle appeared between the High Adept's brows, but he nodded and left the room with an unimpressed air about him. Seyn scowled at his back, realizing the monk likely thought that Seyn had asked for the delay so that he could beg Ksar not to break their bond.

"What is it?" Ksar said, his gaze sharp as his silver-gray eyes scanned the walls.

Seyn inhaled deeply, and for the first time, tried to initiate telepathic communication with Ksar. Without the bond, it should have been impossible, but he *was* a high-level telepath, so he gave it a try. If Ksar could get into his mind and communicate, there was no reason he couldn't do the same.

Reaching Ksar's mind wasn't a problem; the ugly impenetrable barrier blocking the way was. Seyn touched it tentatively, his stomach in knots. He suddenly felt fourteen all over again, bracing himself for rejection.

But the barrier gave in, letting him inside, not deep, but deep enough for communication.

"Do you think it's safe to talk aloud?" he asked, feeling uneasy all of a sudden. Ksar's mind felt disconcertingly familiar. Too familiar.

It took him a moment to realize why. He'd been doing his best not to think about the illicit telepathic merge he'd begged for the last time they'd had sex. But it was hard to pretend it had never happened now that even the shallow touch of their minds made him shiver with eagerness for more.

Fuck, this had been a terrible idea.

"I can't sense anyone else nearby, but communicating telepathically is probably safer," Ksar replied, walking to him. "What do you want?" he said aloud, stopping in front of Seyn. He was so close Seyn could smell the earthy, masculine scent of his aftershave. Ksar's cravat was a little loose.

Seyn moistened his lips with his tongue, his heart beating so fast and hard he felt a little dizzy. "Are you sure we should do this?" he said aloud in case anyone was eavesdropping. *"Are you sure you can handle the High Adept? Are you stronger than him?"*

Ksar's expression changed a little. "I don't know," he said, his gaze intent on Seyn. *"There are whispers among the Council that he achieved his high rank using some very dubious methods. Not to mention that the old High Adept's death certainly raised a few eyebrows. He had been in perfect health, so his sudden death was rather suspicious, even though there was no proof that his successor had anything to do with it."*

Seyn found himself taking an involuntary step closer, his eyes locked with Ksar's.

"Yeah? So you think he's a high-level telepath?"

"It seems likely," Ksar replied, watching him intently. *"You want to suggest something?"*

Seyn looked away before returning his gaze to Ksar. *"You bonded Harry to Leylen without any trouble. Maybe you should...it would make sense for you to bond us now to avoid suspicion."* He bit the inside of his cheek, his stomach clenching as he waited for Ksar's reaction. He hated how insecure he felt. It wasn't as though he was offering something outrageous. It was a perfectly logical thing to do to ensure that everything went smoothly.

Sure, he would be tied by the bond again, but it would be for a very short time until the High Adept broke it officially. It wasn't as though he *wanted* to be bonded to Ksar again.

"No," Ksar said.

Seyn's insecurity shifted into annoyance. *"Why not? It's perfectly reasonable!"*

"We can't risk establishing a deep telepathic connection like the bond."

Seyn lifted his chin stubbornly. *"Enlighten me why not."*

Ksar glared at him. *"Merging minds is dangerous, you little idiot. It can create something akin to addiction."*

Flushing, Seyn glared back. *"I assure you I'm not addicted to your vile mind."*

Ksar stepped even closer, looking at Seyn with intensity that had Seyn's cheeks burning and toes curling. *"Are you absolutely sure that's not why you want me deeper in you right now?"*

Seyn's hands curled into fists. He hissed aloud, "You arrogant ass—"

The door opened, and the High Adept walked back into the room.

Seyn stepped away from Ksar, his hands still trembling with rage.

"My apologies for the interruption, Your Highnesses, but I have other duties waiting for me, so I cannot delay your appointment any longer," the High Adept said neutrally. If he had heard them arguing, he gave no sign of it, his face an emotionless mask.

"That's quite all right," Ksar said. "Let's proceed. I have other matters that require my attention, as well."

The High Adept inclined his head slightly and walked to the ceremonial rug in the middle of the room. "Please kneel beside me and lower your mental shields."

Seyn hesitated but did as he was told. He lowered his shields—after carefully tucking away all the compromising thoughts and memories he had no wish to share. He also dialed down his powers to the best of his ability, trying to pass for the Class 2 telepath he was supposed to be.

Still pissed off, he pointedly didn't look at Ksar, who sat down across from him.

When the High Adept laid his hands over their napes, his thumb pressing against the point just below Seyn's ear—his telepathic center—Seyn braced himself.

He could feel the pressure of a foreign mind pushing into his and had to curb the instinct to throw it out. The High Adept's mind felt invasive, forceful, and alien— wrong. It was strong, too strong, overwhelming and disorientating. It felt like the worst kind of violation, and Seyn fought back the wave of nausea. Ksar's mind had never felt like this. Did that mean the High Adept was a stronger telepath than Ksar?

He didn't know what Ksar's plan was, but it sure as hell wasn't working, because Seyn could feel the moment the mind adept discovered that there was no bond in his mind. The emotionless, cold pressure on his mind changed to suspicion, then anger, then suspicion again—before the invasive presence suddenly disappeared from his mind.

Gasping for breath, Seyn snapped his eyes open. Trying to ignore the splitting headache and nausea, he focused his gaze with some difficulty on what was happening in the room.

The High Adept was kneeling now too, as if his knees had given out. He was shaking faintly, his face deathly pale. His once emotionless eyes were wide with shock and something like horror as he struggled for breath, staring at Ksar.

Ksar, who had a look of intense concentration on his face, a bead of sweat running down his forehead.

Seyn's skin prickled with goosebumps. He could literally feel the *power* pulsing in the room, one mind trying to subdue the other. He could feel that the High Adept was putting up one hell of a fight, his training in mind arts clearly superior to that of Ksar. But it still wasn't enough.

Although Ksar had told Seyn that raw power wasn't everything, it obviously was in that particular case. Seyn could feel the force of Ksar's telepathy crushing the other man's, over and over, one blow after another.

At last, the High Adept whimpered, blood trickling out of his nose as he fainted, slumping to the floor.

Ksar exhaled, his face losing the look of concentration, but his shoulders remained tense as he regarded the unconscious monk with a grim expression in his eyes.

"What did you do?" Seyn whispered, glancing at the door, afraid of someone walking in. If they had been observed, they were screwed.

And then he almost laughed. What was wrong with him? He was afraid of the wrong thing here. If Ksar could reduce even the best mind adept on the planet to a heap on the floor, then he could easily fuck with Seyn's mind ten times over and make him believe anything he wanted. It should have scared him. It didn't. He felt a lot of things around Ksar, but fear wasn't one of them, had never been.

Maybe he *was* an idiot.

Ksar shifted his eyes to him. "Your nose is bleeding," he said in a clipped voice. "Did he hurt you?"

Seyn touched his own nose and wiped the few drops of blood he found. "What happened?"

"I dismantled his defenses while he was distracted, but he was stronger than I expected. He's at least Class 6." Ksar got to his feet and, taking Seyn's wrist, hauled him up. "Does your head hurt?" he said, without looking at him.

Seyn stared at him. "Does it matter to you?"

A muscle flexed in Ksar's jaw. "I wouldn't waste my time asking about something that didn't matter. He's a high-level telepath. A prolonged telepathic contact with one is always dangerous."

"You're a high-level telepath, too," Seyn murmured, watching Ksar curiously. "I've survived having you in me multiple times just fine." Immediately, Seyn regretted his choice of words. Ugh. "He got pretty deep, but I've had you much deeper." Seyn flushed, mortified by the stuff coming out of his mouth. What the hell was wrong with him? Why did he keep reminding Ksar of what they'd shared?

Thankfully, Ksar's still wasn't looking at him, so he didn't see his blush. His gaze was averted, his face hard as stone. Only his grip on Seyn's wrist tightened. "That was different," he said. "He isn't me."

Before Seyn could process what that was supposed to mean, Ksar released Seyn's wrist and walked over to the unconscious man. He pressed his hand below the High Adept's ear and closed his eyes for a moment.

Stroking his own wrist, Seyn stared at Ksar's profile, his eyes trailing over Ksar's strong jaw and the firm, arrogant curve of his lips.

He dragged his gaze away.

"Act a little disoriented and overwhelmed," Ksar said, straightening up. "Like you just had your bond broken."

Before Seyn could say anything, the High Adept opened his eyes and sat up, frowning.

"My apologies, Your Grace," Ksar said, sounding embarrassed, of all things. "I didn't mean to push you away."

The High Adept's face cleared up, as if Ksar's words made total sense. "I understand. I have been told the sudden lack of the bond can be disorienting." A wrinkle suddenly appeared between his brows. He looked between them sharply as he got to his feet.

Seyn's stomach dropped. Did he suspect something, after all?

The High Adept looked at Ksar. "As you are a Lord Chancellor of the MIA, I'm sure I do not need to remind you to retake the Standard Telepathic Test within the next two days, Your Highness."

Ksar nodded. "And I'll make sure that Seyn'ngh'veighli does the same."

The monk looked at Seyn. "Are you well, Your Highness? You look pale."

Seyn winced. "Just a little overwhelmed. Everything feels...so much more."

He must have sounded pretty convincing, because the High Adept actually seemed sympathetic. "It was to be expected," he said. "But if you experience any difficulty handling your heightened senses, you are welcome to return to the High Hronthar. I will make time for you."

"I'm sure it won't be necessary," Ksar said flatly. "Thank you for your time, Your Grace."

Seyn followed Ksar out of the room. He felt the High Adept's unnerving gaze on his back until the door closed behind them.

"I think he suspects something," Seyn whispered.

Ksar didn't say anything.

"Did you hear me?" Seyn said.

"Yes," Ksar said, looking straight ahead.

"And?" Seyn went silent, waiting until the few monks heading the opposite way passed them. "Aren't you worried?"

"It doesn't matter," Ksar said. He still wasn't looking at him.

Seyn glowered at him, starting to get really pissed off. Nothing pissed him off as much as Ksar's ignoring him and making him feel like he didn't matter.

"Why not?" he said, crossing his arms over his chest.

"He won't dare do anything against me," Ksar said. "Even if he is suspecting something, I just got enough dirt on him to make him very agreeable."

"You watched his private memories?" Seyn wasn't sure what it said about him that the emotion he was feeling was exasperation, not outrage or disgust.

"Of course I did," Ksar said, shrugging slightly. "I could hardly miss the opportunity to get leverage against one of the most powerful individuals on the planet. I'm a politician."

"You're a terrible person," Seyn said without much heat.

"Yes."

Seyn chuckled despite himself and turned his head away so that Ksar couldn't see his smile.

He could feel Ksar's eyes on the side of his face. It figured; of course the asshole would look at him now that Seyn didn't want to be looked at.

"You're underestimating him, you know," Seyn said, running a hand through his hair. "He's...extremely powerful. I've never felt anything like that. He's very, very strong."

A flare of annoyance that came off Ksar took Seyn by surprise. Ksar usually had an incredible control over his mental shields, rarely allowing his emotions to be felt—unless Seyn was touching him—so his sudden lapse of control was very surprising.

"I overpowered him easily enough," Ksar said evenly.

"Only because you took him off-guard! He's dangerous."

"No more than me."

Seyn blinked. He cocked his head to the side, eyeing Ksar's stony expression. Was Ksar actually annoyed that Seyn considered him inferior to the High Adept?

"I don't know," Seyn said casually. "He felt a lot stronger than you when he was in me."

Ksar's jaw clenched.

Seyn suppressed a grin, utterly delighted. He couldn't believe Ksar was really getting worked up over something so ridiculous. Like, he knew Ksar strove for perfection in all that he did, but surely he wasn't such a control freak that he wanted to be the very best at everything? It was unrealistic. It was utterly insane.

"He felt stronger only because he didn't know how to handle you," Ksar said in a clipped voice. "Brute force is the easiest route when the mind is unfamiliar. The lack of finesse is hardly something that should be praised."

Seyn almost laughed.

"I wouldn't say he lacked finesse," he said with a shrug. "He was just very, very strong."

Ksar's eyes narrowed. "Are you trying to make me jealous?"

Seyn looked at him blankly.

Jealous? As in jealous over him?

The mere idea of Ksar being jealous over *him* was...utterly ridiculous. He'd spent years flirting outrageously with every semi-attractive person, and Ksar hadn't even batted an eye. Sure, he'd gotten angry with him for acting "unbecomingly," but he'd never been *jealous*. Ksar didn't get jealous over him.

Could he be jealous now? Just because another man had entered Seyn's mind?

Un-fucking-likely.

"Of course not," Seyn said, looking away from Ksar with a crooked smile that felt wooden. "I'm not delusional."

Ksar didn't say anything as he followed Seyn into the t-chamber.

Seyn pursed his lips as something occurred to him. "You said he wouldn't do anything against you. What about me? *I* don't have dirt on him."

"Just keep away from him," Ksar said. "If it's not possible, keep your shields up when you're around him. You're strong enough to hold him off for a while—long enough to contact me. I will deal with him if he bothers you."

Seyn's eyes snapped to him. He frowned in bewilderment. Had he heard that right? Why would Ksar protect him?

"Why?" he said, trying to ignore the stupidly warm feeling in his stomach. Ugh. What was wrong with him? He didn't need to be protected. He could take care of himself.

Ksar's eyes were unreadable. "Just let me know if he approaches you. You have no idea what that man is capable of."

That's not an answer, Seyn almost said, but then he thought better of it.

Why did he care?

Ksar and he were done.

They were going separate ways, nothing binding them together anymore. He was supposed to stop giving a damn about why Ksar did or didn't do something. It wasn't supposed to matter. Ksar didn't matter. The sooner he stopped caring about every little thing in Ksar's behavior, the sooner his...obsession with this man would go away. It had to. Because it was just an obsession. Nothing more. He was entirely capable of not giving a damn about Ksar.

He was.

Let it go. His mother's voice sounded in his mind. *He's nothing to you anymore. Let it go, darling.*

Locking his jaw, Seyn fixed his gaze on the wall. He hated this, hated that he felt...fragile, stretched thin at the edges. He wanted to go home before he could say or do something stupid.

"Are we moving or not?" he said tightly. "I'm sure you have more important matters that require your attention. Drop me off at home first."

In his peripheral vision he could see Ksar press his hand against the console. The t-chamber's doors closed.

But then...nothing.

Ksar didn't tell the computer their destination. He let go of the console and stepped closer, his silver eyes roaming all over Seyn's face.

Seyn licked his lips, his heart thundering somewhere in his throat.

Ksar put his hand on the wall beside Seyn's head and leaned in, his breath brushing against the sensitive spot under Seyn's earlobe. "Do you know how to pass for a low-level telepath on the STT?"

Seyn swallowed.

It was a completely reasonable question. He knew that. But was it really necessary for Ksar to be so close to him? Was it really necessary to whisper the question into his ear? Or was it just a reasonable precaution? Unlike the ancient monastery, the t-chamber could be monitored. Most modern means of transport were.

"I'm not sure," Seyn managed.

He felt rather than heard Ksar sigh. "Fine. Then listen carefully. I will not repeat myself."

Seyn nodded.

Ksar started talking, giving his instructions in a very low voice. The instructions were weirdly long-winded, and Seyn had trouble keeping up. It was hard to focus on Ksar's words when the proximity of him, his voice, and his subtle, masculine scent were quickly overwhelming his senses. Seyn felt like a bundle of nerves ready to go off at any moment, breathing shallowly and staring dazedly at the opposite wall of the t-chamber.

"...think of your telepathic core as a light beacon. You need to learn to dim it at will so that a test program doesn't..." Ksar's lips brushed against Seyn's earlobe and Seyn shivered violently, a whine rising in his throat that he managed to stifle.

"...do you now understand how to do it?"

Seyn blinked a few times. He had no idea what Ksar was talking about.

"Yeah," he managed. "Go on."

Ksar continued. He talked and talked, his voice unbearably low and intimate. They were so close. Close enough that their chests and stomachs brushed. Ksar's cheek was warm against Seyn's, his stubble rough but in a way that wasn't unpleasant at all. He smelled so good that Seyn found himself breathing deeper and deeper, his eyes slipping shut involuntarily. He forced them open when he realized that he was behaving like a crazy person, like an addict greedily getting his fix before it was taken away.

"You suck at giving instructions," Seyn said hoarsely, hating how unsteady his voice sounded, hating how badly he wanted to pull Ksar closer and have Ksar's mouth on his. Just one more kiss. Just one.

Heavens, this was pathetic.

He was pathetic.

Furious, with himself more than with Ksar, Seyn jerked away and slammed his hand on the console. "The Third Royal Palace, second entrance."

The t-chamber started moving.

"Thanks, I think I can figure it out," Seyn said tightly, trying to hide his anger, frustration—and worst of all, formless what-ifs and a hollow sense of longing. Longing he had no business feeling.

The t-chamber opened to the familiar hall of the palace.

Seyn got out.

He came to a halt, his back to Ksar, resisting the urge to run away and hide. He was a scion of the Third Royal House. He was above such immature behavior. He would be damned if he let Ksar see how much this affected him.

With as much dignity as he could muster, Seyn turned around and gave Ksar a shallow, perfectly polite, and perfectly impersonal bow. "Your Highness."

As he straightened up, their eyes met, silver locking with green.

Seyn felt a lump lodge in his throat. They weren't bondmates anymore. They had never been real bondmates, but they had been betrothed for all of Seyn's life. His birthday was two months earlier than it should have been because of Ksar. He'd grown up with the knowledge that this man was his, for better or for worse. He had always been Prince Seyn, the betrothed of Crown Prince Ksar'ngh'chaali.

Did he know how to be just Prince Seyn?

Seyn swallowed hard and the lump lodged in his throat eased, but the hard knot in his chest remained.

He stared at Ksar, feeling utterly lost.

Something flickered in Ksar's eyes. His throat moved, his jaw tightening infinitesimally.

Ksar opened his mouth, and said, "The Second Royal Palace, the left wing."

Seyn had never felt such disappointment in his life.

He didn't watch the t-chamber's doors close.

He turned away and headed for his room.

Once there, he stopped in front of the shiny new table that replaced the one he'd broken. He stared at it unseeingly, feeling a strong sense of déjà vu.

But this time he didn't feel like breaking things.

He wanted to get in his bed, curl up with his pillow, and sleep until he stopped feeling so…hollow. Empty. Wrong.

"This is ridiculous," he whispered. "You hate him. This is what you've always wanted. You're supposed to be happy, you idiot!"

Seyn threw himself on the bed and buried his face in his pillow, groaning as hot, angry tears stung his eyes. What was wrong with him? Why wasn't he happy? He hated Ksar. He loathed him. He hated *everything* about him.

A small, unwelcome thought squirmed its way into his mind,

Do you?

Chapter 19

Calluvian Society Gossip
Intergalactic Union Date: 18768.209

It has been just three days since Crown Prince Ksar'ngh'chaali and Prince Seyn'ngh'veighli had their bonds dissolved, but there are more curious rumors floating around.

It appears our Lord Chancellor left the planet immediately after his bond's breaking, taking his younger brother with him. Prince Harht, who is rumored to be mysteriously ill, had his own bond to his childhood betrothed, Lady Leylen'shni'gul, broken just a day prior to his brother's. It is rumored that Prince Ksar took his ill brother to the pre-TNIT planet Prince Harht visited last year, Sol III [native name: Earth]. What could be the reason?

It is rather curious that their trip coincided with the repeal of the pre-TNIT law. For our readers unfamiliar with intergalactic laws: the recently repealed law regulated the relationship between the citizens of the Union of Planets and planets that have not reached the technological level required for Contact. To be more precise, the pre-TNIT law used to forbid interpersonal relationships such as marriage with citizens of pre-TNIT planets.

Our readers may ask us: What does this have to do with Prince Harht? Perhaps nothing. Perhaps it's nothing but a coincidence. Coincidences can be curious indeed…

* * *

Calluvian Society Gossip
Intergalactic Union Date: 18768.212

Breaking! Crown Prince Ksar'ngh'chaali to wed his own brother's former betrothed!

Councilor Xuvok's soiree last night was unexpectedly eventful as Lady Leylen'shni'gul revealed that she is now engaged to the Crown Prince of the Second Grand Clan.

The implications of this are certainly interesting. We have utmost respect for our esteemed Lord Chancellor, but one wonders how Prince Harht'ngh'chaali feels about his own brother getting engaged to his former bondmate...

As Prince Ksar'ngh'chaali is still reportedly on Earth, he was unavailable for comment.

* * *

"Please, Your Highness."

Ksar's lips thinned. He was starting to reconsider his opinion about Leylen. She was turning out to be a lot more annoying than he had expected.

"I don't have time," he repeated, his eyes on the quarterly budget report of the Ministry.

"But Your Highness," she said, stepping closer to his chair.

It made him twitch.

He didn't like people coming into his personal space uninvited.

"We haven't been seen together since the announcement of our betrothal," she said smoothly. "Lady Zeyneb's ball is the perfect opportunity for our first public appearance."

Ksar lifted his eyes and leveled her with a cold look. "When I say I'm busy, it means I'm busy. Leave, my lady."

She paled.

Ksar knew he was being a right asshole, but he didn't particularly feel like not being one. The girl should be glad that she was still allowed entry into the palace after what she had done.

Ksar had been less than amused upon returning from Earth and finding out that Leylen had told everyone about their engagement while he had been off-planet.

He'd had no intention of making their supposed engagement public so soon, and having his hand forced had been beyond aggravating. It didn't help that he hadn't been in a good mood to begin with—he wasn't happy to leave his brother on Earth—so suddenly being thrust into the middle of a scandal hadn't exactly improved his mood.

He disliked not being in control of the public narrative. He might have made a deal with the girl, but he had never explicitly promised her that he would marry her anytime soon. Now the entire planet was talking about how he effectively stole his own brother's bride. So much for avoiding a scandal.

The Queen was entirely unamused that he had failed to contain the scandal, and Ksar couldn't blame her for that. He was angry with himself, too. He should have noticed how eager Leylen was to elevate her social status. He should have taken time to warn her not to share the news without his permission—instead of wasting the precious little time he'd had on his *former* betrothed.

"Please, Your Highness," Leylen said, looking at him beseechingly. "I know you're displeased with me, but it will be more scandalous if we continue to avoid social functions. We look guilty."

Ksar's first instinct was to throw her out. But the rational part of him knew she was right. The longer he avoided social events, the nastier the gossip would become.

"Fine," he said. "But I will not tolerate more lies."

She inclined her head demurely. "Of course, Your Highness. I told you it wasn't my intention to anger you. I didn't know you would be displeased by what I told people about Prince Seyn."

Ksar pursed his lips. "Go home. I will collect you at nine o'clock."

With a deep bow to him, she left, her hips swaying more than was proper. She still exuded arousal, but at least she seemed to have given up trying to seduce him like a harlot.

Ksar pinched the bridge of his nose, exhaling slowly.

He knew he was being unreasonable.

He wasn't being entirely fair to her. Seyn had behaved far more outrageously in the past, and it had never irritated him that much—or rather, it had irritated him for a different reason.

He should have been more tolerant toward her.

The woman had an admirable self-control. It had been less than ten days, but she was adapting well to her lack of bond. She had far better control of her heightened senses than Seyn had after his bond's dissolution. To be fair to Seyn, he was a stronger telepath than Leylen, so he'd had a harder time than her, but still. Her composure was admirable. Seyn had been a mess of emotions and needs, so damn eager for sex he had looked positively drunk with desire—

Ksar stood and headed out of his study.

He had a ball to get dressed for.

But on his way to his rooms, he was accosted by the King-Consort.

"Ksar, I wanted to speak to you," he said.

Ksar slowed his steps, allowing his father to catch up. "Yes?"

"I want to go to Earth and check on Harry," Zahef said.

"Are you asking for my authorization? You don't need it anymore. The Ministry no longer regulates visits to pre-TNIT planets."

"I am aware of that," Zahef said dryly. "I may not be as interested in politics as your mother and you, but I'm not entirely oblivious. I know I don't need your permission anymore. In any case, I have no interest in talking to the Lord Chancellor. I want to talk to my son."

Ksar grimaced. Sometimes the King-Consort was as naive as Harry.

"I'm all ears, Father," he said, forcing himself to be patient.

"Do you think Harry and…his young man would be pleased to see me?"

"It hasn't even been ten days since I left Harht on Earth," Ksar said, almost smiling at his father's choice of words. "Ten days ago, Adam Crawford didn't even know about the existence of extraterrestrial life. Let him adjust to the fact that his boyfriend is an alien before forcing him to meet an alien father-in-law."

Zahef chuckled. "Indeed, that would probably be too much for the poor human. But I worry. What if Harry isn't being treated well? I know you said Harry's human received the news relatively well, but he might have changed his mind since then—"

"Do you actually think I left my brother unprotected?" Ksar said. "Borg'gorn is monitoring him. I'm receiving updates daily. If Harry is in danger, he'll be teleported home."

There was a short silence before Zahef sighed. "Why didn't you tell me that before?"

"You didn't ask. I didn't know it was of interest to you. I'm entirely capable of handling the issue."

"But you don't have to, Ksar," Zahef said, his voice soft.

"On the contrary, it's my duty."

Heaving another sigh, Zahef said, "It *isn't* your duty. You have parents, Ksar. You aren't the king yet. I know your mother thinks that it's fine to give part of her duties to you prematurely, 'to build character and prepare you,' but it's hardly normal. You have your own duties as the Crown Prince and the planet's Lord Chancellor. Frankly, I'm amazed that you aren't keeling over from exhaustion. You shouldn't think that Harry is your problem to handle, too."

"You're a few years too late for this speech," Ksar said and suppressed a grimace.

He didn't need to look at his father to feel his guilt. Guilt was an unpleasant emotion to feel, even if it was secondhand.

"I know I'm being quite hypocritical," Zahef said, clearing his throat. "I admit that, just like your mother, I relied on you to find a solution for Harry's situation. I'm guilty of expecting you to perform miracles—I won't deny it." He chuckled, self-deprecation written all over his face. "It's a bad habit parents tend to develop when their child never fails at anything. But it doesn't mean I don't worry about you. It doesn't mean I don't see the sacrifices you make. It doesn't mean I don't see how unhappy you are."

Ksar looked straight ahead and walked faster. "I'm not unhappy."

"I haven't seen you smile in months."

"You know I don't smile much."

"No," Zahef said quietly. "You don't."

Ksar let out a sigh, starting to get angry.

A lecture on his life choices was the last thing he needed tonight.

"I'm perfectly happy," he said again. "Almost everything went according to my plans. Harht is free of his bond to Leylen. His health is much better. And since it's so important to you— I believe his human makes him happy."

"And what about you?" Zahef said. "You were saddled with your brother's bondmate instead. I don't remember you being particularly fond of her."

"She will suffice," Ksar said evenly. "I don't need your pity. Cease acting like I have no agency. No one can force me to do what I don't want."

He could feel his father's gaze on his face.

"Is she what you *want*?" Zahef said. "There is a difference between wanting something deeply, with all of your heart, versus wanting something with your brain. When was the last time you did something for yourself? Not because it was the rational thing to do but because you wanted it?"

Ksar's jaw clenched. "I don't have time for this," he said, entering his rooms. "If you'll excuse me, Father." He shut the door unceremoniously in the King-Consort's face and stood still for a moment.

When was the last time you did something for yourself? Because you wanted it?

A harsh chuckle left his mouth. If his father wanted him to act like an irrational, mindless animal, he was out of luck.

The only person capable of making him behave that way was no longer in the picture.

Ksar's lips thinned as he felt a twinge of *something*. Something like raw, gut-wrenching longing.

Ignoring it, he strode toward his wardrobe.

He had a ball to get dressed for and a fiancée to collect.

Chapter 20

Seyn did his best not to tense up outwardly when they announced Ksar's name. But when they announced Leylen's name right after Ksar's, his mask of indifference slipped for a moment.

Seyn hurriedly put it back and didn't look toward the entrance of the ballroom as whispers ran through the crowd. He pretended he couldn't feel the stares and didn't know that people were watching for his reaction to his ex-bondmate and his new fiancée's first public appearance together.

They would be waiting for a long time.

Seyn smiled crookedly at Prince Aedan and murmured, "I feel like an exotic specimen in a zoo."

Aedan shot him a sympathetic look. "It could have been worse."

"You think?" Seyn said with a laugh.

"Your mother could have been trying to whore you out to another planet's king," Aedan said wryly.

Seyn grimaced. Queen-Consort Zeyneb, Aedan's mother, was notoriously known for being eager for her son's marriage to the King of Planet Zicur.

"Do you not like him?" Seyn said, trying to distract himself from the overwhelming desire to look toward the entrance. It was fucking ridiculous. He'd gone longer stretches without seeing Ksar than the nine days that had passed since the official dissolution of their non-existent bond.

But somehow, it felt different this time. More final. The knowledge that there was nothing tying them together anymore made him feel…agitated. It was driving him crazy—this maddening, dissatisfied feeling under his skin—as if he had no purpose in life besides arguing with Ksar, which was fucked up on so many levels Seyn didn't dare mention it to anyone for fear of sounding insane. The only person he trusted enough to talk about it with was Harry, but he was still on Earth with his human. Besides, Harry wasn't exactly impartial where Ksar was concerned.

Aedan shrugged, his dark eyes not quite meeting Seyn's. "He's nice, I suppose. It could have been worse."

Seyn blinked, having already forgotten what he'd asked. "Yeah—I guess," he said. He hoped he didn't look as distracted and self-conscious as he felt.

Judging by the look Aedan shot him, he wasn't fooling anyone.

"You don't have to pretend to be completely fine with the situation, you know," Aedan said. "In fact, if you do, it'll probably be obvious that your indifference is fake. He was your bondmate for your entire life. Some hurt pride is expected, especially after the malicious rumors Leylen has spread about you."

Seyn gave a laugh. "They were nothing but the truth. It's hardly a secret that Ksar always found some fault in everything I did."

Aedan huffed. "She claimed that he'd chosen her because Ksar wanted a 'consort who can behave according to their station,' which is just..." Aedan shook his head. "It's incredibly offensive, both to you and your House. You're a prince yourself. You've been literally taught how to be a King-Consort since before you could walk."

Seyn shrugged. He wasn't particularly offended by the rumors, especially since he was honest enough with himself to admit that there was some truth to them. He hadn't always behaved in a way befitting a prince, much less the future consort of a king; he'd always known that, but he didn't care. Behaving improperly had been a foolproof way to get Ksar to notice his existence.

Granted, it had also earned him Ksar's ire, but truth be told, Seyn had always preferred to be on the receiving end of Ksar's anger to being ignored by him, as if he wasn't worthy of Ksar's attention. Ugh. Even thinking about it made his blood boil, his body tensing for a fight—a fight that wouldn't happen. He and Ksar were nothing to each other. There was no reason to argue with Ksar anymore. No reason to want his attention.

Not that he'd ever *wanted* Ksar's attention.

He'd just hated not having it.

There was a difference. He was sure there was.

"Stop ignoring them so obviously," Aedan said quietly. "People won't stop staring at you until you satisfy their curiosity. Just look at him and then look away."

Aedan was probably right. His indifference probably looked odd. How hard could it possibly be to look at Ksar and then look away, as if Ksar was beneath his notice? He could totally do it. He could.

Seyn turned his head.

The ballroom was huge. There were probably over five hundred people there. His eyes shouldn't have found Ksar as quickly as they did.

Ksar was talking to Queen-Consort Zeyneb, looking regal as usual, not a hair out of place. Seyn stared at him hungrily, his gaze roaming over his firm jaw and sharp cheekbones, and thin, cruel lips that had felt so good on his—

Seyn looked away and grabbed a drink from a passing waiter. He gulped it down greedily, trying to quell the thirst he suddenly felt. It didn't quite work.

Heavens, this was fucked up.

"Don't take it the wrong way," Aedan said, nursing his own drink. He glanced over the rim of his glass in Ksar's direction. "But after having my bond broken, I have a newfound appreciation for Ksar'ngh'chaali." He grinned lewdly. "If you get what I mean."

Seyn scowled. "He's not the most handsome man in this room."

"No," Aedan said agreeably, looking far too amused for Seyn's liking. "You are. But there's something about him that's just..." He licked his lips and smirked. "He looks like he'd be fantastic in the sack."

Seyn pursed his lips and tried not to glare at him.

In all honesty, he could hardly blame Aedan for noticing attractive people—he remembered how horny he'd been the first month after his bond's breaking, so he could definitely understand—but it didn't mean he liked it. He didn't like that Aedan was imagining having sex with Ksar. He didn't like to imagine Ksar having sex with Aedan.

The mere thought was wrong, disgusting, and just—just infuriating.

Dropping his smirk, Aedan actually took a step back. "I was joking, Seyn. Well, mostly." A furrow appeared between his brows. "I thought you hated him."

"I do," Seyn said testily and walked away before Aedan could say anything. He felt absolutely mortified—and horrified—by his completely inappropriate possessiveness. He had no business feeling proprietary over a man who was nothing to him. Over a man he hated. It was none of his business if people wanted to bed Ksar. This vicious possessive feeling was weird and completely fucked up.

Furious with himself, Seyn wasn't looking where he was going.

So of course—of course—out of the hundreds of people in the room, he collided with Leylen.

"Sorry," he said automatically before realizing who it was.

Leylen smiled at him kindly. "Oh, don't worry. It's understandable that you're distracted."

He wanted to hit her.

Immediately, Seyn cringed at the thought. He wasn't a violent person, least of all toward women, no matter how superior and smug they looked. He had been raised by two strong women and had nothing but the utmost respect for them.

But fuck it, Leylen didn't deserve to lick his mothers' shoes, as far as he was concerned.

Isn't that a bit too extreme? his inner voice said quietly.

Seyn had to admit that perhaps he was being a little unfair toward the woman.

He'd never felt such disdain toward her before. She was hardly the epitome of evil.

He still wanted to punch her in the face.

Seyn took a deep breath. He knew people were watching them. The hush that fell around them was unnatural. Making a scene was the last thing he needed after all the rumors Leylen had spread about his inappropriate conduct. So if he were thinking rationally, Seyn would have walked away without saying anything.

He wasn't thinking rationally.

"Your Highness," he said flatly.

She arched an eyebrow. "Pardon?"

"One would think that someone with your impeccable conduct would know how to properly address your betters," Seyn said.

She flushed.

For a moment, she looked mutinous. It was obvious that she already considered herself of a higher rank than him—and she would be, after marrying Ksar.

But she wasn't, not yet. Seyn was a prince of the Third Royal House. She was a member of a minor noble family with more wealth than pedigree.

"Your Highness," Leylen grated out before smiling innocently. "Forgive me, I'm so excited these days that I get distracted and forget my manners. Have you already received your invitation from the Second Royal House?"

Seyn spared a moment to admire her quick mind. She was smart enough to know how to turn the tables on him and make him look pathetic.

Unluckily for her, he had a thicker skin after years of verbal sparring with Ksar, and she had nothing on Ksar's sharp tongue.

Smiling amicably, Seyn leaned closer to her and murmured just for her ears, "Enjoy your excitement while it lasts. You don't know him like *I* do. He will crush you." He nearly face-palmed as soon as he said that. What was wrong with him? Seriously—what was wrong with him? It would have been easy to subtly put her in her place without resorting to such juvenile methods.

Leylen looked as shocked as he was by his open hostility before giving him a haughty look. "Jealousy is so unbecoming, Your Highness," she said, raising her voice.

Scandalized whispers around them got louder.

Seyn winced inwardly, already imagining the headlines.

Stupid, stupid, stupid.

Before he could tell her how ridiculous her words were, a familiar voice said from behind him,

"Is there a problem?"

Seyn's heart skipped a beat.

A nervous look flashed across Leylen's face before she smiled pleasantly. "Not at all, Your Highness. We were just talking."

Distantly aware of the stares and painfully aware of the man behind him, Seyn turned around.

The moment his eyes locked with Ksar's, he felt hot and cold all over, his stomach quivering.

Not wanting to be a hypocrite after criticizing Leylen for her lack of manners, Seyn executed a perfect bow and said politely, "Your Highness."

Ksar gave a clipped nod, his silver eyes fixed on Seyn with a strange expression.

Leylen said with a smile, "Your Highness, we were talking about the—"

"May I have a word with you?" Ksar said, still looking at Seyn. He didn't spare Leylen a glance, and it filled Seyn with vicious satisfaction.

Weirded out by his own emotions, Seyn hesitated. He should probably refuse. Talking to Ksar in private would only make the rumors and speculations worse.

He should refuse.

He should.

But—

But he didn't *want* to. The prospect of being alone with Ksar made his heart beat faster, a strange, almost sickening excitement coursing through his veins.

Seyn found himself nodding before he could stop himself. Idiot. He was an idiot.

The whispers around them became louder as he followed Ksar out onto the nearest balcony.

There were two minor lords on it, but one look from Ksar made them leave. The door shut after the two men, cutting off the noise of the ballroom.

Biting his lip, Seyn braced himself and turned around, determined to act aloof. But his carefully schooled expression was completely wasted.

Ksar wasn't looking at him. His jaw was locked as he stared at the gardens below. If Ksar weren't the one who had asked for a word, Seyn would think Ksar didn't want to be there.

"Well?" Seyn said. "I don't have all night."

"Do you do it on purpose?"

Seyn frowned, genuinely bewildered. "Do what?"

Ksar didn't look at him. "Don't play coy. You always have to be the center of attention. You can't live without making everyone look at you."

Seyn bristled. "Screw you—no one forces you to look at me. Fucking look elsewhere."

Ksar gave a laugh.

"What's so funny?" Seyn said, glowering at Ksar's profile.

Ksar didn't answer.

Instead, he said tersely, "Cease provoking Leylen and making scenes."

Seyn saw red. "Me? She's the one who started it!"

"I don't care who *started* it," Ksar said. "You should be smarter than that. Your reputation is in tatters as it is."

Seyn blinked. Why did Ksar care?

"Yes, thanks to your precious fiancée," he said cuttingly, trying to hide his confusion.

Ksar's lips thinned. "She will stop spreading the rumors. I've already had a word with her."

Seyn snorted. "Clearly it wasn't as effective as you think. She was trying to humiliate me tonight."

"You're hardly an innocent lamb," Ksar said, still looking at the gardens below. "You can take care of yourself. She's just a spoiled girl with overinflated ambitions."

"Charming. I see your opinion of her is as low as your opinion of me."

"She's very different from you."

Seyn cocked his head to the side, studying Ksar. There was something irritated about the way Ksar said it.

"How so?" Seyn said, bracing himself for an insult.

"She doesn't disagree with my every word, for one thing."

Seyn smiled involuntarily at that. "Your ego doesn't need inflating."

Ksar let out a laugh. "You've certainly never inflated it."

Seyn eyed him uncertainly. He was perplexed that Ksar was seemingly content to waste his precious time on him when there was no reason to. Why had he even wanted to talk to Seyn? Just to tell him to stop making a scene? He could have spoken to his *current* fiancée to a better effect. She certainly wouldn't have argued with him. It was puzzling.

"Why aren't you looking at me?" Seyn said, asking about the other thing that had been confusing and bothering him. He'd never handled well not having Ksar's full attention. "Don't you know it's impolite not to look at people when you're talking to them? Stop being a dick."

Ksar finally turned and glared at him.

Seyn wet his lips, holding Ksar's searing gaze.

He didn't know who moved first.

The next moment, their lips collided, and Seyn couldn't stop an embarrassingly loud whimper. Moaning, he opened his mouth eagerly for Ksar's tongue, hands burying in Ksar's hair and trying to pull him closer. Heavens, he wanted to consume him, swallow him whole, suck his dick—anything, just to get Ksar deeper inside him.

He was shaking with want so badly that he didn't know what to do with himself. He sucked on Ksar's tongue, clinging to his hard, muscular body, so familiar and so right, and breathing in Ksar's scent like an oxygen-deprived man would breathe the air.

As if sharing his need to be closer, Ksar pulled him tighter against his body, kissing him deeper and harder until it was no longer possible.

Seyn whined in frustration, grabbing Ksar's face, stroking his lean cheeks with just a hint of stubble, wanting to — wanting to —

Ksar tore his lips away, breathing hard, his eyes like molten silver, bright against the dark fringe of his lashes, intent, hungry, heavy-lidded with primal need. "Damn you," he said before kissing Seyn again.

Moaning, Seyn kissed back. He was so hard it hurt. Try as he might, he couldn't kiss Ksar as deep as he wanted, and the frustration was building, driving him crazy.

He wanted to fuck. He wanted to come. He wanted to — wanted to —

"We can't," Ksar's voice said in his head, his hot mouth trailing down Seyn's chin to his throat. Seyn wasn't sure when Ksar had untied his cravat, but suddenly Ksar's lips were sucking a vicious hickey on his neck and Seyn's mouth was opening in a silent moan.

Heavens, why did this feel so good? It had no right to feel this good, not with this man. The fucked up part was that he couldn't imagine allowing another man to do this to him, especially in such a public place. His parents — and hundreds of high-ranking members of society — were just behind that flimsy door that could open at any moment.

This was crazy.

Absolutely insane.

But he wanted him so badly that at that moment he didn't give a shit if hundreds of people watched them as long as Ksar kept kissing him and touching him.

"Ksar," Seyn breathed out, alternately clutching at Ksar's wide shoulders and running his fingers through Ksar's hair.

"We can't," Ksar said, his hands slipping down and pulling their hips flush. Seyn sucked a breath in, feeling the hard length of Ksar's cock against his.

"Not here," Ksar said, his voice so thick it was unrecognizable. He pulled away and straightened his clothes, not looking at Seyn, a flush high on his cheekbones, his lips wet and shiny. Seyn had never thought it was possible to feel such gut-wrenching want and disappointment. The distance between their bodies felt painful. He hated it.

Finished straightening his clothes, Ksar paused. He looked at Seyn. "I'm leaving the ball. I'll key you into the security system of the palace for tonight."

Seyn could only gape after him as Ksar left.

Ugh, what a presumptuous ass. He was so infuriating! Who did he think he was? Did Ksar think he could just casually tell him to come for a fuck and assume Seyn would just run to him like an overeager, lovesick fool?

Screw Ksar.

He wasn't that pathetic.

* * *

Later that night, as he was spread out under Ksar's heavy, deliciously naked body, Seyn had to admit that apparently he was that pathetic. He had tried to stay home. He had. But it was a lost battle.

So there he was, his legs hooked around Ksar's wide back, fingers clutching at his shoulders as Ksar fucked him so good Seyn could only make hiccupped, strangled groans at every thrust of his cock.

He stared dazedly at the high ceiling above them, feeling like he was floating on a cloud of pleasure. It was hardly the first time they'd had sex, but it was the first time they had it in bed. In Ksar's own bed, in his private rooms Seyn hadn't even seen before.

"Ksar."

"What?" Ksar gritted out, his face tense and his dark brows drawn together as he pulled in and out of Seyn, his biceps bulging with the effort to keep his weight off Seyn.

Seyn kind of wished he didn't do it; he wanted to feel him. He wanted to be crushed under Ksar's body, wanted him closer, tighter, deeper. Fuck, he *wanted* him. The intensity of the feeling scared him so much that it cleared the haze of lust a little.

His pleasure-drunk gaze met Ksar's equally glazed eyes. "What are we doing?" he whispered.

Ksar glared at him and gave a vicious thrust, his cock stabbing against that spot that felt particularly good, and Seyn moaned, his eyes rolling to the back of his head.

"You feel so good in me," he said without thinking. Immediately, he almost cringed. What the hell? Who even said that?

But Ksar didn't mock him. He stared down at him intently, his gaze dark and feverish. "Do I?"

Seyn moistened his lips. They felt sore and puffy from all the kissing they had done since he'd arrived. "Yeah," he said honestly, wondering if Ksar knew what he meant. It was hard to explain. Having Ksar inside him was just...so incredibly satisfying, and not just on a physical level. No matter how defective and one-sided his bond had been, it had been a part of him for all his life. He'd spent years trying and failing to feel Ksar in him.

This—sex—wasn't exactly what he'd had in mind back then, but still, having Ksar inside him was gratifying beyond the physical pleasure of having a thick cock in his hole.

"You feel good in me," he said again, holding Ksar's gaze. "Your cock. You."

Ksar's nostrils flared, his eyes wide open and unblinking, his pupils dilated. Leaning down, he kissed Seyn hard.

Seyn kissed back and tightened his legs around Ksar, digging his heels in as they rocked together, bodies entangled so tightly with each other it was hard to tell where he ended and Ksar began.

But before long, they had to stop kissing, the rhythm of their bodies becoming too fast and hard to make it possible. Ksar was groaning, mouthing the side of his face, his breath hot and unsteady. His mental shields were flickering on and off, as if Ksar couldn't quite control it, and Seyn could feel some of Ksar's thoughts. *You feel perfect, damn you.*

A hoarse laugh left Seyn's mouth. "I think that's the first compliment you've ever paid me, you asshole," he said breathlessly, turning his head to nip at Ksar's stubbled jaw. "And I'm not sure that even counts—you didn't say it aloud."

"If you're still capable of talking, I'm doing something wrong. And I wasn't aware you wanted compliments from me."

"I didn't—I don't," Seyn said, hating how unconvincing it sounded. He whined, pushing back onto Ksar's cock. He was so full of him, but somehow, it still wasn't enough. He wanted him deeper. He wanted more. "Ksar? Can we—you know?"

"That would be highly inadvisable," Ksar gritted out, snapping his hips forward.

Seyn opened his eyes blearily. Ksar looked as drunk on pleasure as he felt.

"So? None of what we're doing is *advisable*," Seyn said. "Get in me. Wanna feel you from the inside."

Ksar's gaze darkened. "You're a menace," he said, but he did dismantle his shields completely and let their minds merge. Either he did it gentler this time, or Seyn was getting used to the sensation. Either way, it felt so good. Seyn sighed in bliss, overwhelmed by the double pleasure.

He could feel how tight he was around Ksar's cock, how good it felt to fuck into him, to press him into the mattress and *have* him. He was a little disgusted by how much pleasure he derived from taking Seyn in his own bed, in his own room, on the sheets that smelled of him. He wasn't a primitive animal. This wasn't his territory. *Seyn* wasn't his territory.

"Stop overthinking it and fuck me," Seyn grated out, pushing back on the hard, deliciously thick length in him. "You can freak out over your caveman tendencies later."

Ksar glared at him, but his glares didn't have quite the same effect when Seyn could feel how much Ksar liked having him under him, how much he wanted to fuck him into the mattress, to *own* him, to fill him up with his come until it was leaking down his thighs.

"I don't have caveman tendencies," Ksar bit off, tightening his grip on Seyn's hips and slamming into him.

They both gasped as Seyn's hole squeezed around his cock.

So fucking tight. So fucking thick.

"Sure," Seyn managed. "That's why you're getting off on having me in your own bed."

Ksar glowered and snapped his hips forward, hitting that spot inside him with the precision that would have been unbelievable if Ksar wasn't literally sharing his mind.

Moaning, Seyn closed his eyes and relaxed against the cool sheets under him, giving himself over to the intense, overwhelming sensation of fucking and being fucked, Ksar's mind enveloping him as tightly as Ksar's heavy body on top of him.

He didn't think he'd ever felt so *good* in his life. So perfect. It felt like he was created for this, to be under this man, to have his cock and his mind inside him. He didn't want this to ever end.

But it ended.

He came embarrassingly fast, but so did Ksar. Seyn could only moan Ksar's name and hold on as waves upon wave of intense pleasure washed over him—over them.

He stared at the high ceiling, panting like he'd just run a marathon, his body still shaking with aftershocks.

Ksar started slipping out of him.

"No," Seyn said, his arms tightening around Ksar. "Don't pull out."

Ksar paused and turned his head to look at him.

Their faces were so close Seyn could count Ksar's every eyelash, could feel Ksar's every breath.

"Are we talking about my cock or the merge?" Ksar said, his voice uncharacteristically slow and lazy—sleepy.

Seyn stared at him in wonder. He'd never seen Ksar sleepy.

It was…strange.

"You would know what I meant if you read my mind," Seyn murmured with a little smile. "It's not like you're shy to read people's minds to get the information you want."

"I don't actually enjoy getting into people's minds and reading their thoughts," Ksar said, his thumb tracing Seyn's smiling lips. "It's not exactly pleasant. Unless the mind is fairly compatible with mine, it's an equivalent of searching for something in a puddle of mud."

Seyn snorted. "Are you seriously going to pretend you don't find my mind pleasant? Seriously?"

"I didn't mean you," Ksar said, sounding faintly amused.

No, he didn't *sound* amused. His voice was the usual flat, cold monotone with no inflection whatsoever. Seyn could feel Ksar's amusement because they were still sharing a shallow merge.

Seyn frowned. "Why do you do this?"

"Do what?" Ksar said, lifting his eyebrows a little.

"Use that emotionless voice and pretend you don't feel shit. It's annoying."

Ksar threaded his fingers through Seyn's long hair, eyeing the silver locks with something that wasn't unlike fascination. "I'm a politician. The less I give away, the less I'm vulnerable to manipulation."

Frankly, Seyn was amazed that Ksar was actually bothering to explain himself. "We're in bed, not in the Council."

Something flickered in Ksar's eyes. "I suppose it's a habit by now."

Seyn could feel that Ksar was telling the truth, but not the full truth.

He was about to question him when Ksar suddenly pulled out of him—out of his body and out of his mind. Seyn pouted, the sudden *emptiness* disorienting and unpleasant.

"Stop looking at me like that," Ksar said tersely, a grimace crossing his face, as if pulling out wasn't pleasant for him, either. "A telepathic merge is illegal for a reason, and prolonging it would be highly irresponsible."

Seyn pursed his lips, a little mollified that Ksar didn't pull away completely— Ksar's large body was still half on top of him. A small part of him was disturbed by how clingy he felt, but Seyn refused to think about it too much. He could freak out later. Much later.

"Have you done it before?" he said.

Ksar shot him a sleepy look that somehow managed to be entirely unimpressed. "Sex?"

Seyn scowled. The reminder that Ksar was a lot more sexually experienced than him irked him for reasons he didn't want to examine too closely. "A telepathic merge during sex."

"Of course not," Ksar said, looking at him as though he was insane. "Even if I wanted to do it during a meaningless sexual encounter, I could hardly risk the other person finding out about the extent of my telepathic abilities. In any case, a telepathic merge isn't something to be taken lightly—it isn't something I'd do without the other party's fully informed consent."

Ksar gave him an unreadable look. "There are very few telepaths insane enough to allow a Class 7 telepath the absolute access to their unprotected minds."

There were several noteworthy things about Ksar's answer.

The most important thing should have been the fact that Ksar had finally admitted that he was Class 7. It wasn't.

Instead, Seyn found himself fixating on one particular thought.

Was this not a meaningless sexual encounter for Ksar?

"I'm not scared of you," he said aloud instead of asking the question. If he did, it would make it obvious that he cared about Ksar's answer—which he didn't.

Except he kind of did. He really, really did.

Fuck.

"I could have done anything to you during the merge," Ksar said.

Seyn shrugged, trying to shake off the panic creeping up his throat. "You didn't."

"You little idiot," Ksar said, taking his chin and forcing Seyn to look at him. "When you allow me a full merge, you let me past all your defenses. Telepathic merges are outlawed for a reason, and that's without taking into account that I'm a Class 7 telepath. If I had been careless during the merge, I could have rendered you brain dead."

Seyn just looked at him for a moment.

Contrary to what Ksar thought of him, he was well aware of the dangers of the merge; every telepath in the galaxy probably had heard the horror stories. Those horror stories still didn't stop some couples from doing it, but it usually required an incredible show of trust in one's partner.

It was terrifying to think that he trusted Ksar to that extent, but the evidence was pretty damn undeniable.

"I'm not afraid of you," Seyn said quietly. "Even when I hated your guts, I never thought you'd hurt me. I guess...I guess I trust you."

Ksar gave him a long, indecipherable look, something conflicted in his eyes. At last, he said, "Hated? Past tense?"

Seyn felt his face become warm. "Hate," he said, but it came out teasing rather than firm. "You're still a dick."

Ksar's gaze was so intense it made goosebumps run over Seyn's skin. Fuck, he loved having Ksar's eyes on him. It was sickeningly exhilarating. It made him feel so damn *alive*.

Heavens, this was really messed up.

"Then why are you clinging to me if you hate me?" Ksar said, his tone amicable and lazy.

Seyn scowled. "Shut up, I'm not," he said, lifting his chin. His arms and legs might be wrapped around Ksar, but it absolutely didn't mean he was *clinging* to him. He simply didn't feel like letting go. The merge was still messing him up. It was hard to go from being one with Ksar to not having him close.

Ksar leaned in and kissed the corner of his mouth, the touch barely there.

Seyn breathed out unsteadily. Why did he still feel so damn hungry for this man? So damn needy? He'd just come, for heaven's sake. He shouldn't feel this way.

"You don't have to be defensive," Ksar said against his mouth. "It's likely a side effect of the merge."

"Yeah?" Seyn murmured. "Do you...do you feel it, too?"

Ksar nodded, nipping at Seyn's bottom lip. "Want to put myself in you and never pull out."

Seyn shivered, his whole being craving the insane intimacy of it again. "Ksar," he whispered, rubbing his cheek against Ksar's, his cock already half-hard. "Let's do it again...just one more time?"

He felt Ksar exhale unsteadily against his cheek. "We really shouldn't. This is dangerous. Not to mention completely pointless."

Seyn's stomach dropped.

He gave a clipped nod.

Ksar pulled back a little to look him in the eye. His expression became somewhat pinched. "Damn you," he said and kissed him, long and endlessly hungry, his mind slipping back into Seyn's.

Seyn sighed in bliss and yanked him closer, everything else disappearing once again.

Chapter 21

As a rule, Ksar didn't sleep with people. He liked sex like any healthy man, but he didn't share a bed after sex — and he definitely didn't take anyone to his own bed. He had never even entertained such an idea. Sex was just a base need that had to be satisfied on a regular basis in order not to let sexual frustration affect his judgment. Sex was for discreet off-world brothels where no one knew who he was. Sex had no place in his private rooms, under the roof he shared with the Queen and the King-Consort.

So it was completely inexplicable that he'd woken up that morning to a warm, naked body curled up next to him and the soft snores of another person.

Ksar eyed Seyn's sleeping form, trying to summon irritation and displeasure he should have been feeling.

But there was nothing.

Seyn was snoring softly, his cheek pressed against Ksar's pillow, his long silver hair spread out all over it like a halo. His normally pale pink lips looked red and swollen after the previous night's activities, ruining the positively angelic impression he gave in his sleep.

He looked good in Ksar's bed.

Like he belonged in it.

Ksar grimaced at the thought, deeply disturbed by how much his judgment was still compromised despite spending most of the night buried to the hilt in Seyn—in more ways than one.

I guess I trust you.

Seyn's words rang in his ears, still as discomfiting and viciously satisfying as they had been last night.

Ksar generally wasn't one to lie to himself. He was well aware he wasn't at his most rational where Seyn was concerned, had never been. He let him get under his skin far too easily—and as a result, had often been unfairly harsh on him.

But it was now obvious that there was another extreme he hadn't experienced before: Seyn's pleasure— and his trust—affected him as strongly as Seyn's hostile, infuriating behavior. He liked it.

He liked it far too much.

As though feeling his gaze on him, Seyn mumbled something sleepily and shifted a little. The dark sheets slipped lower, revealing to Ksar's eyes the smooth, strong expanse of Seyn's back and the dimples above his buttocks.

Ksar wet his dry lips.

This was…perplexing. He'd had four perfectly satisfying orgasms last night. He'd touched and kissed every place on Seyn's body and had been touched everywhere in return. There was no mystery left. At this point, he knew everything there was to know about Seyn's body. A man could come only so much in such a short time.

He should have been feeling nothing but exhaustion and disinterest.

His hands shouldn't be tingling with the desire to touch and his mouth shouldn't feel dry.

He shouldn't feel as eager as an adolescent boy, his cock already thickening.

Sighing in exasperation, Ksar gave in. Pushing the silver locks aside, he leaned in and kissed the soft skin at the back of Seyn's neck. His eyes slipped close as he inhaled deeply.

At least there was no one there to witness his utter lack of self-restraint.

"Ksar," Seyn muttered.

Ksar went still, his lips still pressed against Seyn's nape.

He lifted his head. "Yes?"

Seyn didn't reply, his breathing even once again.

Ksar eyed him. He was still asleep, he realized with a jolt. Seyn was still asleep and he was dreaming of him. Now that he concentrated, he could vaguely feel what Seyn was dreaming about. He was dreaming of having his cock sucked—a perfectly normal, ordinary dream for a healthy young man—except for Seyn the man sucking his cock was none other than Ksar.

Good, something in him said viciously.

Ksar grimaced. These possessive thoughts were getting out of hand. What next? Was he going to piss all over Seyn to make sure the brat smelled of him?

Get a grip, damn you.

"Your Highness?"

Ksar had never heard Borg'gorn sound so awkward.

"Yes?" Ksar said.

"I do not wish to disturb you, but you have a meeting with Councilor Mehur'divani at eight o'clock."

Frowning, Ksar sat up. "What time is it?"

"Eight-point-thirteen, Your Highness."

Swearing quietly, Ksar got out of the bed. He'd never been late in his life. It seemed it was a day of firsts.

"What's happening?"

Stepping onto the shower pad, Ksar looked back toward the bed. Seyn was sitting up, blinking blearily, his green eyes still unfocused, a fetching flush on his cheeks. He was leaning back on his arms, his toned chest and stomach on display.

Ksar wrenched his gaze away and activated the shower with a tap of his fingers.

The unpleasant sensation of dry shower was almost welcome, but it did nothing to quell the desire to walk back to the young man in his bed and kiss the sleepy pout off his lips.

"I'm late for a meeting," he said curtly. "You don't have to get up." Ksar walked toward his wardrobe and pulled out a fresh change of clothes.

Behind him, he heard a small laugh. "Okay, this is surreal."

Zipping up his pants, Ksar looked in the mirror. He found Seyn watching him dress with a vaguely conflicted look on his face.

"What is surreal?" Ksar said.

Seyn shrugged with one shoulder, his lips twisting into a crooked smile. "I just... This is so freakishly normal and weird at the same time, you know? Watching you dress for work. I mean, it would have been normal if we..." He trailed off, looking away.

Ksar felt a twinge of...something.

He knew what Seyn meant.

This felt too normal.

Domestic.

"If we didn't get the bond dissolved and got married as expected, this still wouldn't have been normal," Ksar said, slipping into a white shirt and buttoning it up. "For one thing, I wouldn't have sex with you."

Seyn's brows furrowed. "Why not?"

Ksar shot him a sharp, curious look. Did he actually sound offended? "If you didn't find out about the state of our bond and we got married, that would have meant that I would have had to constantly brainwash you to make you believe that we really had a marriage bond." He met Seyn's eyes in the mirror, tying his cravat. "It seems I'm not evil enough to stomach fucking someone who can't think for himself. A pity."

Seyn actually laughed. "You have no shame."

"Why would I be ashamed?" Ksar said, his lips twitching despite his best efforts not to show his amusement. "It's nothing but the truth. Things would have been so much easier if I didn't have certain misgivings."

Seyn shook his head with a grin, his eyes lighting up with mirth. "You're a terrible person and you don't even bother hiding it."

Ksar stared at his smiling face before tearing his eyes away and reaching for his Ministry cloak. "There's no point in pretending to be something I'm not—not with you. I can hardly be as candid with other people."

He could feel Seyn's gaze on him as he slipped into his cloak.

There was a new tension in the air that didn't precisely feel awkward, but it frayed Ksar's nerves all the same.

He was dressed. He was already very late for his meeting.

There was no reason to loiter around like a green boy hoping for a goodbye kiss.

Disgusted with himself and thoroughly sick of his own irrational behavior around Seyn, Ksar headed for the door.

"Ksar."

He came to a halt, and after a moment, looked back toward the bed. "Yes?"

It seemed Seyn had decided to accept Ksar's suggestion not to get up yet: he was curled up around Ksar's pillow, his gaze lazy and a little heavy with sleep. "Will your meeting take long?"

The wave of want that swept through his senses was almost violent in its intensity.

Ksar closed his eyes for a moment, as if that could stop him from saying what he definitely shouldn't be saying. "It should take an hour at most."

Licking his lips, Seyn dropped his gaze. "Not that I'll be *waiting* for you, but I'm not in a hurry to be anywhere today. That's all I'm saying."

Ksar pursed his lips to keep himself from smiling. "If I don't have any pressing matters that require my attention, I might come back before you leave." He was well aware how much Seyn hated it when he phrased things like that.

Predictably, Seyn glared at him.

This time Ksar couldn't suppress his smile.

Seyn's eyes narrowed before a laugh left his lips. "You're an asshole."

"That's nothing you didn't know before," Ksar said.

Seyn gave him a pinched look. "Please stop smiling. It's freaking me out."

Ksar laughed.

Seyn blinked a few times, looking bewildered, which made Ksar laugh again.

"Please go away," Seyn said, groaning and burying his face in the pillow. "Maybe I woke up in an alternate reality. This isn't happening."

"Closing one's eyes and pretending something isn't real is very childish of you."

Seyn lifted his head with an exaggerated look of relief on his face. "Thank Heaven. I was starting to think someone possessed you. It's good to see you're still my—" He cut himself off, his expression partly disturbed, partly mortified.

Ksar walked back to the bed and hauled him up. "Your what?" he said, genuinely curious about the answer. But if he were honest with himself, it was partly just an excuse to touch Seyn again.

Seyn met his eyes, his expression defiant. "So I got used to you being mine, so what? It doesn't mean I'm in love with you or something."

Ksar stared at him, a strange feeling spreading through his chest and settling in his gut.

"That thought hasn't even occurred to me," he said mildly. "Until now."

The murderous look Seyn gave him was almost comical.

Ksar laughed, feeling more amused than he'd had in years. He'd always enjoyed getting under Seyn's skin and making him fume, but this felt different now, somehow. Lighter.

"Fuck, you're such an ass," Seyn said before yanking Ksar's head down and kissing him wetly.

Ksar kissed back without hesitation, his hand burying in Seyn's hair and holding him still as he devoured his mouth. Fucking hell, he tasted so sweet.

Moaning, Seyn pushed his tongue into Ksar's mouth and all but climbed him. Ksar's hands slipped down to grab Seyn's buttocks, pulling their hips flush—

"Your Highness?" Borg'gorn said.

With a muffled curse, Ksar tore his mouth away and stared at Seyn's flushed face. "Stay here," he said tersely, dropping his hands with some difficulty. "Don't go anywhere."

Seyn nodded, looking dazed and hungry—for *him*.

"Your Highness, you're very late."

Ksar turned swiftly and strode out of the room.

If he didn't leave now, he wouldn't leave at all.

Chapter 22

Later, Seyn would be mortified to realize it, but he'd spent at least half an hour after Ksar left hugging the pillow and thinking about Ksar in a way that could be described as "dreamily." He also might or might not have been breathing in Ksar's scent on the pillow, but that was something he would never admit to anyone, even to himself.

"Ugh," he groaned into the pillow, disgusted with himself. Did he seriously intend to stay in Ksar's bed and wait for him to come home like a...like a good little husband? It was beyond ridiculous. It was insane. No matter how good the sex was, it didn't change anything. It shouldn't change anything. Ksar was nothing to him. A few ill-advised fucks and illicit merges wouldn't change that. Ksar was engaged to Leylen.

"Not to mention that you hate him," Seyn said, hoping that saying it aloud would drive the point home. Since when did he need to remind himself that he hated Ksar? It was one of the indisputable facts of life: his name was Seyn'ngh'veighli, he was a prince of the Third Grand Clan, and he hated Ksar.

But did he, really?

Seyn frowned, pursing his lips. It felt weird to question something that shouldn't even be questioned, but...Did he really hate Ksar anymore? Or was it just a force of habit at this point? He certainly didn't hate kissing him or touching him—or even talking to him. Ksar still drove him crazy, but the difference was, half of the time Seyn wasn't sure whether he wanted to punch him in his arrogant face or shove his tongue down his throat.

The fact that he was no longer sure that he hated Ksar was pretty disturbing in itself. How could he not hate him? Ksar was an asshole. He was a terrible, horrible, no good, very bad person with a very questionable moral compass. Now that Seyn knew the full extent of Ksar's horribleness, he should absolutely despise him. He shouldn't want to have anything to do with him. And he most certainly shouldn't be waiting for Ksar's return in Ksar's bed, naked and eager to pick up where they had left off.

Fuck, he had really lost his mind. After years of wanting to be free of Ksar, how could he want this? He could no longer even blame his constant horniness anymore; he felt perfectly in control of his senses and his libido—unless he and Ksar were in the same room, and then he seemed to lose all control of his higher brain functions.

Ugh. This was horrible.

Maybe he should try to fuck someone else.

Seyn's brows furrowed at the thought. Somehow, he couldn't even imagine doing it—and that was pretty damn alarming, actually.

"Do you think I should sleep with someone else?" was the first thing Seyn said the moment Ksar returned.

Ksar paused in the doorway, still dressed in his official Ministry colors. He looked mouth-wateringly good, but Seyn was determined to ignore it.

He'd spent the last hour pacing Ksar's rooms, getting more disturbed the longer he analyzed his feelings and thoughts. It had soon become obvious that he had no desire whatsoever to have sex with someone else—that he felt vaguely disgusted by the mere idea—and the implications of that were terrifying.

Something needed to be done.

He had to stop this.

He needed to stop being an idiot and get over his fixation on a man he'd hated all his life.

"Pardon?" Ksar said, his eyes narrowing slightly. His gaze swept over Seyn with something like displeasure, as if he'd actually expected to find Seyn still naked.

"I think I should stop sleeping with you and fuck someone else," Seyn said, crossing his arms over his chest.

Although Ksar's face was impassive, Seyn could feel a strong emotion coming off him, something toxic and ugly. It was a most peculiar thing. It seemed the merges they'd done had made him more attuned to Ksar's emotions—that or Ksar didn't keep his shields as perfectly impenetrable as he used to in his presence. Seyn wasn't sure which option unsettled him more.

"Should?" Ksar said. "I know you're new to this, but it's advisable to have sex only if there's a 'want' involved."

Seyn snorted.

If I keep doing what I want, I'll spend all my time under you.

That thought only hardened his resolve, because what the hell, seriously.

"I'm just thinking rationally," Seyn said, taking a cautious step back when Ksar started walking toward him. "You said it yourself: this is pointless. You're engaged. My mothers are also choosing the best suitor out of the proposals I've received."

Something dark reflected on Ksar's face for just a moment before his expression went completely blank. "Proposals? It has been ten days."

Seyn chuckled. "It's been known for a month that our bond was going to be broken. It was more than enough time for me to receive over thirty proposals, mostly from other planets' royalty and politicians." He smiled crookedly. "And before you say something, yes, I'm perfectly aware that most of them are essentially political proposals."

"And you're fine with it?" Ksar said, coming to a halt in front of him.

Seyn took another step back. "Why would I not be? That's what our betrothal was, too."

"I distinctly remember you not being 'fine' with our betrothal."

"I was perfectly fine with it until I met you. I was willing to put in an effort and make our marriage work— until you started treating me like I was an annoying little boy you found lacking." Seyn was proud of how casual he managed to sound.

Something shifted in Ksar's expression. "So you're willing to marry a stranger." His voice was very even. "After telling me for years that you wanted freedom."

Seyn lips twisted. "Not necessarily freedom— freedom of choice. If—when—my mothers narrow the proposals down, I'll be given a choice between them."

"I know that if I don't like any of them, I won't be forced into another unwanted betrothal." Seyn lifted his chin, looking Ksar in the eye. "But eventually I *will* accept one of them. I'm a prince of the Third Grand Clan. Contrary to your beliefs, I know my duty to my clan. I'm not a foolish spoiled boy. I will do what I must to improve our shaken political standing and secure a good alliance for my clan. At least this time it will be my own choice. He, whoever he is, will be *my* choice."

That ugly emotion flared around Ksar again, surrounding him like a cloud of toxic gas. It was amazing how outwardly calm Ksar could look when he clearly felt anything but calm.

"He?" he said tonelessly. "Not a she or an it?"

Seyn shrugged, holding his gaze, "I find that I like cock too much to give it up." It came off as vulgar as he'd hoped. He needed to reduce this—whatever this was—to nothing but carnal desire. Because it was. It *was*, dammit.

A muscle twitched in Ksar's jaw. "I see," he said. He walked toward his desk. "Speaking of marriages..." With his back to Seyn, he picked something up from his desk.

When he turned around, the ugly emotion surrounding Ksar was gone, his shields fully up and impenetrable once again. "I think these haven't been sent out yet, but you may as well take yours now before you leave." He handed the white card to Seyn, his expression closed off completely.

Frowning, Seyn skimmed it with his eyes.

You are hereby invited to the ball that will take place on the 12th of Solctinys to celebrate the occasion of Crown Prince Ksar'ngh'chaali's marriage to Lady Leylen'shni'gul, a daughter of Clan Mihuhr.

Seyn didn't read the rest. He stared blankly at the card—at the wedding invitation.

The 12th of Solctinys? It was barely a month away.

"That soon?" he managed. His throat felt weirdly thick, as if something had lodged in it and he had to speak around it. He didn't know why he was so blindsided by the news. He'd known it was coming. He had. It still hadn't felt real.

Until now.

"Your House isn't the only one that has been damaged by the recent scandals," Ksar said. "In fact, mine has taken a larger blow, especially considering all the speculation about my brother having a relationship with a pre-TNIT citizen. The speculation must be stopped. Harry needs to be reintroduced back into society, and there's no better opportunity to show that he's fine with my marrying his former bondmate than to have him present during our marriage ceremony."

Seyn could barely process his words, his mind still stuck on the fact that in less than a month, Ksar was going to marry Leylen. It seemed unthinkable. Wrong.

Seyn bit the inside of his cheek, hard.

"So Harry is coming back?" he said at last, turning away so that Ksar couldn't see his face.

"Yes. The rumors are getting worse. His continued absence is causing rumors worse than the reality. The sooner he is reintroduced back into society, the better his chances of being able to ever return home without being shunned."

Part of Seyn was almost touched by Ksar's obvious concern for his younger brother's reputation and future.

Almost.

The bigger part of him resented that Ksar hadn't shown the same consideration and care toward *his* reputation.

Rationally, Seyn knew it probably meant that Ksar considered him capable of handling himself, but irrationally, there was a pathetic part of him that wanted to be babied and taken care of in the same way Ksar did with Harry—well, not the *same* way, but…

Seyn cut that train of thought off, grabbed his multi-device from the nightstand, and said, without looking at Ksar, "Let me know if Harry needs help when he's back—no, tell him to call me if he needs me. He's always welcome in my home."

And with that, Seyn headed for the door.

"Seyn."

He paused, his back to Ksar.

"Yes?" Seyn said, as calmly as he could. He was calm. He wasn't going to have a breakdown because a man he hated (yes, *hated*) was marrying someone else.

"Back when we first met, I didn't really find you lacking," Ksar said, his voice quiet and a little stiff. "I was cruel because I had to be, to keep you at arm's length. There was nothing wrong with you. Never has been."

Seyn stared at the door blankly.

His chest hurt.

There was nothing wrong with him. He'd been wanting to hear those words from Ksar all his life, but when he actually got them…he wanted to cry and rage, punch Ksar—and then hide his face against Ksar's chest and feel his arms around him.

He did none of those things.

He said, very evenly, "Thank you for telling me that."

And he strode out of the room, the ache in his throat and his chest worsening with every breath he took until his vision was blurry and he could barely see where he was going.

"The t-chamber is to the left, Your Highness," came Borg'gorn's voice, his tone gentle and kind.

Seyn hated it.

"I know where it is," he said with as much dignity as he could muster.

"Of course, Your Highness."

Seyn managed to get into the t-chamber and sagged back against its wall. It started moving without his command—no doubt Borg'gorn's doing.

Seyn wondered if it was possible for an AI to feel pity.

He laughed, the sound as ugly and empty as the feeling inside him.

* * *

As the sound of Seyn's footsteps receded down the hallway, Ksar's gaze fell on the invitation on the floor. He picked it up and stared at it—at Seyn's name in the wrong place—before crushing it in his fist.

"Permission to speak freely, Your Highness?" Borg'gorn said.

"Denied," Ksar said, walking to the bar and pouring himself a drink.

He downed it in one go. The alcohol burned his throat as it went down, but it did nothing to erase the tight feeling in it.

Chapter 23

Ksar first heard the rumor from Councilor Xuvok, of all people.

"You must be quite relieved, Your Highness," Xuvok said suddenly in the middle of a discussion about trading permits.

"Pardon?" Ksar looked up from the graphs displayed on his screen.

The elderly man clarified, "The...current situation must have been awkward for you—encountering your former bondmate everywhere while you're so close to marrying another person. You must be relieved that Prince Seyn'ngh'veighli is going to move to another planet."

Ksar stared at him. "What."

Xuvok frowned. "Have you not heard the rumors? It is said Prince Seyn has accepted Ambassador Denev's proposal."

Ksar moved his gaze back to the graphs and gazed at them blankly. "Let's return to the subject at hand."

His voice came out strange, but Xuvok didn't seem to notice.

The meeting went as it should.

When the councilor finally left, Ksar sat very still, his hands on his desk.

In the absolute silence of the room, with nothing to distract him, he finally had to accept something he'd been in denial about for years.

People said with great power came great responsibility. They were not wrong. Ksar had always prided himself on being cool-headed enough not to use his telepathic abilities recklessly. He'd done…some morally questionable things in the past, but there had always been the line he'd never allowed himself to cross. He'd never harmed another person.

But now…now he had to admit he was absolutely capable of doing what the horror stories said about the high-level telepaths. Because his first thought upon hearing the news was to find Denev and make sure that he suffered from sudden heart failure. It would be so easy.

So easy.

Sighing, Ksar pinched the bridge of his nose.

He would do no such thing. Denev's only fault was wanting Seyn, and Ksar could hardly blame him for that.

Except Seyn wasn't *Denev's* to want.

"For fuck's sake," he muttered through his teeth.

Seyn wasn't his.

He had never been his.

The only thing they'd ever had was their farce of a bond.

Except the bond had been very real to him. He might not have ever been bonded to Seyn, but he'd had constant access to Seyn's emotions for twenty-four years. Ksar was used to Seyn's presence at the back of his mind, no matter how annoying and distracting it had been at times.

Twenty-four years was a very long time. It was probably natural that at some point he'd started thinking of Seyn as something that was his.

A harsh laugh left Ksar's throat. No, there was nothing fucking natural about it. He should have been *glad* to be rid of the needy presence at the back of his mind. He should have been relieved to no longer feel the guilt that presence had always caused in him.

He had no business feeling this ugly possessiveness twisting his stomach and urging him to crush Denev for daring—

Ksar grimaced. Seyn was a free man now. Seyn was free to choose whomever he wanted. And apparently, it was Denev, the ambassador of a planet half a galaxy away from Calluvia. If Seyn married the man, he would move away—which shouldn't be allowed. Seyn's place was *here*, on Calluvia, where Ksar could see him and look at him even if he couldn't have him.

Ksar stared unseeingly at his desk, disturbed by his own thoughts. Perhaps it was a good thing that Seyn had chosen Denev and would live on another planet. Perhaps it was exactly what Ksar needed to get rid of these…these insane thoughts—especially since he wasn't sure he could handle seeing Seyn with another man without arranging an accident for that man.

Sighing in exasperation and disgust, Ksar ran a hand over his face. This was ridiculous. Seyn wasn't his. Seyn was now engaged to Denev, not him. And there was nothing Ksar could do about it. Seyn was free to choose whomever he wanted.

Whomever he wanted.

Ksar lifted his head.

And then he almost laughed at himself for entertaining such a thought. Seyn would never choose him even if Ksar asked him to. Why would Seyn choose him when being free of him was all he'd ever wanted?

Not to mention the not insignificant fact that Ksar was marrying Leylen in eight days. The invitations had been sent out. The preparations for the wedding were in full force. It would create an enormous scandal if he were to cancel the wedding now. Even his political standing might not recover from it. Entertaining such a thought was beyond reckless and irresponsible. He was the Crown Prince of his grand clan. He was the Lord Chancellor of the planet.

What the man behind those titles wanted was largely irrelevant.

Chapter 24

Harry was nervous.

He hadn't seen his family in over a month. Well, he had seen Ksar once a few Terran weeks ago when his brother had come to check on him, but the visit had been brief and Ksar had seemed distant and distracted, his behavior even colder than usual.

Not that Ksar looked any more approachable now.

Harry eyed his brother with concern, taking in his straight posture, the hard set of his jaw and the *stay away* vibe he radiated.

"Adam is coming with me, Ksar," Harry said, as firmly as he could. He didn't have the combative, stubborn nature his older siblings had, but this wasn't something he was budging on.

"Yes, I am," Adam said in a hard voice, putting his arm around Harry and pulling him closer.

Harry leaned into him, trying to hide the burst of happiness inside him. It was neither the time nor the place to get "saccharine" as Ksar had called them a few weeks ago during his visit.

Harry didn't think they were all that "saccharine" — he was just happy with Adam — but Ksar had been oddly irritated by the mere sight of him and Adam cuddling on the couch while they watched the TV, as if it was a personal offense to him. It had been odd. For all Ksar's standoffishness, he wasn't normally allergic to people's happiness.

Harry hoped Ksar's grumpiness had nothing to do with him, but it probably did. He could only imagine how the society had taken the news of Harry going to Earth and Ksar marrying Leylen.

The latter was something Harry still wasn't sure what to think of. He knew Ksar and Seyn had never been on the best of terms and that Seyn had wanted to break their bond for years, but Harry still felt weird about it — and guilty for saddling Ksar with that burden. Ksar would never admit that it was a sacrifice on his part, but that didn't mean it wasn't. Leylen would never be Ksar's pick if he were given a choice.

Harry wondered if that was the reason for Ksar's dark mood. If it was, Harry could hardly blame him.

"No," Ksar said curtly, tearing Harry away from his musings. "You showing up on my wedding with a member of a pre-TNIT civilization is the last thing we need."

Before Harry could disagree, Adam beat him to it. "I don't care," he said, pulling Harry tighter to him. "I'm not letting Harry go back without me."

Inwardly, Harry winced. Adam was…a little paranoid that someone would force him to stay on Calluvia and never come back to him. Harry could understand: if he didn't come back to Earth, Adam had no means to contact him or go after him.

If something happened to him while he was on Calluvia, Adam would never know. It must be incredibly frustrating for Adam to feel so helpless, and Harry could totally understand why Adam didn't want to let him leave without him.

Harry didn't want to leave without him, either.

"We can make it work," Harry said, looking at his brother pleadingly. "You have told me that there's much speculation about the reason for my stay on Earth and that there are all sorts of nasty rumors about it. Wouldn't it be better to show up with Adam instead of hiding him? You have taught me yourself that if I behave like there's nothing to be ashamed of, people won't shame me for it."

Ksar had a sour expression on his face. "The pre-TNIT law might have been repealed, but it doesn't mean that erased the prejudice society has against relationships with members of pre-TNIT civilizations." He looked at Adam. "You would be treated like a curiosity at best. Can you tolerate being looked down on?"

Adam chuckled. "If I haven't punched you for that, I think I can handle it. Harry is more important to me than the opinion of a bunch of xenophobic snobs."

Ksar gave him a pinched look. "I don't dislike you for being a member of a pre-TNIT civilization. I dislike you for putting my brother in such a position. He will be treated like a curiosity, too."

"I don't regret loving Adam," Harry said, lifting his chin and looking Ksar in the eye. "If you respect me at all, don't blame him for my choices. I love him, and I'm happy with him, and that's the only thing that should matter."

Ksar looked away for a moment, his expression strange.

"You're a fool," he said testily. "But fine. Bring your human with you, become the laughingstock of society. I don't care."

Harry frowned, eyeing his brother thoughtfully. There was something almost fragile about Ksar at that moment, as if he was wound so tight that he was on the verge of snapping. He looked stressed—far more stressed than he usually was. It was strange. Harry couldn't remember his brother looking anything but unflappable, regardless of the insane pressure on him or the amount of duties he had. What happened?

"Good," Adam said, oblivious to Ksar's strange mood. "We have already packed and we're ready to leave if you are."

Ksar just nodded, and Adam left to bring their suitcase from the bedroom.

Harry looked at his brother. "Are you okay? Is everything all right at home?"

A blank look settled over Ksar's features. Harry could literally feel Ksar's mental shields going up until no emotion could leak through. "Everything is as it should be."

Harry shot him a skeptical look, but before he could question him, Adam returned with their suitcase.

Ksar silently laid his hands on their arms and activated the TNIT.

Harry barely managed to shoot an encouraging smile at Adam, who looked a little apprehensive, before the world around them disappeared.

* * *

"Are you sure you want to do it?" Harry said, looking at Adam with a frown as they walked to the t-chamber that would take them to the ball.

Adam gave a wry smile. "Stop worrying about me, love. If I survived meeting your mother, I'll survive some fancy ball."

Harry grimaced a little.

His mother hadn't exactly been warm and friendly when she and Harry's father had met Adam yesterday. She had been perfectly polite, but she had been so extremely cold with Adam, outright rudeness would probably have been preferable.

"They'll all stare at you," Harry said, pursing his lips unhappily. "I don't think there's ever been a pre-TNIT alien on Calluvia." His biggest worry was that everyone would treat Adam as if he were an uncultured barbarian, and since Adam had received a translating chip already, he would understand all their insults.

"At least I'm making history," Adam said dryly.

Harry took his arm, stopping him. "Are you really sure you want to do this?" he said.

Adam looked so confident and handsome, cutting a fine figure in Calluvian clothes, his white cravat complementing his golden skin and firm jaw, but Harry could feel that he was worried, too, though his concern seemed to be primarily for Harry, not himself.

"We don't have to do it," Harry said, leaning into Adam a little and greedily breathing in his scent. It calmed him. "We can go back to Earth. I don't want you to go through this. My people…they can be cruel."

"I can handle it, Haz," Adam said firmly, holding his gaze. "I know we don't have to do it, but this is your home. I don't want you to be shunned by your own people. We're doing this."

Harry smiled at him, feeling so ridiculously in love he felt breathless with it. "I love you."

Adam's dark eyes softened.

"Me, too." Adam leaned in and kissed him, long and deep.

"Hurry up, or we'll be late," said a familiar voice. Ksar.

They pulled apart reluctantly and were met with the sight of Harry's parents pointedly not looking at them. Leylen was eyeing Adam with interest while Ksar just looked impatient and vaguely irritable. He still had the same wound-tight air about him.

Harry looked at them all. "Is Sanyash not joining us?" he said, feeling a little hurt. He missed his sister and had wanted her to meet Adam.

"Your nephew has a fever, Harry," his father said gently. "Sanyash called to say that she would not be attending the ball and that she would come to see you tomorrow."

"Being tardy would hardly help the situation," the Queen said tersely and headed toward the main t-chamber.

Suppressing a sigh, Harry slipped his hand into Adam's hand and followed his mother.

It saddened him that his mother was taking this so badly, but he had expected nothing less. The Queen had a difficult character at the best of times. She wasn't going to be magically fine with the situation. She tolerated it because she loved him, but that didn't mean she had to like it.

"Will Seyn be at the ball?" Harry said, breaking the tense silence as they all got into the t-chamber.

In front of him, he saw Ksar's shoulders stiffen. It wasn't very obvious, but Harry noticed, and wondered.

"Probably," the King-Consort said when Ksar didn't answer. "Speaking of Seyn'ngh'veighli, I have heard that he's gotten engaged as well— I believe to Ambassador Denev. It's a fine match. He's one of the most prominent politicians of his planet, and my sources say he has a high chance of becoming the President. Do you think it's likely, Ksar? You're much better versed in foreign politics than me."

Harry looked back at his brother and noticed that his back was absolutely rigid with tension.

But the t-chamber's doors opened at that moment and Ksar got out without saying a word.

"There's something off about him," Adam murmured into Harry's ear. "He seems really on edge."

Harry nodded, his brows furrowing. If even Adam, who didn't know Ksar all that well, noticed that, something was really wrong.

He eyed Ksar carefully as they joined him at the doors of the main ballroom of the Eleventh Royal Palace, but Ksar's face was a blank mask once again.

Their arrival was finally announced, and Harry braced himself as they entered the ballroom.

Murmurs rippled through the crowd.

Harry could almost physically feel the stares on him and Adam—on their laced fingers. His mother had been against such blatant displays of affection, calling it vulgar, but Ksar had unexpectedly supported it, saying that if they were doing this, it was better to leave no room for ambiguity and speculation.

Harry lifted his head proudly. He was doing nothing wrong. He was with the man he loved. The pre-TNIT law had been repealed. He was no longer bonded to Leylen. All these people had no right to look at them that way.

But prejudice ran deep in their society, and Harry couldn't help noticing the scandalized looks and the sneers. Beside him, Adam's face held an expression of polite interest and nothing else, but Harry could feel the tension in his body. He knew Adam was pissed off. The feeling of being looked at like he was an uncivilized barbarian must have been extremely offensive to Adam: he was a very successful and respected man back on Earth, and he wasn't used to being looked down on. Harry hated it. He didn't care what all these people thought of him, but he cared about Adam. His Adam didn't deserve it. Adam was amazing, and Harry was lucky to be loved by him.

He tried to extend his shields to Adam, hoping to protect him from any telepathic prying, but Ksar shook his head. "I'll handle it," he said shortly, his silver eyes scanning the room. "Don't worry about him."

"Thanks," Harry said, his voice thicker than he would have liked.

"None of that," Ksar said in his head. *"Keep your head high and act like you don't care what they think. He's doing fine, Harry. He's handling it surprisingly well."* A pause. *"Perhaps I was wrong about him."*

Harry smiled at him, feeling happy that someone from his family was finally coming around to accepting Adam. He hadn't expected it to be Ksar. His brother's support meant everything to Harry; it always had.

"Your Majesty," someone said, tearing Harry away from his thoughts.

He looked at the man bowing to his mother and felt his stomach sink. It was Lord Bleyver. He was a widower and a rake who had the reputation for sleeping around. Most worryingly, he was known for his sharp mind and equally sharp tongue. Despite his outrageous behavior, he was well respected, and his opinion had a lot of weight in society.

The Queen inclined her head slightly. "Bleyver," she said neutrally. Bleyver was actually one of her subjects; he was the head of a clan that was part of the Second Grand Clan.

Bleyver turned and bowed to Ksar. "Your Highness," he said, his sharp brown eyes meeting Ksar's cold gaze.

Ksar just nodded before completely dismissing the man and returning his attention to the room at large; Ksar had little patience for rakes.

Harry watched with some trepidation as Bleyver bowed to his father before finally turning to him.

"Your Highness," he said with a smile, bowing slightly. "It's so nice to see you in good health. I see the Terran air was good for you." His gaze shifted to Adam for the first time, sweeping over him from head to toe. "I see you have found a fine native specimen while you were there."

Harry hesitated, unsure how he was supposed to respond to that.

Bleyver wasn't exactly insulting Adam or himself, but there was a condescending edge to his tone that Harry didn't care for.

"The native specimen can speak for himself," Adam said, very dryly. "Yes, I'm an Earth native, and I'm here with Prince Harht'ngh'chaali. Is that all you wanted to know?"

Harry suppressed a smitten smile. Pronouncing Calluvian full names wasn't easy even with the translating chip, but Harry's name had rolled out of Adam's mouth as if he'd been saying it his whole life. Adam must have practiced a lot to achieve such a good pronunciation.

Lord Bleyver stared at Adam for a moment before smiling. "Why, yes. Thank you."

Before Harry could breathe out in relief, Bleyver turned back to him. "Forgive me for being so blunt, Your Highness, but does this mean you do not mind that your brother is marrying your former bondmate?"

Harry smiled uncertainly. He wasn't a very good liar, and he still wasn't sure he approved of Ksar's marrying Leylen in his stead. "I wish my brother nothing but happiness," he said. It wasn't a straight answer, but it was an honest one.

"And I suppose your Terran is the reason for your easy acceptance?" Bleyver said.

Harry hesitated. Strictly speaking, it was none of this man's business, but they had come to the ball to stop all the speculation and try to salvage what was left of his reputation. Harry had no intention of lying about Adam's importance to him. He didn't want anyone to think he wasn't serious about Adam.

"Yes, he is," Harry said. "We're courting." He held his head high as whispers ran through the crowd.

Lord Bleyver smiled. "To be honest, Your Highness," he murmured in a low voice that wasn't low enough not to be heard by everyone listening in. "I didn't think you had it in you, but it seems you really did, in more ways than one."

Harry flushed, absolutely speechless. He had heard of Lord Bleyver's outrageous comments, but he'd never been on the receiving end of them. A glance at Adam confirmed that Adam hadn't quite understood Lord Bleyver's double entendre; the translating chip wasn't perfect and certain nuances of language didn't translate. Harry knew the feeling: there had been so many times humans' turns of speech utterly confused him and made him feel like he'd missed something.

At this moment Harry felt very grateful that the translating chip wasn't perfect. Adam tended to be overprotective of him, and the last thing they needed was for Adam to get offended on his behalf and hit Lord Bleyver.

But Harry forgot that Adam wasn't the only person in the vicinity who could be overprotective of him.

"I find it baffling that you dare speak to your prince in that way," Ksar cut in, his voice like ice, sharp and cold.

Harry blinked and looked at his brother in surprise. Although Lord Bleyver hadn't exactly been as respectful as he should have been toward a prince of his own grand clan, Harry hadn't thought his comment would merit Ksar's attention.

Lord Bleyver was known for his outrageous remarks and scandalous behavior. Ksar usually ignored the man completely, not considering him worthy of his attention.

It was weird that Ksar was getting worked up over a simple risqué comment.

But then again, Harry thought, remembering the strange tension Ksar had been carrying. Maybe it wasn't that weird, after all. Ksar had been on edge lately, and this was likely just the last straw. Lord Bleyver was probably just a convenient outlet for his frustration.

"You misunderstood, Your Highness," Lord Bleyver said smoothly, his sharp eyes fixed warily on Ksar. "I meant no offense."

Ksar's face remained stony.

"You did," he said. "Don't insult my intelligence by pretending otherwise. Apologize."

Harry winced.

At this point, *everyone* in the ballroom was staring at them, listening avidly to the conversation. So much for not causing a scandal. What was Ksar thinking?

It seemed his mother shared his concerns and said, "Ksar."

But Ksar ignored the Queen, still staring Lord Bleyver down. "Apologize to your prince."

Harry could feel that Bleyver didn't feel as calm as his lazy, unbothered stance suggested. He could also feel that while Bleyver was very uneasy about openly defying Ksar, he also didn't want to lose face in public. That would be a blow to his social standing.

Bleyver smiled. "With all due respect, Your Highness, I don't know what I'm supposed to apologize for."

A muscle pulsed in Ksar's jaw, his eyes narrowing. Harry grimaced, bracing himself.

This wasn't going to end well.

The tense energy that he'd felt under Ksar's skin became somehow worse, as if it was moments away from lashing out and crushing something—or someone.

"Ksar," said a familiar voice as a pale hand touched Ksar's arm.

The tension didn't exactly bleed out of Ksar's body, but, impossibly, it settled back under his skin.

Harry's gaze followed Ksar's.

Harry smiled upon seeing Seyn—he'd missed him dearly—but Seyn wasn't looking at him. He was looking at Ksar, a warning in his gaze. "Calm down," he murmured, his voice oddly soft.

Harry had never heard him sound so soft with Ksar. But then again, Seyn was unbonded now and he could likely feel how close to lashing out Ksar was.

What *was* definitely odd was the fact that Seyn was attempting to calm Ksar down at all.

For as long as Harry could remember, Seyn had the opposite effect on Ksar. Hell, Seyn used to be the main source of Ksar's anger.

But apparently, "used to" was the imperative word, because for some reason, it worked.

It *worked*.

The air about Ksar lost its murderous edge, his eyes softening a little as they held Seyn's, though the tension in his body seemed to shift into something else rather than disappear entirely.

"I'm sure Lord Bleyver didn't mean it that way," Seyn said, his gaze still locked with Ksar's. "He would never do such a thing. Isn't that right, Lord Bleyver?"

"Of course, Your Highness, I would never," Lord Bleyver said smoothly, the tension leaving his shoulders.

"And I'm also sure Lord Bleyver will apologize anyway for any offense he might have inadvertently caused," Seyn said pointedly, although he was still looking at no one but Ksar. "Isn't that right, Lord Bleyver?"

After a moment, Bleyver seemed to swallow his pride and bowed to Harry. "Of course. I apologize if I *inadvertently* offended you, Your Highness. It wasn't my intention."

Adam was tense beside him, by now clearly getting the gist of Lord Bleyver's offense.

Harry pasted on a smile and squeezed Adam's hand in warning. "I'm sure it wasn't. You're forgiven anyway."

Lord Bleyver straightened but paused and bowed to Ksar. "Your Highness, I hope you're satisfied now that this misunderstanding has been cleared up," he said cautiously.

Ksar's gaze flicked to him for a moment—long enough for him to give Bleyver a clipped nod—before his gaze returned to Seyn.

Seyn, who seemed to realize that everyone's attention was now on him. It was obvious what was on everyone's mind: why was *Seyn* calming Ksar down while Ksar's current fiancée stood awkwardly a few steps away? Leylen was glaring, not at Seyn, but at Ksar, whose eyes were *still* on Seyn.

Awkward.

Seyn glanced around, his discomfort obvious only to someone who knew him well.

Harry decided to interfere before the situation could get even more awkward.

"I'm so pleased to see you!" he said, stepping forward and reaching out with his mind to hug Seyn's.

He almost flinched when their minds touched.

Seyn's telepathy felt a lot stronger than it had been the last time they hugged, but that wasn't the surprising part.

The surprising part was how downbeat Seyn felt. He was upset about something, genuinely distraught. There was something like anger and desperation too.

Frowning, Harry searched Seyn's face, but it betrayed nothing of the turmoil he felt. Seyn looked as handsome as ever, his silver hair immaculately styled and his clothes impeccable.

Seyn either hadn't noticed his questioning look or pretended not to. "I'm happy to see you, too," Seyn said with a smile before looking at Adam. "How are you liking Calluvia?"

Adam smiled wryly. "The planet is beautiful."

Seyn let out a laugh. "A very diplomatic reply. Please don't judge us all by the doings of a few."

"I don't," Adam said, his gaze flicking to Ksar behind Seyn. "I think my future brother-in-law wants you."

Seyn's smile froze.

Ksar fixed Adam with such a withering look that Harry was actually afraid for Adam's life for a moment.

Adam smiled sheepishly, raking his fingers through his dark hair. "I worded it wrongly again, didn't I? Sorry, I meant that my future brother-in-law seems to want to *talk* to you. My bad."

Harry stared at Adam skeptically. The translating chip wasn't perfect, but it wasn't that bad. Considering that he could feel Adam's poorly veiled amusement, he was clearly having fun at Ksar's expense.

"I do," Ksar said after a moment, his voice very stiff. "Walk with me?"

Seyn's back was still to Ksar, so Ksar couldn't see the conflict in Seyn's eyes.

Harry could, and he wondered.

At last, Seyn said, "Why not?" He headed for the terrace that led to the gardens. After a moment, Ksar followed him.

"Why did you do that?" Harry murmured, turning his confused gaze to Adam. "They'll just fight again."

Adam brushed his knuckles against Harry's cheek and smiled at him. "You're still so naive sometimes, babe."

Harry mock-glared at him but couldn't help smiling. "You love me."

Adam's dark eyes smiled back. "I do."

Chapter 25

The twin moons shone brightly, bathing the gardens in pale light.

"What did you want to talk about?" Seyn said, sitting down on the first unoccupied bench they'd come across, his gaze settling on the blue flowers opposite the bench.

Aware of the other guests that had suddenly decided to take a stroll through the gardens, Ksar took a seat next to Seyn, a palm's length between them.

He stared at the flowers, too, as silence stretched.

A night bird sang a hauntingly beautiful song from one of the trees. Knowing the Regent of the Eleventh Grand Clan, the bird must have cost a small fortune.

Seyn chuckled. "Are we just going to sit here in silence?"

Ksar pursed his lips to stop himself from saying that he wouldn't mind.

Pathetic.

He looked down at his own hands. "Are you really choosing Denev?"

There was silence for a while.

At last, Seyn said, "Yes. He makes the most sense. My mothers approve. And he's nice."

Ksar's lips twisted. No one would describe *him* as nice.

"Is he?" he said flatly.

Beside him, Seyn bristled. "He is. He's handsome, well mannered and—and lovely. He looks at me like I matter."

Ksar laughed.

"What's so funny?"

He looked at Seyn. "You think you didn't matter to me?" His voice sounded hollow even to his own ears, all wrong.

Seyn's lovely lips folded into a scowl.

Gritting his teeth, Ksar looked away.

"You had a funny way of showing it," Seyn said, his tone hostile, even though there was something uncertain about the way he'd said that. "You've never given a damn about me."

"Not giving a damn has never been an issue," Ksar said with a humorless smile. The problem was the opposite.

"Don't do this," Seyn said tightly, resentment coloring his voice. "Don't you dare do this!"

Ksar looked back at him. "Why?" he said. "If you're so happy with your choice, it shouldn't matter what I say. I shouldn't matter."

Seyn glared at him. "Shut up—go away! Leave me alone!"

Ksar looked from Seyn's furious eyes to his trembling lips and back to his eyes. "Is that really what you want? I promise I'll leave you alone and never speak to you again if you say it like you actually mean it."

Seyn continued to glare at him.

He was so damn beautiful when he was angry.

Seyn opened his mouth and closed it. Some emotion appeared in his eyes before Seyn set his jaw and said firmly, "Leave me alone."

Something in him gave a painful twinge, a heavy and unpleasant feeling settling low in his stomach.

Ksar told himself that this was to be expected. It had been ridiculous even to entertain the idea that his…fixation on Seyn might not be completely one-sided. Why would it not be one-sided? He had treated Seyn abominably for years.

This was for the best. He wasn't any good at… emotions. He should stick to what he was good at: his duty to the Ministry, his duty to the throne, and his duty to his family. Emotions and wants were messy. He didn't need them. It was good that Seyn was telling him to leave him alone—Ksar was honest enough with himself to admit that he wouldn't have been able to do so otherwise. Seyn had always been his weakness—the feisty, spirited, argumentative boy that could get under his skin like no other, the only person capable of making him irrational, overly emotional, and reckless. This *was* for the best.

With a clipped nod, Ksar got to his feet, ignoring the hollow feeling in his chest. There was nothing hollow in his chest. He was perfectly healthy. Perfectly fine. It was all in his head.

He was hardly heartbroken.

He was just…

Ksar clenched his jaw and looked down at Seyn for the last time, taking in his bowed silver head and long fingers gripping the edge of the bench. Although Seyn looked fine, he *felt* upset, exuding misery, desperation, and anger.

Ksar's hand twitched toward him and he curled it into a fist. No. Seyn had made his choice. He would respect that. It was a good thing that at least one of them was thinking rationally.

Ksar turned away, but then paused. There was one more thing that needed to be said.

"For all it's worth, I'm sorry," he said. His voice sounded hoarse and unsteady—nothing like him. He didn't think he'd ever apologized in his life, but it felt right to say those words now.

They still felt inadequate.

Everything about this felt inadequate, because a part of him still insisted that the young man he was saying goodbye to was *his and only his, forever.* He wanted to snarl those words out, he wanted to grab Seyn and refuse to let go, he wanted to kiss him and mark him up, so everyone could see whom Seyn belonged to.

Ksar grimaced, utterly disgusted with himself. He had given his word that he would leave Seyn alone if Seyn told him so. He might not be a good man, and he might keep his word only when it suited him, but this time he would. He owed Seyn that much. He refused to be the possessive, controlling ex who couldn't let go when his lover moved on.

He would stop thinking of Seyn as his. He would stop looking for him at every social function—at least he would do his best. He had no right to him. This—whatever that hollow feeling in his chest was—it was of no consequence.

One didn't always get what one wanted; such was life.

He wasn't entitled to happiness.

People like Harry fell in love and got to be happy. People like *him* did their duty. He would marry Leylen, he would tolerate her, and he would treat her with perfect politeness. What he *wanted* was irrelevant.

But no matter what he told himself, making himself leave was still the hardest thing Ksar had ever done. His feet felt heavy, his body reluctant to cooperate, as if it was bound to the young man he was leaving behind with tight, invisible ropes. *Mine*, his body insisted. *Mine*, the feeling in his chest said.

Ksar managed a few steps when a sound stopped him.

A laugh, harsh and a little hysterical.

Ksar turned, and stared.

Seyn was laughing, his hands covering his face as his shoulders shook with laughter. "Sorry? You know where you can shove your fucking apology?" He lifted his head, glaring at him. "You just have to ruin everything, don't you? I don't want to hear your apologies. I don't want to listen to you saying that I mattered to you. I want to hate you, dammit. Let me have that at least!" He slumped forward, running a hand over his face. "I hate you," he whispered, his voice wavering. "Don't take that away from me."

Ksar eyed him with furrowed brows. He took a step closer, and then another, and another, until he was looking down at Seyn's bowed head.

"I..." he said, his hand twitching toward Seyn. He'd never felt so out of his depth. He wanted...he wanted Seyn to stop feeling upset. He wanted to *fix* it. But he didn't know how. He knew what he wanted to do, but it was highly unlikely Seyn would even accept comfort from him.

Seyn heaved a sigh and stared at the blue flowers again. "Have you ever heard of Queen Esme of my clan?"

Ksar frowned, taken aback by the change of subject. "I don't recall her."

"You wouldn't. It happened over five thousand years ago and she ruled for just two years." Seyn touched one of the blue petals. "These are poisonous, you know. They can be used to create a lethal poison—poison that was very popular at the court back then. To protect her daughter from poisoning, Queen Esme's mother fed her small doses of poison from very early childhood, to build up her immunity. But it worked a little too well. By the time Queen Esme ascended the throne, she was completely addicted to it. She was stabbed two years later while she was too high to even notice it."

Seyn lifted his eyes back to Ksar. "It's a story told to all children of our House. The moral of the story is supposed to be that the road to hell is paved with good intentions, but I used to think that my mother just made up that story to stop me from doing something reckless and dangerous."

Seyn gave a crooked smile. "I didn't believe that you could actually grow to need something that hurt you. It seemed really messed up, you know?" He laughed, the sound sharp as broken glass. "It *is* messed up."

Ksar stared at Seyn, his heart beating fast and hard.

"Queen Esme didn't die from that poison," he heard himself say.

"No, she didn't," Seyn agreed, his face raw with emotion that hurt to look at. "She died because she didn't give a shit about anything but her poison. She died because she was too weak to resist it. "

"Isn't that essentially the same thing? She was an idiot. I'm an idiot, too, or I wouldn't hate Ambassador Denev for not being the insufferably arrogant, infuriating, immoral asshole who hurt me all my life." Seyn glared at Ksar, but there was something fragile about his expression, his eyes shining with unshed tears. "What have you done to me? I should hate you."

Slowly, Ksar dropped to one knee, and then the other, until he was kneeling in front of Seyn, who was staring at him, wide-eyed.

Well aware that anyone spying on them could probably see him kneeling on the hard ground, Ksar took Seyn's hand and brought their clasped hands to his right shoulder.

Seyn took in a sharp breath, clearly recognizing the gesture: it had once been used by clan lords to swear fealty to their king. It had gone out of use thousands of years ago; it was considered too demeaning by modern standards.

"I can't promise you that I will never hurt you again," Ksar said, looking Seyn in the eye. "You know me. I'm not—good at emotions. But I can promise you that I will try—as long as you'll have me." He was dismayed by how raw his voice sounded, how desperate he felt—and likely looked.

Crown princes didn't kneel. *He* didn't kneel. But this was more important than his pride. Seyn was owed some groveling after years of rejection and rudeness; Ksar was well aware of that. He wasn't blind to his own faults—he would always be "insufferably arrogant"—but that didn't mean he couldn't suppress his pride and arrogance when it mattered.

And this mattered.

"Stop that, get up," Seyn said tightly, looking away. "What are you even saying? It doesn't matter anyway, does it? It's too late. You are marrying her in four days! And I already said yes to Ambassador Denev."

Ignoring the rush of ugly possessiveness, Ksar took Seyn's chin in his other hand and made Seyn look at him. "Forget about them. If you say yes, I'll handle it."

Seyn let out a laugh, sounding a little hysterical. "Are you out of your mind? It would be political suicide for you! You'd lose all credibility if you suddenly say 'Oops, I've changed my mind' after the Council gave you the permission to break your bond to me, something that just *isn't* done, amendment to the Bonding Law or not. They would crucify you."

"I can handle it," Ksar repeated tersely. "You don't need excuses if you want to say no."

Seyn chuckled, running a hand over his face. "I can't just…" He looked at Ksar with something like frustration, vulnerability, and longing, all mixed in one. "What do you even feel for me? Lust doesn't count."

Ksar sneered a little. "Lust can be dealt with easily enough."

Seyn just looked at him expectantly when that was all he said.

Sighing, Ksar rose to his feet and took the seat beside Seyn again.

He stared at the poisonous flowers, fighting the instinctive urge to deny having any feelings whatsoever.

"I'm not good at this," he said, tugging at his cravat a little.

"I know," Seyn said, very dryly.

Ksar shot him a sideways glare and found Seyn smiling. "I'm glad you find this amusing."

"Sorry," Seyn said, not sounding sorry at all. "Let's hear your grand confession anyway."

There was a faint look of skepticism on his face, as if he still didn't believe Ksar was serious about wanting him. Such insecurity in someone so attractive made Ksar feel like a right bastard—that was entirely his doing, and no one else's.

"I can't do grand confessions," Ksar said, letting his hand graze against Seyn's knuckles. He heard Seyn's breathing hitch and removed his hand before that could escalate.

At this point Ksar was well aware that neither of them could think rationally if they got carried away, and it had been much too long since he'd last touched Seyn. They didn't need distractions, not now.

"But I know what I want." Ksar met Seyn's gaze and held it. "I never really hated you, at least not like you hated me. Even when you irritated me, I wanted to have you. I don't mean just lust. I liked the idea of you being mine— being at my side, in my bed, taking my name, and becoming my King-Consort at some point."

A faint flush appeared on Seyn's cheekbones. But the only thing he said was, "Continue."

"But I knew I could never really have you, not with the way things were. A relationship can't be built on lies and manipulations. So it was…frustrating. The situation made me angry and I took out that anger on you." Ksar averted his eyes. "That's not an excuse, I know. It's the truth. All those offensive things I said, when I insulted your intelligence or your social conduct, it was…"

Ksar grimaced. "Part of it was that I was trying to convince myself that you weren't all that attractive." He snorted. "Though I did like making you fume—you do have a singular talent for making me act like an ass."

"Is that supposed to be your grand confession?" Seyn said, but Ksar could see his lips twitching.

Ksar met his smiling eyes and felt his heart thud almost painfully against his ribs.

He did like making Seyn fume.

But it seemed he liked making him smile even more.

"I can get back on my knees if it's not grand enough for you," he said dryly.

Seyn grinned, glancing around the garden. "I think once is sufficient or all these people hiding behind those bushes might actually have a heart attack."

Ksar made a face. At least it was unlikely that they had been overheard.

"So is that a yes?" he said.

Seyn licked his lips. "I'm..." He sighed, looking at Ksar with a pinched expression. "Fuck it, I guess I'm that crazy."

Ksar's felt his throat constrict. Until that moment, he hadn't realized how much he wanted this—wanted Seyn to choose him, freely.

Aloud, he said, "There's nothing crazy about choosing the Crown Prince of the Second Grand Clan of Calluvia over an ambassador of some irrelevant planet."

As expected, Seyn gave him an exasperated look. "It was probably too much to hope your humility would last." But he sounded *fond*, and the smile on his lips told Ksar everything he needed.

"Let's not pretend you don't like it," Ksar said, taking Seyn's hand again and brushing his lips against his bare wrist. He could actually hear the scandalized gasps from the direction of the trees, but his eyes were only on Seyn's.

"Ksar," Seyn murmured. His gaze was already slightly unfocused, the longing in them mirroring the one under Ksar's skin. "People are watching us."

"Let them," Ksar said, kissing his wrist again. "They will find out soon enough."

Seyn wet his lips, color high on his cheeks. "Come here, then," he said, freeing his wrist and cupping Ksar's jaw. *It's been too long,* came a crystal-clear thought Ksar fully agreed with. It definitely felt like it had been months since he last tasted Seyn's lips and touched him intimately.

It was still a poor excuse for kissing him in such a public place, most likely in full view of several members of high society.

He did it, anyway.

A small moan left Seyn's mouth at the first contact of their lips. Ksar didn't allow himself to deepen the kiss too much—they *were* in a public place—but it took all his willpower not to haul Seyn onto his lap like some uncivilized barbarian. And although he didn't let himself delve into Seyn's mind, either, he could still feel snatches of his thoughts. *I missed this. I missed you. It's so fucked up, but I feel whole only with you.*

"Yes," Ksar said roughly, breaking the kiss and pressing their foreheads together. He knew exactly what Seyn meant. "My sentiments precisely."

Chapter 26

"Have you lost your mind?"

Seyn almost flinched from the anger in the Queen's face, even though that ire wasn't directed at him.

Ksar met his mother's gaze unflinchingly, his face absolutely inscrutable. If he weren't still wearing the same clothes that he'd worn to the ball, Seyn wouldn't have believed that this proud, arrogant man was capable of kneeling for someone.

The mere memory of it made him want to smile, which would hardly be appropriate in this situation.

Queen Tamirs was *furious*. Leylen had been just as furious, but she hadn't returned with them to the Second Royal Palace, leaving the ball with her parents after the scandal had hit.

Unlike his wife, the King-Consort seemed to be torn between shock and confusion. Harry and Adam hadn't been invited to take part in the conversation after they all returned from the ball. Seyn would envy them that, except he didn't really feel like being separated from Ksar. He was embarrassed by how clingy he felt, but despite Ksar's words, there was still a part of him that was sure Ksar would change his mind after talking to Queen Tamirs.

"I'm in full possession of my mental faculties," Ksar said.

"So you're saying that those rumors aren't true and you weren't caught *kissing* your former bondmate?" Queen Tamirs said.

"Being caught implies that we were attempting to hide something," Ksar said, his tone very mild. "It certainly wasn't the case."

Seyn hid a smile.

Queen Tamirs's violet eyes narrowed. "Are you saying you got our House mired in another scandal on purpose?"

Ksar looked at her steadily. "I'm saying that there was no point in trying to hide it when everyone would have found out anyway. I'm not marrying Lady Leylen'shni'gul."

"But Ksar," his father cut in, frowning. "The wedding is in four days. You can't do that. The scandal aside, the poor girl would be humiliated."

"That poor girl has only herself to blame," Ksar said coldly. "She shouldn't have spread the rumors of our imminent marriage without my permission. She cornered me into marrying her. I don't owe her anything."

"To be fair, you did promise to marry her in exchange for her breaking her bond to Harry," Seyn said with an eye roll.

Ksar had a very selective memory when it suited him.

"I keep my promises only to people I care about," Ksar said, meeting his gaze, his eyes softening for a moment before hardening again as he returned his gaze to his father.

Ksar said, "Leylen and her family will be compensated handsomely for their trouble. She'll hardly be heartbroken. She has no fondness for me."

The King-Consort sighed. "I suppose so. But she isn't the main problem."

"Indeed," the Queen said, glaring at Ksar. "The problem is that you are supposed to act like a responsible heir to the throne instead of indulging your selfish whims. You seem to have forgotten what being the Crown Prince entails. You have duties to your clan and to your House, and one of them is to keep your House's reputation unblemished by scandal. I thought I raised you better than this."

Seyn winced on the inside. He didn't know how Ksar managed to look so unbothered by his mother's words.

"Raised better than this?" Ksar repeated with barely any inflection in his voice. "You misspoke, Mother. Borg'gorn has more claim to raising me than you do. You should have said 'I thought I created you better than that.' Perhaps you should have removed my ability to want things for myself when you genetically engineered your perfect heir. I'm sorry, Your Majesty, if I don't behave to your exact specifications."

The Queen paled. The King-Consort turned away, his shoulders slumped.

Seyn bit the inside of his cheek, suppressing the urge to hug Ksar. He knew Ksar wouldn't welcome it, not in front of his parents. Ksar would never show weakness in front of his parents.

What a sad thing this family was. The Queen and the King-Consort weren't inherently bad people. But they weren't good parents, either.

"I told you, Tamirs," the King-Consort said hoarsely. "I told you."

Seyn didn't know what he meant, though he could make a guess from the straight, stiff way the Queen held herself. This clearly had been a subject of contention between the royal couple.

"You should be grateful for what I did," the Queen said tightly. "You were blessed with high intelligence, aesthetically pleasing appearance, exceptional physical strength, leadership qualities—"

"You have no trouble loving Harht for just being him," Ksar said in a very wry tone that about broke Seyn's heart. "Harry can be forgiven for wanting something for himself, for falling in love with a member of a pre-TNIT civilization, someone of no royal blood, but Heaven forbid if I overstep a little. But then again, Harht is the son, not the heir. He deserves happiness."

The Queen looked vaguely sick now. And guilty, as she should be. The double standards were really staggering. Seyn couldn't understand how it was possible to favor one child over the others and treat them so differently. Sure, he knew Harry was the only naturally born child in the family, but it was hardly an excuse. Seyn's mothers loved him unconditionally despite not giving birth to him.

"I would have understood if it was just me, *Mother*," Ksar said in a mocking undertone. "But you barely treated Sanyash any better than me. She used to ask me when we were little why you never hugged her like you hugged Harht. We would have likely hated Harht if he weren't such a disgustingly kind, naive kid who loved everyone." A sardonic smile touched Ksar's lips. "No thanks to you."

"Son," the King-Consort said, but Ksar cut him off.

"I'm not interested in your apologies," he said, still looking at his mother. "I need neither your pity nor your love. Just let me have what I want. I'm not asking for anything more."

There was a long silence.

And then, the Queen nodded, looking weary beyond her years. "If there are problems, you will have my support in the Council," she said tonelessly.

"Thank you, Your Majesty," Ksar said, his voice all business. "We will take our leave now. Good night."

Seyn followed him out of the Queen's office.

They didn't speak until after they reached Ksar's rooms.

"I used her guilt to get what I want," Ksar said without looking at him, loosening his cravat with jerky, angry movements of his fingers.

"Okay," Seyn said softly.

"Stop pitying me."

"I don't pity you," Seyn said, knocking Ksar's hands away and untying his cravat. "Compassion isn't pity." He met Ksar's eyes. "You can look into my mind, you know. I don't mind."

Ksar looked at him intently, his gaze searching, but he didn't delve into his mind. He must have seen everything he needed on Seyn's face, because his shoulders were no longer quite as stiff and his face wasn't a blank mask anymore.

Seyn unfastened Ksar's jacket and pulled it off. Ksar's shirt followed suit, leaving him just in his dark pants.

Slipping out of his own jacket, Seyn took Ksar's hand and pulled him toward the bed.

Ksar let him, watching him with the same weird, intense expression that wasn't quite desire.

Ksar didn't resist when Seyn pushed him to lie on his back, but he did tense a little when Seyn laid his head on his shoulder and slung an arm around his middle.

"I thought we were going to have sex," Ksar said dryly.

"We will," Seyn said, pressing his lips against Ksar's bare shoulder and breathing in his scent. Fuck, he'd missed him. It had been a long month. While he hadn't exactly been wasting away, he'd felt…anchorless, as if he'd been suddenly thrown into a strange, deep sea he had no clue how to navigate. He'd hated it. "But I'm in need of a cuddle first. Indulge me."

"I don't need a cuddle."

"Is there something wrong with your hearing? I said I needed a cuddle, not you. If this relationship is going to work, you'll have to put up with it from time to time."

Ksar sighed, but he seemed amused rather than annoyed. "You're entirely transparent."

"Good," Seyn said, tightening his arm around Ksar and nearly moaning in contentment; it felt so good. Why hadn't they done this before? It felt almost as good as sex. Physical touch was really underrated. "I'm all for transparency and honesty in a relationship."

"Is that a warning?" Ksar murmured against his ear.

Smiling crookedly, Seyn looked at him. "If you need one."

Ksar gazed at him in silence, their faces so close Seyn could feel Ksar's every breath on his cheek.

"No," Ksar said at last. "I don't need such a warning."

Seyn's smile softened. "Good," he said again, burying a hand in Ksar's hair and pulling him down for a shallow kiss. It wasn't meant to be passionate, but it was so satisfying on so many levels that Seyn found himself breathless and eager for more.

When they finally pulled apart, Ksar's gaze was a little unfocused, soft around the edges but endlessly hungry. "Are we done cuddling?"

Seyn gave a sly grin. "Why, is there something else that you want?"

"I have a few ideas," Ksar said, his hand slipping between their bodies to cup Seyn's hard cock.

Much later, as they lay tangled in the sheets and in each other, naked, tired, and sexually sated—for now— Seyn murmured into Ksar's bare chest, "I'm staying the night."

"I wasn't planning to throw you out," Ksar said, his voice already heavy with sleep, his arms tightening around him.

Seyn grinned into Ksar's chest. Embarrassed by his own sappiness, he said, "It's not that I'm feeling needy or something like that." Though, if he were being entirely honest with himself, he did feel needy. Just a tad. It had just been too long, and he didn't really feel like being away from Ksar even for a few hours. "I don't particularly want to go home and face my mothers. And Jamil."

Seyn groaned, imagining his brother's reaction. "Ugh. This is going to be horrible, isn't it? I can only imagine what people are saying right now. Everyone will stare and say all kinds of nasty stuff about us, and it'll be a total shit show—"

"So...nothing you aren't used to," Ksar said dryly.

Seyn lifted his head and grinned, meeting Ksar's eyes. "But this time there won't be a certain top-lofty ass to drive crazy with my improper behavior, so that takes half the fun out of it."

"I always knew that everything you did was for my attention," Ksar murmured with an infuriating smirk.

Seyn gave him a telepathic smack. "Arrogance isn't attractive, you ass."

"Liar," Ksar said. "We've already established that you like it."

Seyn looked at him—at his sex-tousled hair, sleepy eyes and the arrogant set of his jaw—and thought,

I love you so much.

Although sudden, the thought didn't surprise him all that much.

Deep down, he knew it had always been Ksar, one way or another. Ksar was the person he'd always been the most passionate about, be it hatred or love. Even if he'd fallen in love with someone else, he would have never felt as strongly for them. Seyn was glad he hadn't fallen in love with someone else. He'd hate to love someone but not have them as the person that *mattered* the most.

"What?" Ksar said, probably reading something on his face.

Seyn looked at him for a long moment, hesitating.

A small part of him, the one that didn't want to get hurt, didn't want to make himself vulnerable. But he knew that honesty would be the best course of action if he wanted their relationship to work.

Ksar's issues with love were deeper than his. A person who'd never been loved would never recognize love and vocalize it.

So Seyn looked Ksar in the eye and said quietly, "I love you."

Ksar's mouth twitched, as if he wasn't sure what to say or how to react to that. But he didn't need to say anything for Seyn to feel the almost violent rush of foreign happiness and elation mixed with bewilderment and possessiveness.

At last, Ksar said hoarsely, "Let's sleep. It's getting late, and it'll be a long day tomorrow." His arms felt like iron bands around Seyn, holding him so tightly it almost hurt.

Seyn didn't mind.

He felt an odd sort of peace, as if finally admitting his feelings made the war of emotions inside him end. He didn't even mind that Ksar didn't say the words back. He didn't expect him to, not at this point, not before he was ready to say them.

But someday, he would be.

And Seyn would be there.

Epilogue

Four years later

The baby was sleeping.

Seyn smiled, laying a hand against the artificial womb's outer wall and projecting comfort and love. There was no scientific proof that unborn babies could sense emotions coming from the outside world, but that didn't faze him. It wasn't hardship.

The door behind him opened, and instantly, a wonderful sense of wholeness filled Seyn's being. Seyn smiled a little. Although he and Ksar didn't share the traditional bond most Calluvians did, they had something much better: a telepathic bond that had developed naturally over time as the consequence of indulging in too many telepathic merges.

"Councilor Xuvok has been looking for the King-Consort all day, but I see he's shirking his duties," Ksar said wryly.

Seyn pulled a face. "I hate dealing with that stubborn old mule." He shot Ksar a haughty look. "And what do you mean, shirking my duties? I'll have you know I was consulting with my son. I am his Regent, after all."

Ksar walked over and sat down next to him. "You have an answer for everything, don't you?"

Seyn looped his arms around Ksar's neck and grinned at him. "I'll take that as a compliment, Your Majesty." The form of address still felt a little strange on his tongue, even though it had already been a year since Queen Tamirs had abdicated.

It had certainly been an interesting year. Although few had expected the Queen to abdicate so early, her decision hadn't come as much of a surprise to Seyn. Her strained relationship with Ksar hadn't improved over the years despite Harry's continued attempts to make them all love each other. Seyn didn't have the heart to tell Harry that his efforts were pointless and some things couldn't be fixed.

It was obvious that Ksar and his mother's strained relationship had been affecting their ability to present a united front in the Council, so Seyn hadn't been particularly surprised by the Queen's decision: Queen Tamirs might have been a poor mother, but she had always been an excellent queen who cared for the good of her clan. With her abdicating and with Ksar not having an heir, Seyn had to take the second seat in the Council as Ksar's Consort.

Unfortunately, until their son reached his age of majority, Seyn would be the one dealing with old farts like Councilor Xuvok. It was the main downside of being married to Ksar.

Not that their married life was perfect. It might have been emotionally satisfying, but it had been challenging in other ways. Thankfully, the scandal had been forgotten quickly enough, the gossipmongers moving on to a new, much bigger scandal involving Jamil. Seyn hadn't envied his brother, but it had been a relief; they'd had enough challenges as a newly married couple without the added pressure of public scrutiny.

His and Ksar's relationship had never exactly been calm and quiet, and that hadn't changed with their marriage. Ksar still drove him absolutely crazy half of the time. He could be such an asshole to people, ruthless and single-minded when he had a goal in sight. More often than not, Seyn *loved* watching Ksar reduce some self-important ass on the Council to tears, but sometimes Ksar took it too far and it pissed Seyn off.

They had ugly fights every few months, but their fights never lasted long. They were terrible at staying away from each other, always had been, so they always ended up seeking each other out, apologizing, and having sex. Seyn could never stay angry when Ksar kissed him tenderly, need evident in his every touch. Makeup sex was the greatest thing in the world, in Seyn's opinion.

"It *was* a compliment," Ksar said, leaning in and kissing him on the cheek, nuzzling into him slightly. "And you're right: visiting our son is more important than listening to Xuvok."

Seyn beamed at him, not even caring anymore how dopey and besotted his smile probably looked. He *was* besotted with his husband; it was something he'd accepted a long time ago.

"He's just fallen asleep," Seyn said, slipping his hand into Ksar's and turning back to the womb.

"He looks like you," Ksar said, squeezing his hand. "He has your hair."

Seyn wrinkled his nose and looked dubiously at the few wisps of hair on the baby's head. "It might change yet," he said, unsure why Ksar was so insistent that their son looked like Seyn when it clearly wasn't the case. They hadn't used genetic engineering, but Seyn could already tell that the baby was going to be Ksar's little copy, the color of his hair notwithstanding.

"Why do you want him to look like me?" he murmured, putting his head on Ksar's shoulder.

He could feel Ksar's inner turmoil through their bond, but he didn't try to peek. Ksar would tell him when he wanted to.

For a long while, Ksar was silent, playing with Seyn's fingers idly as they watched their unborn son sleep.

"I think it will be easier for me," Ksar said at last, haltingly, "to love him if he looks like you."

Seyn felt his throat constrict. Ksar didn't talk about feelings often—that hadn't changed much over the years—so it never failed to make Seyn feel special whenever Ksar told him that he loved him.

Seyn blinked the tears away and looked at Ksar. "For such an intelligent man, you can be such an idiot sometimes. It's a good thing you have me to tell you when you're being dumb."

Ksar put his other arm around him and pulled him closer. "It's a good thing I have you," he said, his gaze heavy and intense as their eyes met.

Seyn would never get enough of this—this feeling of being the most important thing in Ksar's world—and he couldn't deny how heady it was, even after years together. Fuck, he loved this man, loved him so much. In a way, he could almost understand Ksar's fears. Deep down, Seyn was a little afraid he wouldn't love his children as much as he loved their father, that they would always come second. But rationally, he knew his fears were unfounded. One's capacity for love wasn't limited.

"You're going to be a great father," he said firmly, burying his fingers in Ksar's hair and pulling him down to press their foreheads together. "Trust me."

"I do," Ksar said, kissing the corner of Seyn's mouth, then the other.

Seyn grinned. "Then stop worrying about it and kiss your husband for real, Your Majesty. It's been too long."

Ksar's lips curled. "It's been four hours."

"Exactly. As I said, too long. Kiss me, husband."

Laughing, Ksar did just that.

And as usual, the world around them seemed to disappear, and Ksar was the only thing that mattered.

Just him.

Always.

The End

That Irresistible Poison

About the Author

Alessandra Hazard is the author of the bestselling MM romance series *Straight Guys* and *Calluvia's Royalty*.

Visit Alessandra's website to learn more about her books: http://www.alessandrahazard.com/books/

To be notified when Alessandra's new books become available, you can subscribe to her mailing list: http://www.alessandrahazard.com/subscribe/

You can contact the author at her website or email her at author@alessandrahazard.com.